THE SMALLEST CRACK

By
USA Today Bestselling Author
ROBERTA KAGAN

Book One in A Holocaust Story Series

CONTACT ME

I love hearing from readers, so feel free to drop me an email telling me your thoughts about the book or series.

Email: roberta@robertakagan.com

Please sign up for my mailing list, and you will receive Free short stories including an USA Today award-winning novella as my gift to you!!!!! To sign up…

Check out my website http://www.robertakagan.com.

Come and like my Facebook page!

https://www.facebook.com/roberta.kagan.9

Join my book club

https://www.facebook.com/groups/1494285400798292/?ref=br_rs

Follow me on BookBub to receive automatic emails whenever I am offering a special price, a freebie, a giveaway, or a new release. Just click the link below, then click follow button to the right of my name. Thank you so much for your interest in my work.

https://www.bookbub.com/authors/roberta-kagan.

DISCLAIMER

This is a work of fiction. Names, characters, businesses, places, events, and incidents are either the products of the author's imagination or used in a fictitious manner. Any resemblance to actual persons, living or dead, or actual events is purely coincidental.

TABLE OF CONTENTS

THE SMALLEST CRACK

Berlin, Germany
Spring 1932

Eli Kaetzel paced on the stone steps outside the yeshiva and took a deep breath. He loved the freshness in the spring air as it filled his lungs. Everything about spring made him feel as if the world around him was born anew. The tiny blades of new grass, the flower buds, the crystal-blue cloudless sky. He sighed and looked around. He felt a sense of well-being wash over him. And to make things even better, it was Tuesday, his favorite day of the week. On Tuesday afternoons, when the weather permitted, he and his best friend, Yousef Schwartz, went to the park to study. Instead of being cramped up inside the yeshiva until late afternoon, they sat on a park bench where they ate potato knishes that Eli's mother packed for them and had stimulating discussions about Talmud stories. But that was not the real reason that Eli was so elated and anxious to get to the park today. The real reason was her, the girl in the park. Since the first time he saw her, three weeks ago, he'd thought of little else. She was playing ball with a group of her friends, and when he saw her for the first time, he thought that she might be the most beautiful girl he'd ever seen. All that week he'd hoped to see her on the following Tuesday, and then he thought his heart would burst with joy, when he and Yousef went to the park the following week, and she was there: then, again, the week after. He was mesmerized by her. And even though he knew for certain, by her clothing, that she was not Hasidic, he hoped that at least she was Jewish. Not that his family would have been pleased with him for being attracted to a girl who was not Hasidic. But in his mind, he began creating all kinds of possible scenarios. *Perhaps, she is Jewish, assimilated, but Jewish.* He thought. *And, if by some wonderful miracle I met her and she decided she liked me, she might be willing to join the Hasidic community.*

Today, Yousef was late, but that was nothing new. Yousef could easily get caught up in a heated conversation with his teacher about a story in the Talmud, and a half hour might pass before he realized he'd left Eli waiting. Eli smiled and shook his head thinking about how absentminded his good friend could be.

"Eli!" Yousef called out as he was coming out of the building. "Were you waiting long? I'm sorry. I got tied up discussing today's lesson with the teacher. And you know how intense he can be. Oy! He gets on a subject, and there is just no stopping him. I am so sorry I kept you waiting."

"Don't worry. I wasn't waiting long. And besides, it's so beautiful outside today that I didn't mind at all," Eli said, but he wasn't telling the truth. Inside he was a trembling nervous wreck. He tried to appear calm in order to hide his deepest secret, his attraction to the girl in the park, from Yousef

Eli had known Yousef since they were young boys, and he knew his friend's shortcomings. If he had to place a bet, he would have wagered it was probably Yousef who had been the one who kept the conversation going with the teacher, which made him late. Yousef loved having discussions about Torah.

"Come on, let's go" Eli said.

"Oy, I forgot one of my books. " Yousef looked down at the pile

10

of books in his hands,

"Leave it, you'll get it tomorrow. Let's get going, We want to have time to study don't we? At this rate we won't get there until it's dark."

"I'm sorry Eli. But, I want to read you an important story from this book. I was hoping we could take some time to discuss it. So, I can't leave without my book. I'll be right back. I promise not to get involved in any long conversations with anyone. If anyone tries to stop me to talk I will tell him that Eli Kaetzel the son of the rebbe is waiting and I can't keep him waiting any longer" Yousef winked.

"Stop joking and go and get the book already." Eli said

Eli shook his head. *Yousef should have been my father's son. He's so dedicated to studying. Sometimes I wish I were more like him.*

The two boys, Yousef and Eli, met as seven-year-old children in the yeshiva, their religious school. When they turned thirteen, their bar mitzvahs were a week apart. Even now, memories of Yousef and himself sitting on the hard chairs in the rabbi's study, trying hard to memorize the Torah portions they would recite for their bar mitzvahs, could make Eli smile. The three of them had been so young and so nervous. They knew that everyone in the entire shul would be watching them when they stood up to read their portion of the Torah. Everyone would know if they made a mistake. For Eli, the son of a very well-respected rebbe, making a mistake was just unacceptable. He had to study extra hard so as not to embarrass his father. Each boy would have his own special bar mitzvah day. Following the service, there would be a big celebration, because after all, on the day of their bar mitzvahs, they would become men within their community. It was a very important day indeed. And soon, very soon, they would be expected to take their places in the community as husbands and fathers.

"Come on, let's go," Eli said when he saw Yousef strolling

casually out of the building.

"All right, I'm coming." Yousef said, straightening his kippah, the little head covering he wore out of respect for God, and although he pinned it, was always sliding around on his fine hair. He put on his customary black hat and twisted his long payot around his finger, forming curls.

The two boys walked together toward the park, each carrying a pile of books, their identical, long black coats flapping in the warm breeze. The park was on the outskirts of their neighborhood. Dressed as they were, anyone could easily see they were very religious and came from the Jewish side of town. As they entered the park, a scrappy, young man with blond hair and a strong jawline, wearing a brown leather jacket, was leaning against a tree. He sneered at Eli and Yousef. Then he said loudly, "Dirty Jews."

Yousef and Eli shot each other a quick glance but kept walking. They were not permitted to start a fight even if someone insulted them. The Hasidic way was one of nonviolence. Since he was a child, Eli was taught that even if he were attacked, he was not to fight back. Eli's father would have been furious if Eli came home with evidence that he'd been fighting.

"Eli, perhaps we should leave. It's been getting more and more dangerous at this park for us. They used to whisper the insults about Jews under their breath. They are not hiding their hatred of our people anymore. Maybe we should just go home and stop coming here."

Eli's heart sank. Leave, now? He couldn't leave. He had to see her. He'd waited all week to see her. A wave of guilt came over him. He knew Yousef was right. They should probably go but he couldn't. "Yousef, don't worry so much. It will be all right. Come," Eli said smiling. "Sit down; it will be fine. You'll see. Now, let's eat."

Yousef gave Eli a look of concern, but he nodded and followed his friend.

The two boys sat on the bench under the tree and took off their coats. Underneath, they wore white shirts and black pants. They lay their piles of books on the bench beside them. Eli took out the grease-stained paper bag that held the knishes and handed it to Yousef. Yousef took one then gave the bag back to Eli. Eli bit into the knish and closed his eyes. It was delicious—the crispy dough, the soft potato insides. Taking a deep breath, he opened his eyes and glanced across the park and saw a group of girls playing kickball. Eli quickly lost interest in the food as his eyes searched frantically for the girl. Yousef was speaking to him, but he couldn't hear what Yousef was saying. *Where is she? Is she here?* And then he saw her. She was tall and slender with hair the color of rose gold that was blowing in the wind like the mane of a wild lion. As she was running after the ball, he felt dizzy with desire as he caught a glimpse of her thigh. It was as white as his mother's porcelain china, and in that instant, his heart skipped a beat. She laughed, and he heard her laughter twinkle in the spring air. He thought if the stars in the sky could talk that is how they would sound.

Eli's heart was beating loudly in his throat. He felt had never seen such a free-spirited creature, and her natural beauty left him breathless. Her body was slender and agile, not womanly. She had very small breasts, and her hips were straight rather than curvy. As he watched her playing kickball, he realized that she could run faster and kick harder than any of her teammates.

"What are you looking at?" Yousef asked. "You haven't heard a word I've said since we sat down."

"Nothing."

"Good, and make sure you are not looking over there." Yousef indicated toward the girls playing ball. "You know better than to be looking at them. That is forbidden."

Eli nodded as Yousef handed him his book on Talmud. "Come on, open your book, and let's do some studying," Yousef insisted.

Eli opened his book halfheartedly, then when he was sure Yousef was busy turning pages, he glanced back up at the girl.

"She's pretty, don't you think?" Eli asked. He hadn't meant to say it. Somehow he just blurted it out.

"Prost," Yousef said. "She's prost. Not at all refined."

"She's not prost, not vulgar or cheap. She's lovely and graceful."

"Eli, what's the matter with you? Have you lost your mind looking at a shiksa? Are you looking for trouble? If your father knew, he'd be furious."

"How do you know she's a shiksa?"

"It doesn't matter. She's not one of us. She's not Hasidic. So, she's not for you."

"I'm sorry, Yousef. You're right; we came here to study. And we should stick to strictly business, isn't that right?"

"No, of course not. We're best friends. We can talk about anything. So, since we are taking a little break from studying, I do have to tell you something," Yousef said. "My father wants me to meet this girl. Her name is Miriam Shulman. Do you know her?"

"She's a prospective bride for you, I assume?" Eli asked.

"Yes, why?"

"I met her."

"Your father was considering her for you?"

"Yes."

"And you said no?"

Eli nodded.

"Why? Is she ugly?"

"No, not at all. She's very pretty. And she was nice and refined," Eli said. "I am just not ready to get married, Yousef. It's not that there is anything wrong with Miriam Shulman. She's modest and from a good family. It's just me. I can't see myself as a husband and father yet."

"When, then, will you be ready, Eli? You're seventeen. You're a man. It's time to start your family. And I hate to say it, but if you were married and had a wife to go home to, you wouldn't be so tempted to look over there at the wrong girls."

"But the truth is, I would. I would be looking over there and thinking things I should not think. I would be sinning, committing adultery in my heart. And that's why I should not get married yet. It would be worse," Eli said, feeling a wave of guilt come over him. *Why can't I be more like Yousef? He should have been the son of a rebbe not me. He would have made my father proud.*

"What am I going to do with you? Oy, if you don't stop yearning for forbidden things, you are going to get into trouble for sure."

"Nu? So what should I do? I can't change the way I feel. I try, but I can't," Eli said.

"And it's worse for you because your papa is so important in the community. So, of course, everyone is watching everything you do. Everyone wants you to marry his daughter."

"Yes, I suppose that's true. Not only is my father a rebbe, but we are Kohanes. So, yes, all the old women want me to marry into their families."

"Maybe you should talk to a rabbi. Not your papa, of course. Maybe a rabbi could give you some advice that would help you."

"I doubt it. He'll tell me to follow the rules, and everything else will fall into place. I know because that's what my father tells everyone who comes to see him about their problems."

"Then maybe that's the answer. Maybe it's what you should do," Yousef said.

"Maybe it is. But I can't. I can't just marry some girl and spend the rest of my life with her. I'm just not ready."

They sat in silence for several moments. Yousef put the food down on the bench and stared out looking at nothing. Then he turned a serious face to Eli, and said, "You know that fellow who called us dirty Jews outside the gate to the park today?"

"Yes, what about him?"

"Well, that sort of thing has been happening to me more and more often. And I am quite sure that this Jew-hating sentiment is getting stronger in Germany."

"It'll pass. My father says it will pass."

"You believe him? You think he's right?" Yousef asked.

"I don't know. If it doesn't pass, what are they going to do to us?"

"Who knows? But it scares me. They hate us," Yousef said.

"My father says that pogroms have been going on since the beginning of time, and Jews have always been targeted. This is nothing new; they've always hated us."

"Does he say why?"

"He thinks it's because we are the chosen people."

"Chosen for what?" Yousef said sarcastically.

"I don't know. It's just the way it is, and the way it's always been."

"That doesn't make it right."

"No, it doesn't, but he says you can't change it either."

"How bad do you think it will get?"

"Probably some destruction of our homes and shops and, of course, looting. Then it will be over. It's always been this way for Jews. I hate it too, but I don't know what we can do to stop it," Eli said, shrugging his shoulders.

"I hope you're right. I hope it will be mild and then be over," Yousef answered. "Sometimes, I wish my family would leave

Germany but they won't."

"I know. I have felt the same way. I've talked to my father, but he too refuses to leave. He says Germany is as much our country as it is theirs. He was born here, and his father was born here. He says he won't be driven from his home by a bunch of hoodlums."

"The rioting and fighting that is going on in the streets terrifies me, and the rise of that National Socialist party isn't good for us at all," Yousef moaned.

"I agree with you. But what can we do? Our parents have all our family money. You and I have nothing. We can't possibly leave Germany without their consent. And so far, they aren't consenting. Anyway, if you could leave, where would you go?"

"I don't know." Yousef shook his head.

CHAPTER TWO

The boys studied the Talmud for an hour. The entire time, Eli watched the girls playing out of the corner of his eye. He felt his body tingle when the girl with the red-tinged, honey-colored hair laughed or called out to her friends in her singsong voice.

"It's getting late. We should be going home," Yousef said

Eli nodded in agreement. But he didn't want to leave. He wanted to stay and watch the girl for as long as possible. But he got up and gathered his books together, thinking about the girl as he did so. He heard her laugh and turned to look. When he did, one of his books fell behind the bench. Yousef was already halfway across the park heading toward the exit. Eli was in a hurry to catch up with him, so he never noticed the book that had fallen.

What am I thinking? Eli wondered after he and Yousef split up to go home. *She's beautiful, yes, but she's not a part of my world. If my parents had any idea that I was fascinated by her, my father would drop dead. He has always been so perfect. He finds it easy to follow all the rules. I don't know how he does it. Or how he ever got stuck with a son like me, a son who is restless and uncertain of his faith or his destiny. How can I be so different from my father? I don't think I will ever be able to lead our people the way my father does. He was born to be a rebbe. I wish I that I could be more like him. Everyone admires him. I must be a terrible disappointment to him. I keep putting off marriage. It's too bad Yousef wasn't his son. They could spend hours talking about the Torah, and Yousef would be happy and ready to marry a good Hasidic girl and give him plenty of grandchildren.* Eli continued walking. He felt guilty because he knew he should wipe, the girl with the golden red hair, from his mind, but all he could think about was seeing her again.

Eli walked into the nicely furnished apartment he shared with his parents and his sister, Avigale. His mother was at her usual workstation, the kitchen stove.

"Are you hungry?" she asked.

Eli nodded. He wasn't hungry, his mind was wrapped up in thoughts of the girl, but he knew that his mama felt her sole purpose in life was to feed him. So whenever she asked if he was hungry, he said yes, regardless of whether he was or not. He had to admit the house smelled heavenly.

"I'm going to get cleaned up before dinner," Eli said but he didn't move. He just stood there looking at his mother.

"Nu, what are you waiting for? Go already? Your papa will be here in less than a half hour. He'll want to eat," she said as she stirred the pot on the stove.

Eli studied his mother's face, and again he felt that familiar wave of guilt come over him. His parents were happy. They knew what was expected of them as a Hasidic husband and wife, and they had no problems living according to the laws. They were best friends. They took care of each other. *Why is that not enough for me? Why do I want passion and excitement? Why can I not be satisfied with a good and wholesome life?*

"Eli, go, get cleaned up. Why are you standing there just looking at me?" his mother said, looking at him with a puzzled expression on her face.

Eli nodded. "Yes, Mama."

CHAPTER THREE

Gretchen, the girl in the park with the strawberry-blonde hair, was walking with her friends toward the exit of the park. They weren't good friends, just girls she knew from school who had asked her to play kickball with them when they were short a team member. She hardly had time for friendships; she was too busy studying and taking care of things around the house. Her mother had passed away, and her father was working, so she had a lot of responsibilities at home. As the girls headed toward the exit they passed the bench where Eli and Yousef had been studying. Gretchen glanced over and saw the book. She didn't want to mention it to the others. So as they left the park she turned to them and said, "I am going to go back and run to the washroom. You girls go on."

"Are you sure? I can go with you?" One of the others said.

"Of course, I'm sure. I'll be fine. You head on home."

"All right, then"

Gretchen went into the bathroom and waited until she was sure the others were long gone. Then she walked toward the bench where she had spotted the book. She'd been watching the two boys for the last three Tuesdays as they sat on the bench. She knew one of them had been staring at her the entire time she was playing kickball, and she was intrigued because this was the third time she'd seen them. *They were Hasidic Jews*, she thought, *with their long, black coats and tall, black hats*. From their clothing, she knew they were a part of the religious Jewish community, which, for Gretchen and her friends, had always been shrouded in mystery.

Most of the people she knew were afraid of the Jews. There were rumors that Jews kidnapped Christian babies and used their blood to make the matzos they ate. But Gretchen's father, who was a professor of mathematics at the university and open-minded, said this was nothing but propaganda and was not to be believed.

"I'll tell my friends that this is silly propaganda, and it is just not true," Gretchen told her father.

But he shook his head. "Just leave it alone. Don't declare yourself. It will all be over soon. It's best if you just ignore it."

She picked up the book, knowing that one of the two Jewish boys had left it there. All of her friends had left the park. She was alone and knew she should get home, but she took a moment to sit down and look inside the book. The book was not written in German. In fact, the letters didn't look like any she'd ever seen before. She scanned through the pages until she got to the back where written in large black letters it said in German, "If found, please return this book to Eli Kaetzel at 1627 Augsburger Strabe. You will receive a reward for your kindness."

A reward? Well, Papa and I could use any extra money we can get our hands on. If we had a little extra, I might be able to buy something nice for Papa. Some cake perhaps.

Gretchen tucked the book under her arm and headed for the address written inside. She knew it would be located within the Jewish community, and although her father had tried to convince her that the scary horror stories she had heard from her friends and neighbors were untrue, she was still a little fearful of entering the Jewish sector of town. However, she knew that her father would be happy to have the reward money she would get for returning the book. The money would allow them to buy some extra food this month.

She mustered all her courage and entered the Jewish sector. Looking around her, Gretchen saw Jewish-owned shops standing right beside those of their non-Jewish neighbors. Gretchen passed the Jewish old people's home and the school for Jewish boys. Then she turned down Sundgauer Strausse and walked until she crossed the street on to Rathus. She walked quickly past the city hall then veered right on to Klosterter Strausse. She knew that her father wouldn't be home for at least an hour. He had department meetings at the university on Tuesday nights.

The streets were filled with people dressed in what she knew to be the clothing worn by religious Jews. Some of the men had long, curly sideburns and beards. Some wore fedoras, and some wore tall, black hats, while other men wore only skull caps. Women hurried along the busy streets wearing long, full skirts, with long-sleeved blouses, their heads covered by scarves. Her heart raced a little, and a bead of sweat formed on her brow. Two men walked past her wearing fur hats; they were engrossed in conversation, not seeming to notice her. These people looked very different from the people she knew, and she felt odd and out of place walking all alone in their neighborhood. Could her father have been wrong? Might they be dangerous to non-Jews? She shuddered at the thought but kept walking until she found the address written inside the book.

As she approached the address that was written inside the book, she noticed the window shades were open. She could not help but catch a quick glance inside the dining room as she walked to the front door. A young girl with her head uncovered was carrying plates to a table. *What pretty hair she has. I wonder if it bothers her to cover it all the time? If I had such thick, wavy hair, I would want to show it off.*

But then she recalled that she'd seen young girls with their heads uncovered. It must only be the old ones or maybe just the married women who covered their heads. Gretchen mustered her courage and knocked on the door. It opened. There he stood, the boy from the park. He wore no hat; only a small, round skullcap covered his thick, black, wavy hair. He was beardless, but his sideburns were a single, long curl that looked strange to her. Still, even with the sideburns, there was no denying that he was handsome. More handsome than any man she knew, with his deep- coal-black eyes in which she was sure she saw both wisdom and tenderness.

Eli felt as if he were dreaming. Or as if he were experiencing some sort of a modern-day miracle. So many times he'd fantasized that he would somehow open his door, and the girl with the rosy, golden hair would be there. And now, here she was. Was it possible? Was this really real? His heart fluttered. She was even more beautiful close-up than she'd been when he'd admired her from a far.

Through the open door she saw a man who looked ancient, with salt-and-pepper hair, a long, graying beard, and wearing black pants with suspenders, walk into the dining room. He kissed the top of his daughter's head and took his place at the head of the table.

Eli was at a loss for words. He could hardly breathe. There were so many things he longed to say. So many things she should know. If he could speak freely he would tell her how he'd thought of nothing else but her since the first time he'd seen her. He would tell her that she was the most beautiful, graceful creature he'd ever . . .

I'm here because you left this in the park, and I found it when I was leaving." Gretchen cleared her throat and handed him the book.

"Oh," he said, taking the book and not knowing what else to say, but not wanting to let her go. "Thank goodness you found it. And thank you for bringing it to me."

She had forgotten the reward. All she could think of was that he was beyond handsome, with his dark, soulful eyes, and his voice was so soft and deep. *What more can I say to him? I've given him the book. I should go.* But her feet felt glued to the ground. She couldn't move. His eyes held her captive. *I could get lost in his eyes, and stay there forever.* But then the older man with the beard came to the door.

He said something to the boy in a language that sounded a lot like German, but it wasn't German. Gretchen thought she understood a few words, but she wasn't sure. Her father had told her about that language, and she had sometimes overheard it spoken when the Jews passed her on the street. *Yiddish,* she thought. *The language of the very religious Jews.*

"Nothing is going on here, Papa," the boy answered his father in German. "This nice young lady found my Talmud book. I accidentally left it in the park where Yousef and I were studying."

"Give it to me, Eli," his father said, speaking half in German, half in Yiddish. The boy handed the book to his father, who wiped it with a white-and-black shawl that he wore around his shoulders and then kissed it. Turning to the girl at the door, Eli's father said in German in a kind voice, "Thank you so much for returning my son's book. We very much appreciate your kindness." The old man smiled and then added, " Goodbye now. Have a safe evening." Softly, he closed the door.

A feeling of wild excitement passed through Gretchen. She'd never felt this way about anyone before. This boy was mesmerizing. His eyes were as dark as coal, yet they were kind and gentle. His lips were full and soft, and she wondered what it might feel like to kiss him. Turning the corner, Gretchen realized it was getting dark. She began to walk as quickly as she could out of the area. The street was quiet, overly quiet. There were no cars on the road, no honking, no people outside. Just the night settling in. An owl hooted, sending a disturbing signal to all other night creatures.

Gretchen looked around her. *I don't feel comfortable here in this neighborhood at all, I am an obvious outsider. Who knows if those old wives' tales are true? My father is a scholar, but he doesn't know everything. He just thinks he does. And a lot of people say the Jews are dangerous. Why would they say it if there weren't some truth to it? That old man at the house looked so scary with his long, gray beard, and he was so mean.* Gretchen shivered. She heard footsteps behind her. Her heart began to race as her feet took flight. She was running as fast as she could.

"Wait!"

Gretchen heard a man's voice behind her. It wasn't the voice of an old man. It was the voice of a young man. She ran faster. But within minutes, her pursuer caught up with her.

"Wait. Please, I have something for you," the young Jewish man said. He stood beside her, breathing heavily from the effort of running. Gretchen stopped and turned. She looked up into his eyes. It was him. *Oh my gosh,* she thought. *It's him.*

She bent over just a little in order to catch her breath.

"I'm sorry. I didn't mean to startle you," he said, looking down at the ground, not meeting her eyes. "But you certainly do run fast."

She was still trying to catch her breath. "I suppose I do."

"I owe you this," he said, handing her a bunch of change in a cloth pouch. "I promised a reward if my book was lost and returned. Here is the reward money."

"Oh, thank you," Gretchen said, taking the money. She smiled remembering that there had been the promise of a reward. But, her thoughts were only of the man and how he had left her spellbound.

She waited for him to speak.

Eli stood still for several moments not knowing what to do or say next. Then Gretchen began to walk away. He knew if he did not speak, he would never have the opportunity to speak to her again. She was not a part of his world, and within the next few seconds, she would be out of his life and gone forever. It was forbidden for him to talk to girls. Even more forbidden to talk to girls who were not Jewish. But something inside Eli was nudging him hard. By nature, he was not a rule breaker. However, he could not let her go. Not now. Not yet, so he took a step out of his well-defined life and said, "It's getting dark outside. Perhaps I should walk you home. I would like to ensure your safety."

Gretchen looked intently at him, studying him, trying to understand him and his ways. He was handsome; that was for certain, and he certainly was different from anyone she ever knew. But what she found very odd was that she was not afraid of him at all. Something inside her wanted to know more about him, more about his strange clothing and his odd lifestyle.

"Yes," she stammered. "I would be grateful to you if you would accompany me home. I was feeling a little uneasy out in the darkness, being alone and all." Her words sounded clumsy even to her own ears.

"Of course," he said without hesitation. Even though he knew what he was doing was out of character for him. *I am talking to a girl,* he thought. *A shiksa. My father would die if he knew. And yet, my whole body is tingling. My heart is fluttering. What is this odd and magnificent feeling? It feels a little like becoming lost in prayer. It's ecstasy. Hashem, forgive me for my impudence. I don't understand what is happening to me. I am so filled with emotions that I cannot explain.*

"I'm Gretchen Schmidt," the girl said.

"Eli Kaetzel."

As they walked through the streets, Eli noticed that a few of his neighbors were peering out of their windows. By tomorrow, his father would have a full report of the walk his son had taken with a shiksa through their little sector of town. The neighbors would tell him everything and, of course, embellish it. They always did. His father was going to be very angry with him; he knew that. Once the news spread that he was seen walking down the street with a shiksa, it was going to be difficult for his father to arrange a match for him. But at that moment in time, with the sun setting behind the buildings casting golden rays on the earth, Eli Kaetzel didn't care about anything. He was walking on concrete, but it felt like he was walking on air. *Perhaps she's Jewish,* he thought. *Perhaps she could be my b'sheirt. My one true love. Wouldn't that be something wonderful?*

"What language is that book written in, the book I brought back to you? I noticed it wasn't German," Gretchen asked.

"Aramaic. It's a text on the Talmud."

"Talmud?"

"It's a sacred book. It's something I study.

"What is it exactly? A Jewish book?"

"Yes, a Jewish book." He smiled ruefully. *She's not Jewish,* he thought, his heart sinking in his chest like a hunk of lead. "A religious text."

"Like the Bible?"

"In a way. I suppose you could say that," he said, looking down at her. She was a full head shorter. Gretchen smiled. When she did, he noticed a sprinkle of tiny freckles under her bright blue eyes.

"I guess you speak two languages, then?"

"Oh no. I speak far more than two. I speak Hebrew and Yiddish. Of course, I speak German. And my father's brother lives in Poland, so when he brings his family to visit we speak a mixture of Polish and Yiddish. But the Talmud is written in both ancient Hebrew and the language I just mentioned, Aramaic."

"My father would find you fascinating," Gretchen said, and then she smiled.

"Oh?" he said. "I'm not so sure. I wonder what he would think of you walking and talking with a Jewish man."

"We are not doing anything wrong, so I don't know why it would be something he would disapprove of."

"Then somehow you don't know how non-Jews feel about Jews, do you?" There was a note of sad cynicism in his voice.

She avoided answering. His question made her uncomfortable. She was quite well aware of the hatred of Jewish people. The dislike of Jews was no secret among her friends. They told jokes about the horrible, moneygrubbing Jews. They talked about a Jew-free Germany. And of course, there were the scary rumors too. But she couldn't bring herself to discuss any of this with him. He didn't press the question, and they walked without speaking for several minutes. Then, to break the silence, she asked, "What is the language that you speak daily, German? Because your German is perfect."

"Oh, thank you. Yes, I speak German when I leave my neighborhood for any reason at all, but when I am at home, or in our little Jewish sector of town, it's always Yiddish. We believe that Yiddish is the language of God. So, when I want to speak to God, I speak in Yiddish."

"If you say so." She shook her head.

"You don't believe that, do you?"

"When it comes to God and religion, I don't know what I believe. All I know is that religion causes problems between people."

"Hmmm. So you think it's a bad thing, then?"

"Yes, I do." She nodded. "I don't believe in all that stuff. I guess I don't even really believe in God. I can't believe in anything I can't see."

"That's where faith comes in."

"Well, I don't have faith in any kind of a supreme being."

"Oh?"

"No, I don't," she said, crossing her arms over her chest. "I've seen far too much evil in the world to believe there is a God. And anyway, if there happens to be one, he just might be the cruelest entity of all."

"You're so angry and bitter. How old are you? You look so young."

"I'm old enough."

"And what age is that exactly?"

"Sixteen."

"Well, you are still very young."

"Don't act like such a sage. You can't be much older."

"I'm not." He smiled looking down at her. "It's just hard to understand why someone so young could be so cynical."

"My mother died when I was born. I never knew her. What kind of God does that? What kind of God leaves a child without a mother? You tell me."

"I am sorry about your mother."

She shrugged, trying not to cry. "Well, like I said, I never really knew her, so I never felt the loss. Not directly, anyway. I had a good enough childhood, even though my father raised me alone. He's a very special man."

"But a girl needs a mother. There is so much a father would not know how to teach a daughter."

"My father did all right. He tried his best." Tears were forming in the corners of her eyes. "However, since you're a religious man, I have a question for you." A single tear slid down her cheek.

"I am not sure I have an answer, but I'll do my best."

"Well . . . if there really is a God, and you believe there is, don't you?"

"Yes, I do."

"Then tell me, wise-and-brilliant Eli Kaetzel, if there is a God, and he is powerful, then how could he let a mother die when she still had a young child to raise? A helpless, little girl who will someday need advice from her mother? A little girl who's body will someday change into that of a woman. And when it does she will not understand what is happening to her but be too embarrassed to talk to her father about it? So, for three months, she is quite sure she is dying until finally her aunt comes to visit, and she has a chance to tell her aunt that she is bleeding from her most private parts. And finally, her aunt explains? What kind of a God leaves a child with such uncertainty?"

Eli hesitated. He could hear the pain in her voice. He wished he had a magic wand that could bring her mother back. But he didn't. All he had was the wisdom that was in his heart. "She loves you. Your mother does. She watches over you, Gretchen. And I believe she is always with you. She may not be alive, but she watches over you." He saw that she was crying. It was forbidden for him to touch her. But he wiped a tear from her cheek.

"Do you?" I've often tried to talk to her when I lay in bed before going to sleep. But I never feel that she is with me."

"But she is. And some day you will know it."

"You're so sure of this."

"I am," he said.

She looked up at him, her eyes illuminated with tears, and then she continued. "I still think of my mother often. Not as much as I did as a child, but often. I have a picture of her. That's all I have. And I have never told anyone this, but sometimes, when I am alone, I stare at that picture, and I wonder what she would have been like had I known her. Was she kind? Was she smart? I often wonder. Anyway, my father says I look like her, but I don't think so."

"If you look like her then she must have been very beautiful," Eli said surprised at his own moxie. *What nerve I have*, he thought.

Gretchen let out a short laugh—an embarrassed and self-conscious laugh. "Beautiful, me? That's funny," she said.

"I mean it." His voice cracked.

"I like your necklace," she said trying to change the subject quickly.

His hand went up to touch the Star of David that hung loosely around his neck. "Oh, this is a Star of David," he said. "Would you like to know an interesting fact about the Star of David?"

"Yes, sure. Why not?"

"Well, every single letter that is in the Hebrew alphabet is contained within this Star of David."

"Really?"

"Yes."

"How is that possible?"

"Do you have a pencil and paper? If you do, I will show you."

"I have a pencil." She reached in her purse and took it out.

He remembered that he had a note that Yousef had left for him in class the day before. It was nothing important, just a reminder to tell his mother to pack the knishes. He pulled the paper out of his pants pocket. He took the pencil.

Leaning against the side of a building, he began to draw all the letters, explaining how each one fit into the Star of David. By the time he had finished, she was smiling.

"That's rather clever," she said.

"Oh, I don't know about clever. It's important."

She nodded, and they began to walk again. They were silent for a while then she asked, "You said that book that I found is a book about the Talmud. I was just wondering, is the Talmud the same as the Kabbalah?"

He stopped walking and turned to look at her. "How do you know of Kabbalah? Are you Jewish?" A glimmer of hope flashed through him. Could he have been wrong?

"No, I'm not. But my father's a professor, and since I am his only child, he's always teaching me things."

"And your father studies Kabbalah?" he said, disappointed that she wasn't Jewish, even though he knew when he asked the chances were slim.

"I'm not sure that he studies it. Or how much he knows about it. But he told me that it's a mystical text that is studied by religious Jews. Men only. Is that true?"

"Yes, actually. He is right."

"Why only men?"

"It's the way we have always done it. Women raise the children, men study."

"I suppose it's the same for us in many ways. Women are expected to take care of the home and children. It's not as important for a woman to learn as it is for a man. However, I think that's rather sad. I mean, women are as smart as men . . . some may be even smarter. And yet because we are women our intelligence is overlooked," she said.

"Oh, I believe that wholeheartedly. I know that women are definitely smarter. They are born knowing all the secrets of the universe, so they actually have no need for study. You see, God gives that gift to them so that they are able to naturally become mothers and instinctively know what to do to care for a child. Their purpose in life, which is to bring forth life, is the highest purpose of all. They must know a great deal in order to raise a child properly. And the bringing up of children is the most important thing in the world. So perhaps you could say that, in many ways, women are superior. They create life, with God's help, of course. But perhaps that makes them closer to God. What do you think?"

"Truthfully, I think that you have a rather strange way of looking at things. But I do have to admit you're interesting. I've never talked to anyone who thought the way that you do."

"You have never met a religious Jew before?"

"I've seen people on the streets who wear those same long sideburns and big hats like you do. But I've never talked to any of them. They keep to themselves."

"Yes, you're right. They do. It's part of the way we live and the way we believe."

"You believe that you should keep to yourselves and not associate with non-Jews? Do you think that's perhaps why people dislike Jews?"

"It's possible. But we believe that it is best for our people to stick with their own kind. Do you know what I mean? We believe that Jews should marry other Jews. And we should stay in our own neighborhoods, around people who understand our customs. You see, we are afraid that if we assimilate into society we will lose the purity of our people." He shrugged, not sure if he believed that this was right.

"That sounds like the Nazi Party to me. It sounds like the propaganda I heard when I was in the Bund."

"The Bund?"

"Yes, the Hitler Youth group for girls."

"You were in that group?"

34

"I was. I didn't know any better when I joined. And besides, it's required. But I didn't say I agreed with their teachings. All I said is that I heard them. And that all this nonsense of keeping races pure, in my opinion, is just that: nonsense. Thinking in this way gives people a reason to hate each other rather than bringing people together. Whether they are Nazi's or Jews." She sneered.

He quickly glanced at her. Realizing that he hurt her feelings, he added boldly, "But . . . I am really glad that you found my book and were kind enough to bring it back to me. I've really enjoyed talking to you. I guess I am saying that I am very happy that we met. In fact, you are quite different from anyone I have ever talked with. However, I have to admit that I haven't had a conversation with a girl before. And . . . I'm sorry if I offended you. I didn't mean to."

There were several moments of silence. Then Gretchen said, "It's all right. I am glad we can talk about these things." She hesitated, then she smiled and continued. "You've never talked to a girl? Really? That's very odd."

"Not the way we are talking now. I am sure you would find it odd. But it's our way. I have spoken with girls, but always with other people around. I have never been alone with a female and talked to her the way we have spoken today. And quite frankly, I probably won't be alone again with a girl until I get married. Then I will be allowed to talk to my wife. But our conversations will be mostly about our children and our home. Women don't have intellectual conversations with men."

"That's so strange, Eli."

She said my name, he thought, and he felt a tingle run from his head to his toes. "Well, let's just say that this walk has been most interesting. Most interesting indeed," he said. Then he added, shaking his head, "And perhaps a little dangerous."

"You sound like our short walk together was something bad for you. Dangerous? Why? Do you really feel that I am dangerous?" She let out a laugh.

"Time will tell," he said. "I don't know . . ."

"You don't know if you're glad you met me?" She was shocked. "I've never had a boy say he wasn't sure if he was glad he met me. I guess I am insulted. Well, you are certainly a strange fellow, aren't you?"

He shrugged. "I suppose to you, I am." *You are so forbidden, and I am so attracted to you. I've never been attracted to any of the girls my father has introduced me to.* He stopped walking and looked down at her. Then he smiled and said, "Actually, I cannot deny it. I am very happy to have met you, Gretchen."

"I'm glad to have met you too, Eli Kaetzel. You intrigue me."

Gretchen was bold and outspoken. She was exciting, intelligent, and beautiful. He had to admit he was captivated.

They arrived at the door to a tall apartment building in a middle-income area. The homes were modest but well kept. The streets were clean, and unlike the poorer neighborhoods, there was no garbage on the walkways.

"I live here. In this building," Gretchen said. "Thank you for walking me home."

"Thank you for bringing my book back to me," he said. She began to walk up the stairs. His heart raced. He knew if he didn't say something she would disappear behind the door of her building and back into her world. Chances were that he would never see her again. He knew he should let her go. But he couldn't. He wanted to see her again, and his longing was stronger than his desire to follow the rules. He was terrified of his willingness to break the rules, to commit what his father would surely see as a sin. It took all the courage he could muster, for even as he said the words, he could hear his father grunting in disapproval in the background.

"Maybe we could see each other again? Maybe we could talk like this again? Perhaps, sometime?" He cringed as he heard his own voice. How foolish he sounded, and how wrong it all was. Yet, his heart thundered in his chest as he waited for her answer. Hoping she wouldn't say no, yet knowing it would be best if she did.

She turned to look up at him. Then she smiled. "I would like that. How about after school on Friday? I get out at four."

"Friday is the Sabbath. I can't. I'm sorry." He suddenly felt a wave of guilt. What was he doing? What was he thinking? He should turn and go. Run away as if he had to, but get away from these forbidden feelings he was having.

"I should go," he said, but she gave him a big smile, and his heart melted.

"How about Monday, then?" she asked.

"Yes, Monday," he heard himself answer. It was as if he had stepped outside of his body and was observing himself. "Yes, Monday," he repeated. "But where shall we meet? I am afraid that the park is too dangerous for us."

"I know of an abandoned warehouse on the edge of town. Do you know where I mean?"

"Yes, actually I do. You mean the old textile warehouse? It's been empty for years"

"Yes." She nodded "We used to play there as children. Four o'clock at the warehouse? I'll meet you?"

"Yes." He nodded, swallowing hard, knowing it was wrong yet unable to stop himself.

"Good. Well, I'll see you then," she said and walked into the building. The door closed quietly behind her.

CHAPTER FOUR

Eli couldn't believe what he'd done. As he walked home, he imagined his father's face wearing a mask of disapproval. It was bad enough he'd rejected every one of the prospective brides his father had introduced him to, including Sarah Kaufman. She was the daughter of a Kohane, a high priest in the Jewish religion. Eli also came from a long line of Kohanes. He knew that his father would have been so proud if Eli had chosen Sarah as his wife. But like all the others, she was tongue-tied in Eli's presence, afraid to speak directly to him. She was a sweet girl, and pretty too, and he knew she was doing what she had been taught to do. She was trying very hard to please him.

But Eli felt strange in her presence, as he did with all those girls. It was as if he were hiring a servant rather than searching for a life partner. How wonderful it would be to have a wife with whom he might talk about anything. Perhaps even the Torah, although that would be very radical.

There was something about Gretchen that made him believe that if he knew her better, they could discuss all matters easily. She was not afraid of him. Her bright blue eyes sparkled with intelligence, and he somehow felt that she could hold her own if she were given an opportunity to read holy books. The very idea filled him with a pang of fear. If his father had the slightest inkling of what Eli was thinking, then Eli would never outlive the old man's anger.

It was growing darker by the minute. Eli turned the corner on his way back to his neighborhood only to run into a group of boys wearing leather jackets, huddled in an alleyway. A spasm of fear struck Eli like a bolt of lightning. He wasn't a small man, and unlike most of the other yeshiva boys, he always engaged in plenty of physical activities. But he had never been involved in a fistfight. To make matters worse, there were five of them and one of him.

As he walked along, he noticed his thin wrists. Food was so expensive these days that there never seemed to be enough. His mother didn't let on that she was eating less to ensure that Eli and his father always had a larger portion. But Eli knew that she would rather feed her family than take care of herself, and he wouldn't take her share. So, he always left the table hungry, claiming he couldn't eat another bite. His sister too, tried to give him some of hers, declaring that she didn't need as much. He knew she was only trying to help him, but he always refused. Eli continued to walk, trying not to hurry, in the hope that the boys would ignore him.

But he knew better.

Since January, when that strange little man, Adolf Hitler, with his angry voice and peculiar-looking mustache, began trying to become chancellor of Germany, anti-Semitism had grown like a giant octopus, its tentacles reaching out and squeezing every inch of Germany. Not that the hatred of Jews was ever nonexistent, but now it was growing more and more acceptable to hate Jews openly. Every time Eli tried to discuss leaving Germany with his father, his father silenced him.

"I'm not going to run away," his father said. "I am as German as they are. I was born here. My father was born here. And his father before him."

His father refused to discuss this Adolf Hitler. The old rebbe ignored Hitler's frightening speeches about the Jews. When Eli insisted that his father open his eyes before it was too late and that he consider moving the family out of Germany, the rebbe's face turned scarlet. He slammed his fist on the table, turned to his son, and banned Eli from saying the name "Adolf Hitler" in their home ever again.

"As long as I am alive you will not utter that man's name in our home. You will never suggest that we leave Germany again. Do you understand me?"

Eli was angry with his father, but he did not dare raise his voice to him. When the old rebbe was angry, Eli thought he looked like Moses coming down from Mount Sinai.

As he walked along, trying not to hear the thugs coming up behind him, Eli was forced out of his thoughts and back into the present moment. One of the thugs called out to him, "Hey, kike!"

Eli felt his heartbeat quicken. His breath grew shallow, but he kept walking. A bead of sweat trickled down his face, and he shivered lightly. There were several of them, but it was dark, and he wasn't sure how many. If he turned to look at them long enough to count them, they would know he was aware of them and that he was afraid. He knew from past experience when animals smelled fear, they attacked.

"What's with the curls on the side of your face? You a faggot? Are you some kind of a little girl? You sure look like one to me," one of the boys said. The rest of them let out hearty laughter.

Eli picked up speed. But like dogs, the thugs sensed his fear. They came out from the darkness of the alleyway and began to circle him. He dared not run. If he did, he knew that whatever they did to him would be worse.

"Eric, take your knife and cut off those curls. I want them for my collection of Jew stuff," said a boy who seemed to be the leader.

Eric took a knife out of his pocket and approached Eli. Eli had been taught never to fight. No matter what was said to him, he was to be passive. However, at that moment, Eli's instincts took over, and he smacked the knife out of the boy's hand. He pushed his way through the group of angry, red-faced boys hungry for his blood.

For a second, he almost believed they were going to let him go. He walked several steps ahead, and they did not pursue him. Every nerve in his body wanted to take flight and run as fast as he could, but he dared not.

Walk, he told himself, but his feet seemed unable to move quickly enough to satisfy his mind. His body was trembling with fear.

Could it be possible that they would let him get away this easily? This painlessly? He began to thank God. But then the leader said in a loud bellowing voice, "Get him."

In an instant, five strong young boys were upon him. He punched and kicked, but there were too many of them. Although they were kicking him and punching him, Eli strangely felt no pain. He was too fired up with anger. Then Eric, the leader's right-hand man, grabbed Eli's head and slammed it hard on the concrete. This time the blow was so harsh that Eli felt a sharp and unbearable pain shoot through his entire body. His vision blurred. He passed out.

When Eli awakened, he was covered in blood. His face was sore, and his head ached. He reached up to touch his bruised cheek and found that his sideburns were gone. They had been cut. Looking across the lawn he saw them. His hat had been hurled across the grass, and his coat was torn. When he tried to sit up, he was dizzy, and a strong bout of nausea overcame him. He curled over and vomited.

Afterward, he forced himself to stand up. Eli gathered his hat and his payot, which he put into his pants pocket. Then slowly, he began walking home. He'd never felt so much pain. Every inch of his body hurt. But what worried him the most was what his father would say when he saw him. Eli had run out of his house to walk the girl home. A non-Jewish girl, and this was what happened. His father would be furious with him. That was for certain. He would blame Eli for having contact with people outside of their neighborhood. And right now, Eli was thinking that perhaps his father was right.

But despite what just happened, Eli still couldn't help wanting to know more about Gretchen. What an interesting girl she was. He finally met a girl who was not in awe of him just because he was a man, and his father was the rebbe. She was not only ravishingly beautiful, but she was smart and wanted to learn about things other than cooking and childcare. According to every teacher he ever had, that was wrong for a woman. But it enticed him.

Eli knew that even though he'd been beaten up, and it was probably a sign that he was on the wrong path, he would still show up for his meeting with Gretchen. Oddly enough, when he thought about her, his limbs tingled with pleasure, and all the pain in his body disappeared.

Oh, what power the human mind possesses, he thought smiling.

On his way home he stopped at the bathroom in the park to wash away the blood. He knew his parents would be upset when they saw him. He did the best he could, but there was no hiding that he had been beaten, and his payot had been cut.

"What happened to you?" his mother said when he walked into the house.

"I'm all right," Eli answered.

"You're not all right. Look at you! Oy vey! You're bruised and bleeding. Asher, come quickly. Eli has been hurt," his mother yelled to his father who was in his study in the back of the house.

"I'm coming, Chenya," his father answered. Slowly, the rebbe walked into the room. When he saw his son, he shook his head. "You went out after that shiksa, didn't you? What happened? Did her father or brother beat you up?"

"No."

"I am sure you know that I was disappointed that you went out of the house after her. I called for you to come back. Didn't you hear me?"

"I wrote inside my book that if it were ever lost, I would reward the person who returned it. I wanted to give her the reward money that I promised."

"You were gone a lot longer than the five minutes it should have taken you. You could have handed her the money and come right back inside, but you didn't. You went somewhere."

"Papa, it's dangerous for a girl to walk home alone in the dark. She did me a favor returning my very precious and expensive book. I thought that walking her home was the least I could do."

The old rebbe studied his son. For several moments he didn't speak. Then he put his arms around Eli and held him for a long time. "Thanks be to Hasheem that you are alive," he whispered.

"Yes, Father," Eli said, thinking that his father's reaction was not what he expected. He thought his father would be angry, but he seemed frightened. "Stay away from the goyim, Eli. You are going to get into trouble. Look what happened to you. Need I say more? Your cheek is cut; your eyes are bloodshot. They cut off your payot. I hope this is over with you and that shiksa now. You're a smart boy, so I know you are not going to see her again, are you?"

"No, Papa," Eli lied and felt a wave of guilt come over him. He could feel the power of his father's love for him. And he wished he could be the son his father deserved. But regardless of what happened, Eli knew he would not stop seeing Gretchen, the girl who wasn't afraid to speak to him.

"See to it that you don't ever talk to that girl again or any other shiksas. Do you understand me?"

"I understand you, Father," Eli said.

CHAPTER FIVE

That night, as Eli lay in bed, he overheard his parents talking in their room.

"It's time he should be married, Chenya. He's going to get into trouble as sure as I am standing here. Shiksas are trouble, and one of them has her sinful eye on our son. We have to find him a wife, so his natural desires don't take over and get him involved in something he shouldn't be involved in. He's getting too old to be without a wife."

"But he doesn't accept any of the girls you bring. He is so stubborn."

"I don't care what he wants anymore. He will do as I say. I know what is best for that boy. After all, he is my son."

"You are going to force him to marry?"

"I am. I am going to force him because it is what is best for him. And I know the girl that I will choose as his wife."

CHAPTER SIX

Rebecca Kesselman was peeling potatoes when her father came home early from the shul. He smiled at her.

"Hello, Tate," she said, happy as always to see him. She still called him Tate, her childhood name for him.

"Hello, my angel," he said. "Where is your mother?"

"She went to the butcher shop."

"Nu, so what are you cooking?"

"A potato kugel. Mama is going to try and get some chicken fat to make chopped liver. Are you hungry? We have a small piece of strudel that you could have. It would hold you until dinner."

"You didn't eat your piece last night. I saw."

"I saved it for you, Tate. You love sweets. I know this about you, and I don't care much for them."

"What a good daughter you are. I have good news for you. I was going to tell your mother first, but since she isn't home, I'll tell you."

Rebecca pulled the plate with the small piece of strudel out of the pantry and took a fork from the cabinet. She set them both down in front of her father. "You want some tea?"

"No, no, this is plenty good," her father said as he lifted a fork full of the strudel.

"Well, Tate . . . tell me. What's the news?"

"Patience, my child." He laughed.

"Come on, Tate . . ."

"All right. All right. Sit, I'll tell you."

As an unmarried woman, Rebecca was not required to cover her head. But she covered it most of the time anyway. Tonight, while she was cooking, her scarf fell back, and several strands of her light-blonde hair fell out. She pushed them back under her scarf and sat on the stool beside her father. "Tell me, please?" She smiled at him.

"You have been chosen to be a bride. Eli Kaetzel, Rabbi Kaetzel's only son, is interested in you, my beautiful daughter."

Rebecca turned as white as the dove outside her window. This was not good news at all. She wanted to be happy. She really did. But she was only fifteen, and she had hoped that her father wouldn't find her a match for another year. But, of course, if the boy was considered a good match, and this one was, then fifteen was a perfect age. If a girl wanted to be respectable, she should marry by seventeen. But Rebecca loved her home, her parents, and her sweet little sister. If she got married, she could no longer live with her family. She would have to move in with his. She didn't want to leave her home, not yet. She wanted to wait as long as possible. She looked at her father and for his sake, tried to look happy.

"You are not pleased?" he asked.

She nodded. "I am, Tate. I am," she said, but tears began to well in the corners of her eyes.

"How about you meet him, and then we decide? How does that sound? If you don't like him, you will refuse."

Her father was such a kind and good man. He would never force her, but she loved her father so much that she would never want to disappoint him. So if he liked this boy, Eli, she would marry him. She

47

would do what was expected of her. She always did what was required. For as long as she could remember, Rebecca knew the day would come when her marriage would be arranged. And because she was a Kohane, she was a good catch. She would be sought after by many fathers of prospective chazens, grooms. It was an honor for a man to marry his son off to the daughter of a Kohane, a high priest of the Jewish faith.

Up until now, her father had rejected all possible suitors, and she began to hope that she could spend one more year as a single girl in the warm, protective home of her parents. But the rebbe's son was not just a good match—it was probably the best match any girl could hope for. Looking into her father's eyes, Rebecca knew that he was excited about the possibility of her marriage to the rebbe's son. She would go along with his choice even though the thought of getting married and leaving her family made her sick to her stomach.

"I'll do as you say, Tate. Whatever you decide."

"You've always been such a good girl. Like I said before, we won't make any quick decisions. We'll wait until you meet him, then we'll decide together."

She nodded. "Yes."

After her father finished his small piece of strudel, he got up and left the room.

"I'm going to lie down for a little while before dinner."

"Go on, Tate," Rebecca said, and she mustered a wry smile. But as soon as she was alone in the kitchen, tears fell down her cheeks. *A husband. I don't want to get married. I wish I could just stay a little girl forever. I don't know anything about this boy. He could be fat; he could be ugly or mean. But the worst of it is, once I am married, I can never return to my old way of life.*

Rebecca couldn't bear the news of this possible match all alone. She longed to speak to someone she could trust, someone she could share her honest feelings with. She walked out of her family's apartment and dashed up the stairs to the flat where her best friend, Esther, lived. She knocked on the door and tried to catch her breath before Esther's mother opened it.

"Rivka!" Esther's mother called Rebecca by her Hebrew name. "You look disheveled. Nu? What's wrong?"

"Nothing." Rebecca tried to smile. "Is Esther here?"

"Of course, where else would she be?" Esther's mother looked at Rebecca suspiciously. "Nothing is wrong? You look like you have been crying, and you're out of breath. Nu? What is it?" she asked again.

"Nothing is wrong. I was carrying a heavy basket of laundry, so I am out of breath a little bit. I don't know why my eyes are tearing."

"All right, then, Rivka. Come on in," Esther's mother said. "Esther, Rivka is here."

Esther came running out of one of the rooms in the back of the flat. "Rivka!" She hugged her friend. "Come sit with me while I do my work. I am washing the floors in the back of the house."

Rebecca smiled at Esther, but she couldn't help noticing the bruise that was turning yellow on Esther's cheek.

"I'll help you," Rebecca said.

Esther's mother nodded in approval, and both girls headed back toward the bedroom.

"I've missed you so much," Esther said. "You haven't been here to see me for almost a week."

"I know. I am sorry. I couldn't get out. My parents had a million chores for me to do," Rebecca said as she squeezed Esther's hand. "I missed you too. I missed you so much. You're the closest person in the world to me. The only person I completely trust."

"Me too," Esther said.

"What happened to your face?" Rebecca asked gently touching the bruise.

Esther shrugged.

"Come on, you can tell me. I'm your best friend."

"My papa hit me again. He was in a rage. He said it was because I am so ugly. He said he can't find me a husband."

"You are not ugly. You're beautiful. He can't find you a husband because he has a reputation for being a drunk. He's blaming you."

"Yes, I know. But I am not in any hurry to get married. I am afraid a husband might be as bad as my father, or worse yet."

"You don't have to tell me, Esther. I know he hits your mother too."

"He does." She sighed. "I wouldn't ever tell anyone else but you, Rivka. You're the only person I know I can trust with our terrible family secrets."

"Oh, Esther! Of course, you can always trust me."

"You look sad today. Is it because of me? I hate to make you sad," Esther said.

"It's not you, Esther. Although it breaks my heart to see your lovely face bruised. I hate to think that your father has hurt you. But the truth is, I have terrible news of my own today."

"What is it?" Esther said, closing the door to the back bedroom.

"My Tate has found me a husband. I am sure he will insist I marry this boy. Then I will be going away from here. I don't know where I will be going or how far away I will be from you. I don't even know when I will be able to see you."

"No!"

Rebecca nodded as tears began to form in the corners of her eyes.

Esther put her arms around Rebecca and held her close. "Rivka, no matter who they make me marry, you will always be my one true love."

"I know, Esther. I know. But your feelings for me are forbidden."

"That doesn't mean I can stop feeling them, does it?"

Rebecca shook her head. "Esther, I love you too. But your feelings for me are different than mine for you. I can't love you the way you want me to. I can't love you the way a man and woman love each other. I am not made that way."

"I wish I were a man, then I could marry you."

"I know you do, Esther. But you're not."

"I wish you could love me. I wish you could love me as a woman."

"For your sake, I wish so too. But I can't. And what I do know is that right now I am scared of marriage to a complete stranger. I am scared of failing my new husband and how much that would disappoint my Tate. And sweet Esther, my oldest and dearest friend . . . I am terrified of hurting you, of breaking your heart. That's the last thing I would ever want to do."

CHAPTER SEVEN

Eli could hardly wait until his next meeting with Gretchen. He thought of her outspokenness and her bold, sparkling blue eyes while he was in class at the yeshiva. Just the thought of her brought a smile to his face. Just thinking of her intrigued him. No girl from his community would ever question the existence of God. They would never ask him questions about the Talmud or the Torah either. If he had spoken to any of the girls he knew the way he spoke to Gretchen, they would listen quietly and agree with anything he said. But Gretchen had voiced her opinion as if she were a boy. He thought of her pretty hair, the way the golden strands were tinted with just a hint of rose. How would it feel to run his hands through her locks? He remembered how her eyes looked like blue topaz in the rays of the setting sun.

"I have good news, Eli," Rabbi Kaetzel said when he returned from the shul late that afternoon. "I have arranged for you to meet a potential bride tonight. She will be coming to our home with her parents for dinner. Her name is Rebecca Kesselman. Do you know of her?"

"No, Father. I am sorry. I don't."

"Well, that doesn't matter. Of course, you wouldn't have heard of her. You're at the yeshiva all day. How would you meet any girls? I don't know why I even asked you that. Well, never mind. Anyway, she's a good girl from a good family. She would be quite a match for you. She's the daughter of a Kohane. Her father is a well-respected man. I hope she likes you. Be on your best behavior. Do you understand me?" The rabbi's face was stern, and the wrinkles in his brow were deep.

Eli knew his father well enough to realize the old man's mind was set. His father had chosen this girl, and chances were good that she was probably going to be his bride. The only way out of marrying her was to run away. But Eli had no trade, no way of earning a living. Since he was a child he was being trained to follow his father and become a rebbe. Where would he go? What could he do? He spent all of his days studying the Torah, and now he was completely dependent upon his father for everything. *Best not to argue*, he thought, nodding his head. Most of the time he admired his papa, but there were times that, although he wished he didn't, he resented him.

CHAPTER EIGHT

Eli washed his face and hands and put on clean clothes, but there was no disguising his black eye or bruised cheek. He knew that the girl's family would notice his payot was gone. Perhaps the terrible beating he suffered would save him from having to marry. *Sometimes things happen, and you don't understand why*, he thought. *But in the long run, they turn out for the best. When this girl's father sees my bruises and missing sideburns, he will think twice about me as a husband for his daughter. Consequently, this could very well be my way out.*

CHAPTER NINE

Gretchen sat in her bedroom thinking about the strange boy she'd met. When she saw him in the park earlier that day, and before she heard the gentle tone of his voice, his unusual way of dressing had put her off. Yet when she was walking beside him, and he looked into her eyes, she saw a depth in his gaze that was missing in the boys she knew from school and the neighborhood. Eli was so serious, so intense. His voice was soft and kind, and she had to admit, he was so darn handsome. There was no flirtation in his smile, only sincere admiration. She could tell from the way he looked at her that he found her beautiful, and to her, this revelation was mesmerizing.

She had purchased an entire bag of potatoes and carrots with the money she'd received from Eli. It was now stored in the cellar beneath her apartment. Gretchen felt good to know she had the extra vegetables available in case they ran short.

But to her surprise, the reward money was not the only benefit. She also met Eli. He was such a gentleman to offer to walk her home, so she wouldn't have to walk alone in the dark. How could she not find him charming? Of course, she did. However, as they first began to walk side by side, she was a little frightened. She realized that in spite of her father's thoughts she had absorbed some of the propaganda that stated Jews were dangerous to Christians. Yet as she walked beside him and they began to talk, she relaxed. Then as they continued to walk, Gretchen found him interesting and their conversation thought provoking.

By the time she got home, she was not afraid of him at all. She no longer believed any of the propaganda she'd heard about Jews. Instinctively, she knew all of it was nothing but lies. The boys she grew up with were not half as deep or intellectual. They only wanted to talk about Hitler, and how they hoped he would be appointed chancellor of Germany. Once he was, they would rant and rave that Hitler was going to restore Germany to her rightful place in the world. They lived on a practical plane of existence. They were concerned with the end of unemployment and the glory of the Nazi Party. There was no talk of God.

Most of them made sexual passes at her, hoping she would give them a sign that she was interested and willing. But not Eli; he was philosophical. He had not made any sexual passes during their walk, and he seemed so willing to listen with interest to her views on everything.

However, she ventured to guess that her father would not approve of her getting to know Eli Kaetzel better. If her father knew she was planning a meeting with Eli, he would discourage her because he was always careful when it came to her. It wasn't that he had a dislike for Jews, but he would say that with all this Jew hatred on the rise, why get involved? She could hear him say that anyone who befriended a Jew was setting himself up for a lot of unnecessary trouble.

Knowing her father well, Gretchen decided she would not say anything about Eli. However, she was counting the days until she saw Eli again. She could hardly wait.

CHAPTER TEN

Rebecca and her parents arrived at the home of Rebbe Kaetzel at exactly seven o'clock. Chenya Kaetzel, Eli's mother, welcomed them into her home. Although it cost the Kaetzels what seemed like a small fortune to buy the food and spices that Chenya needed, she dipped into the family's savings and prepared as nice a dinner as possible. Because her husband was the rebbe, she was able to buy a small chicken. It wasn't as meaty as she would have liked, but it made a nice impression anyway.

"Come in, and welcome to our home," Chenya said to her son's potential in-laws. "We are so pleased that you could come tonight."

Mr. Kesselman smiled and nodded. Rebecca's mother, Deborah, smiled and said, "Thank you for inviting us. I brought you a vinegar-and-raisin strudel."

"Oh, you didn't have to bring anything. But thank you so much," Chenya said, taking the strudel and realizing it had probably cost the Kesselman family a pretty penny to buy all the sugar needed to prepare this lovely dessert. "Please, sit down. The rebbe and our son will be here shortly."

The Kesselman family sat in a row on the plush sofa in the Kaetzel's living room. Eli walked into the room. "This is our son,

Eli," the rebbe said with a smile.

"A pleasure to meet you, Eli," Rebecca's father answered.

"My pleasure, sir," Eli responded. Then he sat down on a chair by the window.

Mrs. Kesselman tried not to stare, but she stole several glances at the boy, Eli, her daughter's potential groom. She couldn't help but notice how handsome he was. Unlike most young boys who spent all day in the yeshiva, this boy's skin was not pasty white. He had a bit of a golden hue to his coloring as if he spent a nice amount of time outside. She wondered how and when he found time for such a thing. After all, he was supposed to spend his days engrossed in the studies of the Jewish text.

Still, no matter how he got his slightly tanned skin, his coloring was attractive, and she hoped that her daughter would be pleased. His hair was thick and black with a deep wave, and his eyes were dark and deep but not cruel. They were soft, kind, and intelligent, but also inviting. And he was tall, taller than most of the men in their neighborhood. She would have pegged him at six feet at least, perhaps a little taller. His build was solid and not too skinny. Of all the potential husbands her husband had presented to Rebecca, this was the first one that might have a chance of winning her daughter's approval.

The rebbe studied Rebecca for a moment. Her long, wheat-blonde hair was pulled away from her face and clipped back with a small hair ornament that had a single pearl. She wore a modest, brown dress that covered her from her collarbone to below her knees. Even though it was a warm night, her sleeves covered her arms down to her delicate wrists. Rebecca's eyes were cast down, but when Eli welcomed her and her parents to their home, she smiled warmly. Eli saw her quickly glance up at her father. He nodded back at her with his approval.

"My daughter Rebecca. She's a good girl," Rebecca's father said.

Chenya Kaetzel got up and began to bring the dishes out to the table.

"May I please help you?" Rebecca asked.

"I would like that," Eli's mother said.

"I would like to help too," Rebecca's mother chimed in.

The three women went into the kitchen and began bringing the dinner to the table. Without saying a word, Rebecca obeyed as her future mother-in-law instructed her which platters and serving pieces to use. She followed her mother and Mrs. Kaetzel in and out of the kitchen as they carried platters of food to the table.

When Mrs. Kaetzel was occupied, Rebecca's mother whispered in her daughter's ear, "He's handsome."

"Yes, I suppose he is," Rebecca said.

"Do you like him?"

Rebecca shrugged. "I don't know. I don't know him, Mama." She had spent her entire life being obedient, never speaking her mind. So now that her mother was asking for her opinion on the most important decision of her life, Rebecca found herself at a loss for words. All she could say was, "If Papa likes him, I will learn to like him too."

But inside, her heart was breaking. Not because she didn't want to marry this strange but handsome boy, with a bruised eye and no side curls, but because once she was married, she could no longer live at home with her parents and sister. She would see them, of course, but not nearly as often.

She would no longer be a child; it would be time to fulfill her role in life as a wife and mother. The idea was terrifying. In her father's house, she always had someone to ask for help, but she had no idea if that would be true once she moved into her husband's home.

They all sat at the table. The men talked of the Torah, and the mothers spoke about babies and how to stretch their budgets. Rebecca did not speak at all. She kept her head down and was careful not to overeat lest she looked like a glutton.

Eli began to speak, and Rebecca quickly glanced up at her father to see what he thought. It was easy for her to read her beloved father's face. Her Tate was listening intently. She could see that he was impressed with Eli's knowledge.

He is well studied, Rebecca thought. *And he is handsome. What more could I possibly ask? There is a calm about him, so I don't think he will have a temper. But who knows? He could. I really know nothing about him.*

Her stomach turned, and she suddenly felt nauseated. She put her fork down. Rebecca couldn't eat another bite. *Oh Hashem, if only I could stay a child in my father's house forever. Marriage!*

CHAPTER ELEVEN

The evening felt as if it would never end. But finally, Rebecca and her parents were on their way home. As they walked the familiar streets of their small neighborhood, Rebecca's father asked, "Nu? So, do you like him?"

"I don't know him, Tate. Do you like him?"

"Very much. His father is a rebbe. What a learned man! This boy Eli certainly comes from a good family. He's bright, and he's articulate. What a speaker! Didn't you think so?"

Rebecca nodded.

"What's wrong?" her father asked.

"Nothing, Tate . . . nothing."

"You're afraid, my little girl?"

"Yes, Tate. I am very afraid. Marriage is frightening."

"I know. And if it were up to me, you would stay at home with your mama and me forever. But it's not right. You shouldn't be an old maid. You should have a house full of laughter and children. You should have a good husband to care for you. Your mama and I would have had more children if we could have. We would have had a dozen. But that was not meant to be for us. We were fortunate that Hashem blessed us with you and your sister. But for you, I hope you have a house full of babies. And I hope that they are all just like you. What a good-natured child you have always been. Such a blessing for our mama and me! You never argued and never gave us any tsuris. No aggravation at all, like some other people's children. You are such a pretty girl. I swelled with pride when I saw the rebbe look at you. My girl is so delicate and mild mannered. Such a good, modest child. That's why I want to be sure you like this Eli Kaetzel before I agree to the match. I want you to be happy."

Rebecca swallowed. Her head was swimming, and she felt dizzy. She could see in her father's shining eyes that he wanted her to say yes. So, as she had done her entire life, Rebecca smiled and did exactly what was expected of her.

"Yes, Tate. Make the match. I will marry him."

CHAPTER TWELVE

Eli could not deny that Rebecca was a beauty: a diamond of a girl as his mother liked to say. She was tall and slender with ample hips and bosom. Her eyes were gold like the sun on a summer day, and her hair was an unusually pale, soft beige, like the hair of an angel. He'd never seen a Jewish girl with hair that shade before. She had a long, straight nose, high, prominent cheekbones, and a delicate chin with full, rose-colored lips.

At dinner the next day, Rebbe Kaetzel was insistent that the match go forward, but Eli protested. He tried to convince his father that he wasn't ready. But his father liked Rebecca, explaining that she was perfect not only because she was modest and lovely, but also because she came from a line of Kohanes. No matter what Eli said, his father wasn't taking no for an answer.

Eli could see his destiny being written. Unable to change his father's mind, Eli began to resent Rebecca. He knew it was not her fault. She was as much a pawn as he was in their parents' matchmaking game. But still, the very idea that he had no say in his future infuriated Eli and made him want to push Rebecca away.

The days passed. Eli's parents talked about the match constantly. They were excited about planning the wedding, but all Eli could think of was Gretchen. He dreamed of her at night, and he thought of her hair with its red undertones the color of a wildfire. Eli knew his thoughts and feelings for Gretchen were wrong. He knew that Gretchen's outspoken audacity would repulse all of his male friends. They would be appalled if they knew he was on the brink of getting married, but his heart and mind were not with his modest and beautiful Jewish fiancée. No. The fire of Gretchen, a beautiful woman whom he couldn't erase from his mine consumed his thoughts. A charming, perhaps a little dangerous, but also terribly exciting girl. Eli realized that his strong feelings for Gretchen would put a damper on his marriage to Rebecca. The union could never be what a good marriage should be.

CHAPTER THIRTEEN

Gretchen was full of questions for her father when he returned from teaching at the university that night. She prepared him a minimal meal and sat beside him while he ate.

"Papa, do you remember telling me about the Kabbalah? The Jewish Kabbalah?"

"I don't remember telling you about it, but what would you like to know?"

"Well, I heard that it's not the only Jewish study book. There is also the Torah and Talmud. Do you know anything about these books?"

"A little. But what I do know, Gretchen, is that the country is not looking kindly upon Jews right now. I personally don't think it's right how Germany is treating the Jews. But with the hatred of Jews on the rise, I would rather you didn't explore an interest in Judaism. Your safety is my utmost concern. I would die if anything happened to you. What makes you so interested in it anyway?"

"Maybe because of the growing hatred of Jewish people that has consumed Germany. Everywhere you go you hear people say all kinds of things, like the Jews have all the money, and the Jews are the reason we lost the war. It seems that everything bad is being blamed on them. And I guess I would like to know more about the Jews, so I can make up my own mind."

"Ahhh. Well...?" He scratched his scruffy chin. His hair was thick, and although he shaved every morning, by afternoon there was enough growth to give his chin a dark shadow.

"I can't be too critical of you because you are certainly my daughter." He let out a loud laugh. "A purely intellectual pursuit? I understand that. I've had plenty of purely intellectual interests in my time. And I don't blame you for wanting to know things. But it's too dangerous. The last thing you want is to draw attention to yourself."

"Papa!" she persisted "You always said that it was a good thing to be intellectually curious. Since I was a child you taught me to study things that interested me and to learn and explore. All I want to do is to know more about the Jews. What is so wrong with that?"

"Gretchen"—he sighed, frustrated—"I know it's all very interesting. But we live in dangerous times. Now, don't get me wrong, I think it's wonderful that you have an inquisitive nature. But for God's sake, this is not something you want to pursue right now. There is nothing you can do to stop what is happening to the Jews. You are only one person, and besides that, you are all I have in the world. Please Gretchen, forget about all this."

Gretchen saw the pleading in his eyes. He was clearly worried, and nothing she said or did would convince him to discuss anything having to do with Jews. She hated to see him upset, so she decided to change the subject.

"You want some more soup, Papa?" Gretchen asked.

"Did you eat?" He looked at her.

"Of course, I did."

"I don't think you did, Gretchen. You're so skinny. I know you try to give me the largest portions. But you are a growing girl, and you have to eat."

"I know, Papa. I do eat."

"Not enough. Come on now; have a bowl of soup with me." He tore the heel of bread she'd given him in half. "And eat this too."

"Oh, Papa. You are a man. You need to eat more than I do," Gretchen said, but she took the bread. The truth was, she was hungry. Her monthly periods did not come regularly. She went to the doctor to find out why. The doctor said it was because she was very physically active but also not eating enough.

Gretchen filled the ladle and poured the soup into her father's bowl, making sure to give him the potato. She got a bowl down and poured some for herself.

"What do you think about this Adolf Hitler?" he asked her. "The fellow who wants to be our chancellor?"

"He says he is going to save Germany," she said. "Maybe if he is appointed, we can finally get rid of unemployment. That's what everyone says."

"Perhaps. More steady employment would be nice. But I think this Hitler fellow could be dangerous too."

Gretchen didn't pay much attention to politics. She knew there were plenty of conflicts between the different parties, and sometimes there were fights in the streets. But none of it seemed very important to her. She didn't care who was chancellor. All she knew was that she was always hungry, and there was never enough food.

Sometimes she would have a little extra money available to her, but when she went to the stores, they were out of goods. The bottom line was that everything was very expensive and sometimes scarce. Perhaps she might afford an extra egg. But what good was a single egg? It was considered a treasure, but it couldn't satisfy two people, especially if those two people were a full-grown man and a very physically active teenage girl.

Gretchen was an active girl. She tried to sit still, but she loved to run and play ball. Her father warned her that running around burned calories—calories she could not replace fast enough with food. That was why her periods were not regular.

When she looked in the mirror, she felt sick at how painfully skinny and underdeveloped she was. Her period started very late: she was sixteen the first time. She had begun to wonder if it was ever going to come. Gretchen was afraid it would be difficult for her to conceive a child when the time was right. She tried not to think about it. However, when people talked about Hitler getting rid of unemployment and hyperinflation, she was all for his becoming chancellor.

Everyone knew he was a raging Jew hater. But what difference could that make? In the long run, all that mattered to her was that she and her father would be able to acquire more food.

CHAPTER FOURTEEN

On the Monday that Eli was to meet Gretchen at the abandoned warehouse, he woke up nervous and excited. He knew that by defying his father's wishes, he was committing a sin. "Honor thy father and thy mother" was one of the Ten Commandments. He shivered when he thought about it but forced it out of his mind. The sun cast a bright yellow glow over the earth. The trees were blossoming. Eli was filled with anticipation. All day, as he sat in the yeshiva, he thought about Gretchen, the girl with the sprinkle of freckles beneath her bright, inquisitive, blue eyes. He couldn't concentrate on his studies. At break time, Yousef came up to him to share his bread and butter.

"Here, eat," Yousef said, handing him a chunk of challah. "My mother made this last night. She bought some extra flour from the money she got from selling my grandmother's carved picture frame."

Eli took the bread, grateful to his friend. "I forgot to bring any food today."

"You forgot? Nu? What's the matter with you? You've been looking distracted all day."

"Eh? I don't know what it is. Maybe it's that my father is insisting that I marry this girl he chose."

"He found you a match?" Yousef asked, his mouth stuffed with bread.

"Yes, he did."

"NU? Who is it?"

"Her name is Rebecca Kesselman. Her father is a Kohane. My father likes that, of course."

"What? You don't like her?"

"I don't know her, Yousef. I met her, but she hardly said a word."

"Of course. They never speak. Did you expect her to?"

"No, of course not. But still, I don't know . . ."

"Is she ugly? Fat?"

"Neither. In fact, she's quite beautiful."

"You should be happy. I met my future bride. I wouldn't say she's beautiful, but she is pleasant looking. My parents like her because she's from a good family, so we will marry."

"And you are happy with this?"

"I will be happy, Eli, because I want to be happy. My parents say that I will learn to love her."

"Sometimes our traditions are hard to swallow," Eli said.

Yousef nodded. "You know it's hard for the girls too. When I met my future wife, I could see how nervous she was. Her hands were trembling. I felt sorry for her. I want to make her happy if I can."

"You're a good man, Yousef. A good person," Eli said.

"I'll meet you after class to walk home."

"I can't today. I have to go into town to pick up something for my father," Eli lied. *Another sin. Now I've lied to Yousef. What am I doing?*

But before he could give it any more thought, the boys were called back to class. After school ended, Eli walked as quickly as he could, checking to make sure no one he knew was behind him, especially not Yousef. He didn't want to have to justify his lie. But to his relief, no one was following him. Eli was alone. Once he turned the corner to the warehouse he knew that Yousef would not be anywhere near.

It was a bright sunny afternoon. As he approached, his eyes quickly scanned the area. He didn't see Gretchen anywhere. *She has more sense than you,* Eli told himself. *Of course she didn't come. You are a Jew; she is a shiksa. She knows better, and so should you.*

He tried desperately to rationalize his feelings, but he was overcome with disappointment. He'd waited almost a whole week for that afternoon and thought of little else. And now, he realized their meeting was not important to Gretchen at all. If it were, she would be waiting for him. What if she realized just how dangerous it was for her to associate with a Hasidic Jew? What if she'd decided he wasn't worth the risk?

He began to feel a wave of panic settling into the pit of his belly. *I have to go to her house. I have no other choice. I don't want her to think that I didn't show up for our meeting. What if I've hurt her feelings?* He stood up and began walking toward Gretchen's apartment with his head bent when he heard her call his name.

"Eli!"

He turned quickly. For a single second, a twinge of fear shot through him. He wondered what he would do if someone from his neighborhood saw him. But at the same time, Eli was elated. Gretchen had come to meet him. *What a mess I am,* he thought.

He called back, "Hello."

She ran toward him, as graceful as a fawn. He smiled. He knew that he should have left before she arrived. He should have run away when he had the chance. If Hashem was testing him, he was ashamed to admit that he was failing miserably. Even with all of his studying, his attraction to this young shiksa was proving more powerful than his faith.

The secret meeting with Gretchen was like a strange and

irresistible waltz with danger. In his protected world, few men would dare to flirt with such things. In his world, men didn't dance with women. Women danced with women, and men danced with men. Men and women didn't sit together in synagogue when they went to pray. They were separated. Great care was taken to prevent a man's temptation to sin. Even though he feared his desire to sin was stronger than his power to control it, he never felt as elated as he did when he saw Gretchen walking toward him.

"Hello," she said, a little breathless. "I came here earlier when school let out, and you weren't here, so I left. I thought you might have had second thoughts about meeting me. But then I thought about it, and I just wasn't willing to believe that. So I decided to find out what time your Jewish school let out for the day."

"How did you ever do that?"

She laughed. "I guess I have to admit I was spying on you! I went over to your school building, and I peered in the window. I saw the classrooms were still full, so I knew you hadn't been released yet."

"Smart girl!" He laughed. "Bold too!"

"You don't like it?"

"Like what?"

"That I am smart and bold."

"Actually, I do. I like it too much."

"What's happened to you?" she said, reaching up and touching his face. "You're all bruised. You've been hurt. And your side curls are gone," she said.

He nodded

"You were beaten up?"

"Yes."

The look of concern in her eyes touched his soul. He wanted to take her in his arms and kiss her. He wanted to tell her she was the most wonderful, kind, and compassionate being in the world. But he knew he must not. Instead he must tell her everything before things went any further. He didn't want to tell her. He didn't want it to be true. "I suppose I must tell you that I have some news. My father has arranged a marriage for me."

"You are getting married?"

"Yes," he said, hanging his head.

"Oh." She crossed her arms in front of her chest. "I didn't know you had a girlfriend." Gretchen felt like she was dying inside. She tried to stay composed. She didn't want to cry, but the tears were welling up in the backs of her eyes.

"It's not like that. I wouldn't call her a girlfriend. I've only met her once. But because my father wills it, she is my betrothed. She and I have never been alone together. We have never had a private conversation like the way you and I are talking now."

"I don't understand."

"Let me explain it to you," he said, and he began. He explained that he would not be alone with his future wife until they were married. He explained that all he knew about Rebecca was her name and that her father was a Kohane.

"I suppose we shouldn't meet here again," Gretchen said.

"I guess not." He felt his heart sink as he said it, but he knew it was for the best.

"Well, if we aren't ever going to meet again, then . . ." She looked into his eyes. He thought she was going to get up and leave. He wished there were something he could say or do to change his fate, but he knew it was impossible. Gretchen stood up and turned to go. Eli felt as if the door to a bright and happy life was closing on him, and he was going to be left forever in darkness. But then she turned and walked back toward him. Leaning down, she gently kissed his lips.

A multitude of conflicting emotions washed over him, drowning his sense of right and wrong. He stood up, tall and handsome and pulled her into his arms, kissing her hard and passionately. She sighed. He held her for a moment then released her.

Then he turned and left the warehouse.

Gretchen stood alone watching him as he walked away.

CHAPTER FIFTEEN

This is for the best, Eli told himself over and over as he walked home. *I have done the right thing by separating myself from Gretchen. No good could ever come from it.* He always did what was expected of him, but this time, his heart could not accept his choice. He turned his thoughts to his future bride. Rebecca was a lovely girl. Her mother made a point of telling his family that her daughter was obedient and an excellent cook. All the while, Rebecca sat like a statue with her head down, never looking up and never saying a word. Of course, that was what was expected of her, and she followed protocol perfectly. This was what he was supposed to want in a bride; it just didn't fulfill him.

So, Papa, I will do as you wish. I will marry the lovely and perfect Rebecca Kesselman. She will never question any decision I make. I will rule as the man of the house, just as it should be. My wife will know her place. She will keep our house kosher and, of course, keep the Sabbath. Together, we will give you many beautiful grandchildren. And you will be happy, Papa. I will be the son who makes you proud. The son you can brag about to all of your friends. Our children will be the shining product of a rebbe's son and a Kohane's daughter. And you will have such nachas, such joy.

But me? Oh, Papa, if you only knew the truth in my heart. I wish I didn't feel so strongly about Gretchen, but I do. I know I will always remember Gretchen as the spirited girl, with the sprinkle of freckles and eyes the color of a blue jay's wing, for the rest of my life.

CHAPTER SIXTEEN

Rebecca had just returned from the mikvah, the ritual bath house for Jewish women, where she had her ritual bath. Tonight, she and Eli would be married. As required, she had bathed and been made ready for her wedding night. Her nails were cut and her hair washed. It was embarrassing to stand naked in front of the old women at the mikvah, but she knew she had better get used to it. Once she was married, she was required to bathe after every menstrual period before physically reconnecting with her husband. According to Jewish law, a bleeding woman was considered unclean. Her husband was not even permitted to touch her hand until the blood stopped, and she had to bathe at the mikvah, before being declared clean enough to lie with her husband once again.

Slowly and methodically, Rebecca filled her small suitcase with all of her possessions. She didn't own very much, so there wasn't much to pack. Her heart was heavy, knowing that after tonight she would never live in her childhood home again. She would live in the rebbe's house with his son. From this day forward, she would no longer be the carefree young girl she'd always been; she would be the wife of Eli Kaetzel.

She tried hard to rationalize. *My father has been kind in his choice of husband. At least Eli is a handsome boy. I just wish I could turn back time and be a child again.* She ran her fingers through her lovely pale hair. She always thought it was her prettiest feature. But for a married Jewish woman, there was no room for such vanity. Her wedding ceremony would be the last time she would be permitted to show her hair to anyone outside of her family.

After she was married, she would not leave her house without her head covered. Even worse, tomorrow morning her mother would come to her new home and shave her head to make sure that no hair escaped her head scarf. If Eli were kind, she would be allowed to grow her hair back, probably not as long as it was now, but at least not shaved. However, if he were very strict, she would be required to shave her head each month. And, of course, she would be obedient. Rebecca was always obedient.

When her father asked if she were happy about her upcoming marriage, instead of telling him the truth that she didn't want to marry, she said, "Yes, Tate. I am happy." Rebecca knew it was what her father wanted to hear. He nodded and smiled at her, and before she knew it, it was her wedding day. Rebecca felt her shoulders slump in defeat. What could she do except go forward with the plan her parents had put into motion? She could only pray to Hashem that her new husband would be gentle and kind, and that, somehow, she would find a way to be happy.

CHAPTER SEVENTEEN

The wedding was lovely. It was held in the shul that the rebbe had attended since he was a child. It was the same shul his father had attended and his father before him. Because both sets of parents had many friends in the community, many guests came to see the couple joined. The men sat on one side, the women on the other, and the music began. The audience uttered a collective gasp as the bride entered the hall. Eli waited in front of the rabbi as his new bride-to-be walked toward him accompanied by her father. She circled him seven times, as was tradition and then stopped at his side for the rabbi to begin the ceremony.

What a beautiful couple they made! Eli Kaetzel, tall and well built, with his dark, wavy hair and deep, mysterious eyes, provided a stunning contrast to his striking wife, Rebecca Kesselman, with her soft, curvy figure, pale hair, and bright yellow-green eyes the color of a cat's. The vows were spoken, the rings exchanged, and then the couple shared a glass of wine. Once the glass was empty, the rabbi wrapped the glass carefully in a cloth and put it down in front of Eli's foot. The room was silent as Eli raised his foot. He stomped on the glass, and the breaking sound elicited a hearty "Mazel tov" from the guests. The marriage was now sealed.

Rebecca trembled at the sound of the breaking glass. At that very instant, her life changed forever. But what she didn't yet know was how it would change.

CHAPTER EIGHTEEN

The young couple was escorted to a private room where they were allowed to speak alone together for the first time. Eli closed the door softly, but Rebecca heard the click of the door magnified in her ears. She felt her heart beating hard and fast in her chest. She was so nervous that she had been unable to eat anything that day, and now she was dizzy and nauseated. She knew so little about this handsome, young man whose ring she now wore on the first finger of her right hand. Quickly, she glanced at the gold band. *This man is my husband,* she thought, feeling a little overwhelmed as if she might faint.

"Hello," he said, sitting down beside her and folding his hands in his lap.

She looked at him for a second and gave him a quick and nervous smile. She mustered up a "Hello." *He has nice hands,* she thought. *His fingers are long and thin. His nails are clean. Of course, his hands are clean and smooth. He doesn't do any manual labor. He is the son of a rebbe; he studies all day.*

"You look very lovely tonight," Eli said.

"Thank you."

"We are married." It was an awkward statement from him. But after all, what could she expect? *He must be very nervous too,* she realized.

She nodded, not finding any appropriate words to say.

"The ceremony was very nice," he added.

"Yes," she choked out.

Relief came when the door to the room opened, and the couple was invited back to the reception to celebrate their marriage with their guests.

Esther was the first to greet Rebecca when she entered the woman's side of the shul. "You're married," she said almost as if she couldn't believe it. "Mazel tov is in order, I suppose."

"Thank you," Rebecca said.

"I want you to be happy, my friend," Esther said.

"I know that. I am trying, Esther. But I am scared. It's strange. We have spent our whole entire lives being raised for the day when we would be married and have children of our own. Yet when it happens, well, at least for me, I feel as if my life is over instead of beginning."

"I know. I feel the same way about marriage. In fact, I wanted to tell you my father has made a match for me. I am dreading it so much. I met him. He's very fat, and his nose is red, like my father's. I am afraid he drinks too much. And when I glimpse his eyes, he looks angry."

"He might be nice. You don't know him yet."

"I know; you're right. My father says I have no choice."

"Oh Esther, I hope it all works out for you."

Esther squeezed Rebecca's hand and asked, "Are you staying here in Berlin with your husband, or are you moving?"

"So far, I think we are staying here. I haven't heard otherwise. How about you?" Rebecca asked.

"I think we are staying here too. My future husband is a watchmaker. He owns a little shop in town, so I don't see why we would leave. But of course, they never consult us women. We just go along with whatever our husbands or fathers demand. I hate it. You know that though."

"Yes, I know you do, Esther."

"Tell me you don't? Tell me truthfully that you don't wish you had some say in your future, in your life?"

Rebecca nodded. "Of course, I do. But it does me no good to think about it. Come, eat, dance. At least for the moment, Esther, try to be happy." Rebecca took her friend's hand, leading her onto the dance floor.

The dancing went on well into the night. The men danced on one side, the women on the other. Every time Rebecca glanced over to the men's side, she saw men congratulating her new husband. He was laughing and talking with his friends and with their fathers. It seemed he was never looking in her direction. *I wonder if he is not pleased with me? Is there something I should be doing differently? Should I have said or done something more when we were alone? But what? No one told me what to say or do, and I didn't want to do the wrong thing. My Tate wants me to make my husband happy, but I don't know how.* She felt a wave of anxiety wash over her. Her mother had already told her what to expect later, once she and Eli were alone. The idea of this man she hardly knew touching her most private places seemed horrific. How was she to endure this? No man except her father had ever even kissed her, and he had only kissed her on her forehead in a fatherly way. But now she was expected to allow her new husband complete access to her body. *I wish I could just run away. Or fly away like a bird*, Rebecca thought. But then she looked over at Eli, and he glanced back at her and smiled. He leaned against the table, and his wine glass fell to the floor. It shattered, and the wine pooled like blood around the broken glass. Eli stood frozen in shock. For a single instant, she was mesmerized by the deep crimson color of the wine, and a shadow of dread came over her. A cold finger ran up her spine. She looked up from the mess on the floor, and her eyes met Eli's. He looked away quickly as if he were embarrassed at being so clumsy. It brought her out of her trance. *Perhaps he is as nervous about the coming night as I am. Maybe he feels as uncomfortable as I do. And just maybe, everything will be all right.* But she couldn't help feeling that the bloody-looking wine and the broken glass were some kind of a premonition.

Once the guests departed, the newlyweds retired to Eli's room in his father's home. Rebecca sat on the edge of her twin bed with her head down. Eli's parents had purchased twin beds for the couple once the marriage had been arranged. Eli and Rebecca would not share a bed. When they joined together as man and wife to produce an offspring, Eli would come to her bed. She couldn't meet Eli's eyes. She knew if she did, he would see how frightened she was and how much she wished she could run home to her parents and forget that this marriage had ever happened.

"I suppose we should get ready for bed," Eli said.

Rebecca nodded.

"I'll go and leave you to get undressed. I'll be back soon," he said walking clumsily out of the room, tucking his hands in and out of his pants pockets as if they were not a part of him, and he had no idea what do with them.

As she took off her mother's wedding dress, Rebecca could hear her heart beating. If she thought too long or hard about all that would change tonight, she knew she would throw herself on the bed and weep. *What would Eli think if he came back into this room and found me crying? He would think I wasn't raised as a proper Jewish wife. I would bring shame upon my family.*

She turned off the light and climbed into bed. The room was pitch black save for a sliver of moonlight that came through the window.

The crisp cotton bed sheets felt cold and foreign. Her whole body shivered under the blankets even though it was a warm night. Soon her husband would enter the room, and his body would be beside her in the bed. This man she hardly knew, this man whose name and bed she would share for the rest of her days: Eli Kaetzel. He would explore the most sacred and private places of her body. All this must be endured so she could fulfill her most important role, which was to become pregnant and bring forth a child. No matter what happened. No matter how much it hurt, she knew she must lie still, allow it, and not scream.

The door creaked open, and Rebecca felt the bile rise in her throat. She forced herself to swallow. The floorboards groaned as Eli made his way to her bed. He got in beside her but was careful not to brush against her. His presence so close to her body felt strange; she could feel the warmth of another living being. The bed moved with his trembling.

"I don't want to hurt you," he said, his voice barely a whisper.

"Thank you." Several moments of silence followed, then Eli cleared his throat.

"I am afraid that I am new at this too," he said. She could tell by his tone of voice that he was trying to put her at ease. He continued, "I am going to start, all right?"

"Yes," she croaked.

"If I hurt you please tell me. Promise me you will."

"Yes, I promise."

It wasn't as bad as she thought it would be. Eli was gentle and very considerate. Rebecca couldn't honestly say she liked it, but she could tolerate it if it brought her a gift from God, a mitzvah, a blessing, a child.

Once Eli finished, he got out of Rebecca's small bed and went to his own. She curled up into herself, relieved to be alone, but feeling chilled and a little lost. It would have been nice to get up and clean herself but she didn't. Instead, she allowed the tears to flow silently down her cheeks. Tonight she became a wife, and she was on the path to fulfilling what her parents had always told her was her life's purpose. Trembling and alone, she tried to think of the blessing God would send. A child. If she endured this humiliating thing that her husband must do, a thing that must be endured by all women, then God might see fit to send her the greatest gift he could ever give a woman, a baby. She lay there unable to sleep. Her body was cold, but she remained silent as she watched the moon through her window, waiting for the first light of dawn.

As expected, her mother arrived early the following morning. Rebecca and her mother went into the bedroom she shared with Eli. They were alone. Rebecca touched her lush, thick, blonde hair with her fingers and felt the loss even before her mother began to shave her head.

"How was last night?" her mother asked. "Are you all right?"

Rebecca nodded, swallowing the loneliness she felt. She dared not speak because if she did, she was afraid she might beg her mother to leave her hair alone and to take her back home.

With trembling but purposeful hands, her mother shaved Rebecca's head. Rebecca watched the golden locks fall on the wood floor. Then before she could see herself in a mirror, Rebecca's mother covered her daughter's head with a pretty scarf that she brought as a gift for her.

"Do you like the scarf?" Judith, Rebecca's mother, asked. "I saved it for you for years."

"It's very pretty, Mama."

"You've always looked good in pink."

"Thank you. Thank you for everything," Rebecca said, but she could no longer hold back the tears.

"What is it, my baby, my sweet daughter? What is it?"

"I don't know, Mama . . ."

"I know. I understand. Shaa . . . shaa . . . Don't cry. The beginning of a marriage is always hard for the girl. It was hard for me too when I first married your Tate, but we are happy now. And you'll be happy with Eli. You'll see."

Rebecca nodded.

"Now go, wash your face because we have to join the rest of your new family for breakfast."

"Yes, Mama. I will."

Rebecca splashed her face with cold water and peeked under the scarf. Her stomach dropped when she saw her bald head. She tried to push it out of her mind. She knew everyone was waiting in the living room for her, so she steadied herself and walked out of the bathroom.

"Come," Eli's father said to Rebecca and her mother. "Let's have breakfast. My wife baked a fresh challah for the occasion."

Eli, his sister, his parents, Rebecca, and her mother all sat around a heavy, round, wooden table. The rebbe cleaned his hands ceremoniously in a bowl of water. Then he took the golden, brown bread and broke off a piece for himself before passing it around the table. When the challah came to Rebecca, she tore off a small piece and began to nibble. She was so sad that it was difficult to swallow, and the dough caught in her throat. Keeping her eyes cast down at the plate in front of her, she listened as the rebbe spoke to her mother.

"It was a beautiful wedding. May our families be blessed with many grandchildren," he said.

"Halevi. It should only be so," Rebecca's mother said.

The rebbe nodded and smiled.

Rebecca found it very difficult to sit at the table with the families. She couldn't help but think that everyone at that table knew exactly what had happened between her and Eli the night before. She was so glad her father wasn't there. Facing him was going to be embarrassing, even though everything was exactly as it was supposed to be. Even so, right now, she felt self-conscious with everyone there. She couldn't meet their eyes. Finally, breakfast was over. Without a word, and keeping her eyes cast down, Rebecca helped clear the table and then cleaned the kitchen. Once her mother had gone, Eli came up behind her. He whispered in her ear so no one else could hear, "I don't mind if you let your hair grow back. I mean, it's up to you, of course. But if you want to, it's all right with me. Of course you will have to keep your head covered when you are outside."

"Thank you. That's very kind of you," she said.

"I want you to be happy with me. I want us to have a good marriage and a happy family. I am not sure what to do to please a wife, but I will try."

His kind and sincere words touched her heart. Tears began to form in the corners of her eyes. She didn't know what to say. She wanted to talk to him, to tell him everything she was feeling. Rebecca wanted to make him happy too, but she didn't know how. All she could think to say to him was, "Thank you."

CHAPTER NINETEEN

March 1934

Eli was content with his wife, but he could not say he was truly
happy. Anyone who saw her would say Rebecca was very pretty. Eli
had to admit she was a good cook, and her sewing skills were
competent. She was a tremendous help to his mother in keeping the
house clean and kosher, never complaining. His father was proud to
have her as his son's wife. The old rebbe often told Eli that he
impressed with Rebecca's quiet and modest ways. Eli told himself
every day that he should be thrilled. Any of his friends from the
yeshiva would certainly be overjoyed. But for Eli Kaetzel, something
was missing. Although he'd been married over a year, he still hardly
knew his pretty, slender, young wife. There was nothing he could put
his finger on to complain about, but Rebecca was emotionless, almost
like a well-made machine. She did everything right yet Eli still found
himself thinking about the other girl. Although he hardly knew her,
Gretchen had made a deep and lasting impression on him. She had
shown him that women could be exciting and challenging. Gretchen
had the audacity to speak to him as an equal. If he were honest, he
would have to admit that Gretchen was not nearly as pretty as

Rebecca. But she intrigued him, and he couldn't forget her.

Meanwhile, everyone at the shul was talking about the rise in the hatred of Jewish people. It was no secret that the new chancellor, Adolf Hitler, was a strong Jew hater. Even though the entire congregation seemed worried, Eli's father wasn't concerned. He refused to accept fear or danger. But Eli was frightened. After his marriage, Eli began teaching the younger boys at the yeshiva. At least once a week, one of his students would arrive at school with a black eye or a broken nose, the result of a beating by Hitler's youth gangs. When Eli addressed his concerns with his father, his father just shook his head. He insisted that this strong wave of Jewish hatred would pass.

"It always does, Eli." The old rebbe nodded and smiled sadly to his son.

"I hope so, Father. But I am worried about the country. Very worried," Eli answered.

Rebbe Kaetzel just waved his hand.

Eli tried to talk his father into listening to the radio, but his father refused. The rebbe, like the others of his religious sect, did not pay attention to the world outside his small Jewish community. However, Eli's friend Yousef purchased a radio. He and Eli set it up in the old tree house that they had built together when they were children. Often, when the rebbe thought Eli and Yousef were studying in the tree house, they were, in fact, listening to Adolf Hitler speak.

"Every day I get more and more concerned about this hatred of our people. No good can come of it," Eli told Yousef. "Just listen to that crazy man. He promises the German people everything they want, and he is blaming all the problems in Germany on the Jews. I have a feeling that this won't be good for us."

"No. It won't. That's for sure. I have been feeling the same way for quite a while now," Yousef said. "I am thinking about taking my wife and moving to America to live with my father's cousin."

"Your family would go with you?"

"My parents would, yes, but not Sarah's. They have two younger children, and they don't want to uproot them."

Yousef had married a few months after Eli. *Although his wife is not nearly as attractive as mine, Yousef is happy,* Eli thought, studying his old friend. Marriage agreed with Yousef. His complexion had cleared up; he was no longer a pimply kid. He had turned into a mature, handsome man. Eli was glad that his friend had settled into the life expected of him, and he envied him. Eli was still so restless.

Some days, when he got off work, he would walk alone by the park where he had met Gretchen. He was secretly hoping to see her again, but he never did. Sometimes he would drop by the warehouse where they'd met secretly. He would enter the dull dark building and sit down, wishing he could bring back the moments that he shared with Gretchen. Each time he returned home, he would constantly remind himself that it was for the best. Meeting with her would mean nothing but trouble. Still, sometimes he daydreamed about going to her home and knocking on the door. What would she say when she saw him, he wondered. But he was a married man and the son of a respected rebbe. He dared not ever do such a foolish thing.

CHAPTER TWENTY

Gretchen Schmidt wore her long strawberry-blonde hair in a twist at the back of her neck. She had grown into a lovely young woman with an athletic build and long sleek legs. In the six months since Hitler had been appointed chancellor, she had secured a part-time job working two nights a week after school at a factory that produced pharmaceuticals. She had taken a class in shorthand and another in typing, and her uncle, who was a prominent member of the Nazi Party, was able to help her find work. The pay she earned would make their lives easier.

Gretchen enjoyed her job. She liked the camaraderie of working as part of a team.   Every day while she and the other girls she worked with ate the lunches they brought from home, they looked through magazines and talked about boys and fashions.   Then one afternoon Gretchen met a coworker named Hilde Dusel. Hilde had lived in the same area for many years, and she seemed to know everyone. But they were acquaintances, never friends. Hilde had always been an outsider looking in, she was not one of the popular girls. So, Hilde was ecstatic when Gretchen accepted her friendship, and she latched on to Gretchen, wanting to spend as much time as possible with her. Hilde's father was originally from Germany, but he lived in Austria for several years where he met his wife, who was also of German descent. The Dusel family had moved to Germany when Hilde was twelve, and her younger sister was eight. Hilde was a solid girl, heavyset with thick legs and heavy breasts. She had thin but wavy, light brown hair, which never seemed to stay in place, and pale blue eyes. She wasn't pretty by anyone's standards, but Gretchen, who was kind and always looked for the good in everyone, loved Hilde's quick wit and clever sense of humor. She could always find something to say that would make Gretchen laugh. From the first time they met, Hilde made it clear that her father was a strong supporter of Hitler. She was a member of the Bund Deutscher Maedels, sometimes called the Bund—the League of German Girls' branch of the Hitler Youth—and she strongly urged Gretchen to join.

"It's so much fun," Hilde promised. "Most of the girls are very nice. We do a lot of different things, like nature hikes and campouts. We play competitive sports on the weekends. I've learned so many things, like how to build a campfire, how to cook and bake. Sometimes we help mothers that have a lot of children. And whenever we have a meeting, we sing lots of songs. But that's not all. The most exciting thing is the boys. Our group is affiliated with a group of boys called the Hitler Youth. Some of them are just dreamy. I know you must have heard all about the Bund at school. I have to say that I am so surprised you haven't joined yet."

Gretchen laughed. "I have heard about it, but I was so concerned with getting a job that I didn't really think about joining. My father is a professor, and we are surviving, but the truth is we would like to have more, so I couldn't even consider joining the Bund. I figured it was best to find a job."

"Well, you have the Jews to thank for that."

"For what?"

"If there weren't so many Jewish professors stealing from the system, your father would be earning plenty of money."

"My father's never mentioned anything like that to me."

"Then you should be listening to the speeches the führer makes over the radio. If you did, you would realize that the Jews are to blame for all of it. They are evil, you know?"

Gretchen said nothing; she was remembering Eli.

"Well, I can assure you that Jews cannot be trusted. You'll learn more when you join the Bund."

"I've heard that you spend a lot of time learning Nazi doctrine in the Bund. Is it true?"

"You mean all the stuff we learn about being perfect Aryan wives?"

"Yes, all of that," Gretchen said, "What is the doctrine, for instance?"

"It's nothing strange."

"Just give me an idea," Gretchen persisted.

"They stress being good wives and mothers. The more children pure German girls have for the Reich, the better. They want us to be devoted to our families and Hitler. That's really all there is to it. And, of course, they warn us about the Jews because they want us to stay safe. After all, the Jewish bankers brought our country to her knees in the Great War. After what the Jews did to us, we would never have been able to rise again if it weren't for our führer."

"I am not sure what you mean about the Jews and the war. My father was in the war," Gretchen said.

"Let's not get all bogged down with politics. The leaders make it fun. It's not like school or anything. Besides, when you see the boys in the Hitler Youth you'll want to be the perfect Aryan girl, so you can marry one of them. When the Bund and the Hitler Youth join together and have a dance, you will see all the handsome boys dressed up. You'll see German men at their best. And all I can say is, you'll be proud of your heritage and excited to learn more of our doctrine."

At seventeen, Gretchen was more interested in the boys than she was in the cookouts and camping.

I am telling you that the boys in the Hitler Youth are so handsome you won't be thinking of much else. The Hitler Youth makes sure that the boys get plenty of exercise and fresh air. And it pays off. What good-looking men they are. Aryan men are the most handsome men in the world. They are superior, after all."

"All right. All right." Gretchen giggled.

"So you'll join?"

"I'll join." Gretchen shrugged her shoulders and smiled.

"Well, then, let's get you subscribed to the *Mädelschaft.*"

"What's that?"

"It's the magazine for girls in the BDM. It's a wonderful publication filled with all kinds of lovely ideas that can help a girl be a good German housewife. There are recipes and all sorts of fun ideas. You'll enjoy it."

"The BDM?"

"Yes, silly, the Bund. Everyone calls it that."

"Then let's go and get me subscribed. I just can't wait to read another recipe book."

"Stop it, Gretchen; you're being sarcastic!"

"I guess I am."

"I am telling you that you are going to love this group. We'll have so much fun that in a few months you will be thanking me. By the way, in the summer they say we will all be able to go to a wonderful summer camp, all expenses paid. And maybe next winter we can all go skiing. Again, all expenses will be paid. Just imagine, you and I getting away from our parents' watchful eyes for several weeks. Now that has to sound like fun."

"Yes. I'll admit that it does." Gretchen gave her friend a big smile. "But what about work? Will the factory let us go to summer camp and on skiing holiday without firing us?"

"Of course. They have to. They have no choice. They must show their allegiance to the führer, right?"

CHAPTER TWENTY-ONE

The girls in the BDM wore pretty, little, white smocks that showed off their young figures, especially their shapely legs. When Gretchen tried her uniform on, she didn't feel like she fit in. Except for Hilde, she felt the other girls were all prettier than she was.

"You look adorable," Hilde said.

"I don't think so," Gretchen frowned. "I look dumpy. I'm too skinny, and I have no figure."

"You do not. You're tall, and slender, and lovely."

Gretchen studied herself in the mirror, less than pleased. She glanced outside the window at a group of girls lined up to take a hike together. She caught a glimpse of a tall, blonde girl with the brightest blue eyes Gretchen had ever seen. It made her want to quit and go home.

"Look at that one," Gretchen said.

"Oh, yes, of course. That's Thea, Hilde said. "Everyone considers her to be the prettiest girl in the BDM."

"She's beautiful."

"I know. Everyone wants to be her friend, and all the boys want to take her out."

"What's she like?"

"Vain. She thinks she is better than the rest of us."

"You don't like her, do you?"

"Not really, no. I've tried to befriend her, but she wants no part of me."

They watched Thea straighten her uniform and put her long blonde hair into a ponytail.

CHAPTER TWENTY-TWO

The next meeting of the Bund was on the following Saturday afternoon. The girls changed into their uniforms in the school locker room and then met outside on the field.

They had formed small groups by the time Thea arrived. Everyone wanted Thea to join her group.

"Hello, Thea!" someone yelled as Thea walked onto the field, the bright sunlight illuminating her hair. "Come and join us."

"No, Thea, come join us," another girl called.

Thea smiled at both of the girls, but she didn't join either group. Instead, she walked over to the fence at the side of the field and waited alone for the Bund leader to arrive. Thea knew the leader would place her in a group.

She leaned against the fence and stretched her long, shapely legs. Thea knew she was pretty. Every day, no matter where she went, people told her how attractive she was. Many of the boys asked Thea out, but she refused them. She had her sights set on only one boy. His name was Hann Meier, and he was as handsome as she was beautiful. When the two were together, they looked like a poster for the perfect Aryan couple.

The leader arrived, and she sent several girls to set up the gymnastic equipment and then assigned Thea to a group. The activities began. The girls walked the balance beam and practiced their high jumps. Not only was Thea a beauty, but she was a wonderful athlete as well.

Even though Gretchen was sporty, she still felt out of place. Hilde introduced her to everyone, but the other girls seemed to have established bonds, and being new, Gretchen felt left out. It was easy to see there was a hierarchy. Blondes, with light-wheat-colored hair, were considered the top of the line. Gretchen, with her strawberry-blonde hair and freckles, felt a little unattractive. Hilde had brown hair, and she wasn't nearly as nice looking as Gretchen, but Hilde seemed to be accepted by the others. As the day wore on, Gretchen began to feel more comfortable, and as she relaxed, the others began to warm up to her. By the end of the day, Gretchen decided that she liked the group.

The leader set the girls up to run a mile race, and Thea immediately took the lead. Her legs were long and muscular, and she looked like a beautiful animal when she ran—something gorgeous and blonde, perhaps a lioness. Gretchen was athletic but she didn't excel at running, so she admired Thea's grace and speed.

Thea was several yards in front of everyone when Judith, one of the clumsier girls, tripped and twisted her ankle, letting out a scream. The other girls turned to see what happened but kept running. The only one who turned around and gave up her lead was Thea. Thea ran to Judith and carefully lifted the heavy girl, helping her to the sideline.

"Did you see that?" Gretchen asked Hilde after the race was over. "If Thea would not have turned back to help Judith, she would have won."

"I know. Thea's done things like that before. She's a fool if you ask me," Hilde said.

"She is, but she is so kind."

"That's why she's a fool," Hilde said. "Kindness is a weakness. Don't you know that?"

Gretchen shrugged. She wasn't sure how to answer.

On Monday, after school, Gretchen went into work. When they took their meal break, Hilde told Gretchen all the gossip about every girl in the Bund. Judith was sickly; Anna had pimples on her back, and Marlene had a reputation for being very promiscuous. It seemed that Hilde knew something private about everyone except Thea. All Hilde said about Thea was that she and a boy named Hann Meier were seen together quite often. Everyone thought Thea and Hann would become engaged as soon as they finished school.

"I'm a little jealous. He is so handsome," Hilde said. "Some girls get everything. You know what I mean? Looks, the right boys, everything . . ."

"You'll meet someone nice. You'll see," Gretchen said.

"Have you ever secretly wished that you could be someone else?"

"What do you mean?"

"I mean, have you ever wanted to trade everything about yourself and replace it with another person's qualities? I guess what I am saying is that I wish I were Thea instead of me."

"Oh, Hilde, don't feel that way. You are a wonderful person," Gretchen said. "You're very pretty in your own right."

"You know you're lying," Hilde said. "No one could honestly call me pretty."

Gretchen didn't know how to answer, so she said nothing.

On Tuesday evening, Gretchen was to attend her third Bund at the home of one of the other BDM members.

"Come to my flat before the meeting. We can get dressed

together. My parents are always out; they're never home," Hilde said. "My father doesn't always come right home after work, if you know what I mean. Sometimes he's gone for days at a time. He's had girlfriends for as long as I can remember. And my mutti? Now she's a real case. She'll probably be at the neighbor's flat, drinking and complaining about my father. But if for some crazy reason she happens to be home, chances are she'll be drunk and asleep. So no one will disturb us while we're getting ready. I live only a few streets away from Anna's flat where they are holding the meeting. Once we're ready, we can quickly walk over together. By the way, don't eat. We always have a cooking class on Tuesday, so we will both have a nice meal."

"Really?"

"Yes!"

"I'll have to prepare something that I can leave for my father's evening meal before I go out. He's terrible at taking care of himself, but it won't take me long. I am pretty good at throwing something together quickly after work. Once I've made his dinner, I'll come over. I'll bring all my things and get dressed at your place."

"That will be perfect. And by the way, I have a surprise. I have a tube of red lipstick. I'll let you try it."

"You do? How did you get it?"

"Never mind how I got it. I have it! Anyway, stop asking so many questions. Do you want to try it on or not? It's a wonderful shade of red that will look just gorgeous on you." Hilde said, winking at Gretchen.

"Of course, I want to try it," Gretchen said.

"Then make sure you put your father's dinner together quickly and come over to my flat just as soon as you can."

"I will."

Gretchen made a stew that was mostly potatoes and carrots with a little broth. She left a note on the table for her father explaining where she was going, packed a small bag, and left.

Hilde and Gretchen got dressed quickly. Hilde pulled out the coveted tube of lipstick, and with a smile, she handed it to Gretchen.

"Here. Try it on."

Gretchen carefully applied the lipstick. "This is so pretty," Gretchen said. "I feel so glamorous—like a movie star."

"I know. Don't you? I just love it too."

Both girls stared at themselves in the mirror, then they broke out into giggles.

"We can't wear this red lipstick to the meeting, or we'll get in trouble," Hilde said. They blotted the lipstick until it was barely visible, so they would not be forced to wash it off entirely.

Once they were both ready, they left Hilde's flat to walk to Anna's house. On the way, they talked about the boys they knew from work, giggling conspiratorially. When they arrived at Anna's, all the girls from the Bund were there. They were planning to prepare a meal together. Surprisingly, there were plenty of eggs to go around and enough sugar to bake a luscious cake. They were told to pair up with another girl and given plenty of cooking instructions. Hilde and Gretchen paired up. When everyone was ready, Frau Lundschmidt, the group leader, turned to Thea and said, "Thea, if anyone needs help, would you please help her?"

"Of course, Frau Lundschmidt," Thea said. "I would be happy to help."

"Can you believe Frau Lundschmidt asked Thea to help everyone? Is there anything that Thea isn't perfect at?" Hilde whispered in Gretchen's ear.

"I'm sure there is something. No one is perfect at everything,"

Gretchen said trying to comfort her friend.

'Well, I sure wish I knew what it was. Then I would not feel as defective as I do," Hilde moaned.

Even though she was on a team with another girl, Thea made sure to go around the room and help others several times.

After they finished eating, all the girls sat around the table with full bellies, sipping coffee, and talking about the importance of being a good German wife and mother.

"She must be virtuous, strong, and able to stand behind her husband. She should be modest, and a woman that all can admire," Frau Lundschmidt said. The girls nodded in agreement. "Look at Thea. She is the perfect example of an Aryan girl. She's beautiful, virtuous, and capable. She will make some man the perfect wife. Now, let's all thank her for her help today."

"Thank you, Thea," they said in singsong unison.

Next, the leader went around the table and asked each girl to tell a story about something that had happened to her the previous week.

At the end of the meeting, the girls sang a song written by a man Gretchen didn't know. His name was Horst Wessel. Gretchen sat silently because she didn't know the words. . But things happened so fast that once the girls finished singing, Hilde whispered in Gretchen's ear, "Don't worry, I'll teach you the song tomorrow at work so you'll know it by the next meeting."

Gretchen gave Hilde a quick, uneasy smile. Then all the girls were hugging each other and saying goodbye.

As they walked home, Hilde and Gretchen talked about the meeting. The sun had set, and the temperature dropped. It was getting chilly, and Gretchen pulled her sweater tighter around her body.

"So what did you think of the meeting?" Hilde asked.

"It was fun. The food was wonderful. I couldn't believe how much there was. I have never had an omelet made from two eggs before. And that cake …" Gretchen said.

"It was delicious, right?"

"Yes, it certainly was."

"You know, once the führer restores Germany to her rightful place in the world and gets rid of all the undesirables, like the Jews and the Gypsies, there will be plenty of everything left for the rest of us. No more rationing. Won't that be nice?"

Gretchen nodded. "If tonight's dinner is any indication of the future then yes, it will be very nice."

They walked for another block in silence. A soft wind rustled the trees, and although she said nothing, Gretchen wondered what Hitler planned to do with all the people he had deemed undesirable.

CHAPTER TWENTY-THREE

The first time Hilde saw Thea and Hann walking together holding hands, she felt as if the world had stopped. The green of the trees was a little less vibrant, the colors of the flowers were not nearly as lovely, and although it was late spring, she felt as frozen as if it were the middle of winter. She first saw them on a Saturday. Hilde was on her way to the market when she saw Thea and Hann directly across the street. Thea saw Hilde too, and called out, "Hello there, Hilde!"

Hilde stared directly at Thea and forced the biggest smile she could muster.

"Hello, Thea!" But even as she tried to be friendly, her heart was black with jealousy. If only she could be as beautiful and as popular as Thea. If only she had a boyfriend who was handsome and popular like Hann. Then she too could be the envy of every girl in the Bund. Thea was everything Hilde always wanted to be. It wasn't that Hilde didn't have friends—she did—but Hilde was not popular the way Thea was. No one admired Hilde or treated her like she was something special. Then again, she knew she wasn't special. Hilde was not a leader; she was a follower in every way. She joined the BDM and became a staunch supporter of the Nazi cause because it was the accepted thing to do. Her hair and clothes were always copies of the most popular styles. And although she never told anyone, she always knew that she wasn't pretty. When she looked in the mirror, she saw an average-looking girl with mousy brown hair and a strained smile. She felt most comfortable with girls who were not beautiful either—average girls who lacked the spark Thea had from birth. That was, of course, except for Gretchen. Gretchen had a way of making Hilde feel like she too was beautiful and Hilde loved her for it. Hilde was too ashamed of her feelings to share them with anyone, not even her best friend, Gretchen. She secretly wished that if she couldn't be just like Thea, then she'd like to find a way to destroy her. But of course, that was impossible. Thea was the brightest star in their group of girls and it seemed to Hilde that Thea had everyone's admiration.

The next meeting of the Bund was at Thea's house. Hilde was shocked to find that Thea's mother was as pretty and charming as her daughter. She was a perfect hostess, not crude and fat like Hilde's mother who drank too much, belched, and often embarrassed her. The girls baked a raisin and vinegar strudel. Once it was baked, each girl took a slice and sat around a wooden table discussing the importance of Nazi holidays. They spoke with enthusiasm of all the different celebrations, each girl eager to please Frau Lundschmidt.

"When I get married and have children," one of the girls said, "I am going to make sure that my children know the importance of all the holidays. We will celebrate Tag der Arbeit, Labor Day, and of course, we will have a special celebration for Erntedankfest, the harvest festival."

"That's very good," Frau Lundschmidt said. "And now, I have something very exciting to tell all of you. We have a very important holiday coming right up. Does anyone know what that special day is?"

"Yes," Thea raised her slender arm.

"Go on and tell us then, Thea."

"It's Führergeburtstag, our führer's birthday."

"That's right. And does anyone know the date?"

Judith raised her hand. "April twentieth."

"Correct. And since that very special day is coming right up, our group is going to join with the boys in the Hitler Jugend for a celebration. We will have a spring dance party."

The girls let out gasps, and some giggled. An excited buzz of whispering filled the room.

"Quiet down now, girls," Frau Lundschmidt said, trying to be stern. Then she shook her head and smiled. "Oh well, there's really no need to be silent. Go on and chatter; this is a very exciting celebration. But even so, you must keep your voices down. We are in someone's home, and we must be respectful. After all, ladies, we must never forget who we are. We are superior women, Deutche maidels. The future of our beloved fatherland. So it is essential that we always show some decorum."

Many of the girls nodded.

Hilde reached over and squeezed Gretchen's arm gently. "I'm so happy. This will be so much fun," she whispered.

Gretchen smiled.

It was Gretchen's first BDM dance. Because it was a celebration for Hitler's birthday, all the schools and businesses were closed. The girls would have the entire day to get ready. However, Gretchen was not planning to attend because she didn't own a party dress. Her father never had enough money to spare. Until now, she hadn't cared because she never needed one.

After the meeting ended, Hilde and Gretchen walked home together.

"You are going to really love this dance. This is only the second one I have attended, but they are so much fun," Hilde exclaimed.

"Hilde," Gretchen said. "I'm not going."

"What? Why not? Of course, you're going."

"I can't."

"Tell me why."

Gretchen hesitated. She was embarrassed. "I don't have a party dress. I only have two dresses, and they are suitable for work and school but not for a party."

"Is that all?" Hilde said, shaking her head. "Why don't you come to my house and look through my closet? I know I'll have something that will look ravishing on you. You can borrow it. You are rather slender so we might have to alter the size with a belt, but we'll sort it all out. Don't worry."

"Are you sure you don't mind?"

"Quite sure. So, you'll come over?"

"Of course," Gretchen said smiling at her dear friend.

"How about you come by my house tomorrow after work?"

"All right. I'll tell my father I am going to be late coming home."

After the girls parted, Gretchen went home, but Hilde didn't. She took a bus five miles to the Jewish sector of town where she found a woman's dress shop. She went inside and began to look around. A very thin, older woman with a slight hump in her back wearing an elegant tailored, black dress walked up to her.

"Can I help you, dear?" she asked.

"Oh, no thank you. I'm just looking," Hilde answered. She selected several dresses off the rack and carried them into the dressing room.

"Well, if you need anything, just call. I'm right here, and I'd be happy to assist you."

Hilde found it easy to steal from Jews. She'd been caught once when she took the lipstick from a Jewish shop. The owner was furious, but when Hilde threatened to tell the German police that he had molested her, he let her go without reporting the theft. The best part was that she still kept the tube of lipstick.

The shopkeeper was not watching Hilde intently, making it easy for her to put two dresses on underneath the dress she was wearing. She hung the others back on the hangers and handed them to the shopkeeper.

"I'm sorry. I didn't find anything," Hilde said. *These Jews have been stealing from us good Germans for a very long time. So what if I get a little of it back?* Hilde thought.

"Well, good luck to you. I hope you find what you're looking for," the shopkeeper said as she began to straighten the dresses on the hangers.

Hilde left the store and ran home. She carefully removed the price tags and hung the stolen goods on hangers. She marveled at her conquest. One dress was pale pink, and the other was pale yellow. Either one would be perfect for a spring dance. They fit Hilde, so she knew both dresses would be too big for Gretchen. Since Hilde liked both frocks equally, she decided she would let Gretchen choose first then she'd wear the other one. Once Gretchen chose her favorite, Hilde would help her add a belt at the waist to make it fit.

Sitting on her bed with her back against the wall, Hilde smiled. She was excited about the dance. Perhaps, by some miracle, with her new dress and her red lipstick, she would be able to attract Hann's attention. She could hardly wait until the dance. It was two weeks away, and she was counting the days.

CHAPTER TWENTY-FOUR

Two days after Hilde stole the dresses, she decided she also needed a fancy handbag. Carrying an old worn bag with a pretty dress would not do. She had no money, but that didn't worry her. Since the führer had taken power, getting what she wanted or needed was easy. *You just have to know how to make the best of a situation*, Hilde thought smiling to herself.

She knew there was a leather shop in the Jewish neighborhood. She had walked by it several times and had seen its owner, an old shoemaker. Hilde had no doubt that she could scare him into giving her a bag by saying she would report him for trying to molest her. This tactic was working so well on the male Jewish shop owners that she was beginning to feel powerful like she could have any material thing her heart desired.

She was quite sure the old shoemaker would be no different. After all, no Jew in his right mind would risk arrest. From what she had heard, those who did suffered pure hell. And, of course, the Jew would know that the police would take the word of an Aryan girl over his. He would, no doubt, give her a bag. Perhaps she could get two—one for herself and one for Gretchen. Gretchen would surely enjoy a new bag.

Even though Hilde considered Gretchen her best friend, she would never take her along on such a mission. *It wasn't smart to trust anyone too much. Things can always go wrong.* So rather than share her plans with Gretchen, she decided to handle things on her own.

After work the following day, Hilde walked to the Jewish sector of town. She turned onto the street where Dreifuss and Company, the handbag and accessory shop, was located and began to window shop. Since discovering her new scare tactic, she felt like a rich woman. *I can demand anything of a male Jewish shop owner, and he would be a damn fool not to give it to me without causing a problem.* She was looking for a dress store owned by a man. She didn't want a dressy dress like the ones she'd stolen the other day but thought it would be nice to have a few new, casual frocks to wear to work.

As she sauntered down the shop-lined streets, she happened to recognize Thea's mother. Hilde was sure it was her; she remembered her from the Bund meeting. But what was she doing in the Jewish sector of town? Hilde had to know. There might just be a secret here, one she could use to destroy Thea. Careful not to be seen she followed Thea's mother and watched as she entered a building. The window blinds were down, but there was a small crack where Hilde could see inside. She stopped and stared through the crack. It was only a few minutes before Thea's mother entered the room. Hilde's mouth fell open when she saw Thea's mother taking off her blouse. Then Thea's mother sat down on the examining table wearing nothing but a bra and her skirt. Hilde read the sign above the storefront: Doctor Benjamin Fineberg.

Fineberg! Of course, he's a Jew. We are in the Jewish sector of town; what else would he be? A smile came over Hilde's face. She watched the doctor lean over Thea's mother. *Did I see him kiss her?* she asked herself, knowing full well that she had not but wanting to believe that she did

112

see it. *He kissed her. The Jewish doctor kissed Thea's mother, and Thea's mother was naked.*

Hilde spoke the lie that was forming in her mind, out loud, hoping that doing so would make it true. *He kissed her, and I saw them; they were starting to make love.* The more she said it to herself, the more she began to believe it. Hilde quickly lost all interest in finding a handbag. She was too excited to worry about a purse. All she wanted was to get home and figure out what to do with this new information. Her heart was pounding fast. The more she thought about what she saw, the more real it became in her mind. She knew that she would find Anna and Judith, the Zimmer sisters, at the market. They were a year apart in age and had been schoolmates since Hilde started school. Both were also in the BDM. The two Zimmer sisters could always be found at the market after school, helping their father clean the family bakery.

Hilde tried to mess her hair and look as if she'd been running as she walked into the store. Mr. Zimmer was sweeping, and he turned and said, "Hello, Hilde. I don't have any bread left. I'm sorry. But the girls are in the back washing the pans."

"May I go back and see them?" Hilde asked in her sweetest voice.

"Of course. But you look a little frazzled. Are you all right?"

"Yes, yes, I'm fine," Hilde said, and she walked into the back of the bakery.

"Hilde's here," Judith said, wiping her hands on her apron.

"Here, have a cookie. Papa saved a few for us," Anna said.

Hilde took a cookie then sat down on a stool. "I have something that I need to talk to someone about. I don't know who to turn to."

"You can talk to us," Judith said.

"Yes, of course you can," Anna chimed in.

"Well, I saw something today that really frightened me."

"What?"

"I don't want to cause trouble. But I have to tell someone . . ."

"Go on . . . tell us," Anna said.

"Well . . ." Hilde hesitated for dramatic effect. The Zimmer sisters were listening intently. "I saw Thea's mother and the old Jew doctor in town." Hilde told the girls how she saw Thea's mother kissing Dr. Fineberg through an opening in the blinds in his office. "She was naked and so was he." The story grew as Hilde went on. "And have you noticed? There's a small bump in Thea's nose, and I think I've seen her dark roots. I am fairly sure she bleaches her hair. Do you think it's possible that Dr. Fineberg is her real father? Maybe she's half Jew."

None of the girls really liked Thea; she was too pretty, too perfect. So the two Zimmer girls easily swallowed the tale that Hilde was spinning. By the end of the week, the rumor had spread through the girls in the BDM like an aggressive cancer. By the following week, not only the girls in the BDM knew the story, but even the girls' parents were talking.

One afternoon when the BDM girls were showering after running the track, Hilde stood back a few minutes. She looked around carefully to be sure no one else saw her. Once she was sure she was alone, she took her tube of lipstick and dropped it into Thea's handbag. She quickly ran into the shower before anyone realized she was missing.

Afterward, while the girls were getting dressed, Hilde let out a cry of panic. Everyone gathered around her. "I just found my lipstick in Thea's handbag. Her handbag was open on the bench, and I saw it in there. I wasn't sure it was mine, so I checked my purse, and sure enough, my lipstick is missing. She must have stolen it. Isn't that just like a Jew to steal? I told you she was a Jew."

"Let me see inside your purse," Anna said to Thea.

"No. You don't need to see inside my purse," Thea said, shaking her head.

"Then Hilde's telling the truth. You stole her lipstick," another girl said.

"I did not."

"Then why are you afraid to let us see inside your handbag? If you didn't take it, it won't be there," Anna said.

"Here. Go ahead and look." Thea thrust her handbag at Anna.

Anna fished through the contents and easily found the tortoiseshell tube. She took it out and opened it. "Is this your lipstick?"

"No. It's not mine. I don't know how it got into my bag," Thea said. "I don't own any lipstick."

"It's mine, and you stole it. Thea, you are a dirty, lying Jew," Hilde said.

"I'm not Jewish. I swear it. And I didn't take that lipstick. I don't know how it got into my purse."

The other girls shook their heads.

"Please, you have to believe me."

"This is a crime. We have a responsibility to tell Frau Lundschmidt," Judith said.

"But I didn't do it. I swear to you; I didn't."

The girls refused to listen to Thea. A band of them got together and took the tube of lipstick to Frau Lundschmidt.

"You are expelled from the group until further investigation," Frau Lundschmidt told Thea in a stern voice. "This is a terrible thing you did, Thea. I have always liked you, and I would never have expected such behavior from you. But lately, I have heard some very disturbing things about you."

"They are not true," Thea said.

"We shall get to the bottom of this. But until we do, you will not be able to go to the dance this weekend."

"Oh no, please. I didn't steal anything. I didn't do anything wrong. I swear to you that I didn't." Thea began to cry, but the other girls didn't pay any attention. They left her standing alone in the locker room with tears running down her cheeks. It was very difficult, but Hilde had to exercise strong self-control to keep the smirk off her face.

CHAPTER TWENTY-FIVE

Gretchen walked to Hilde's flat on the afternoon of the dance, expecting to be disappointed. She was hoping that Hilde would have a dress that she could borrow, but she knew that Hilde was much bigger than her, and the chances were slim that any dress of Hilde's would look presentable on her. Gretchen was prepared to go home disappointed instead of going to the dance to celebrate the führer's birthday.

She would never tell anyone, but she didn't care much for the führer. All this nonsense about Jews was a waste of time. Sometimes it got on her nerves. It seemed pointless. Instead of creating fear and hatred inside of her, it was a constant reminder of how much she had enjoyed the company of the Jewish boy, Eli. She thought of his kind but dark and mysterious eyes. She remembered the thoughtful words he said about her mother and the way he made her feel. It was something she never dared tell anyone.

Gretchen knocked on the door to Hilde's flat. Hilde opened the door smiling and said, "Come on in. I got some bread and a little cheese for us. Are you hungry?"

She anticipated Gretchen coming over, and she wanted to be able to offer her something to eat. So as soon as school was over, Hilde ran to the bus stop and caught the first bus to the Jewish bakery on the other side of town. She waited until the shop was empty and then threatened the Jewish baker. She said she would go to the police and tell them that the baker had tried to rape her. It worked. The man's son, who was working with him, was so upset that he went to the showcase and put the last three loaves into a brown paper bag and handed them to her. The baker made a face, but he said nothing.

Hilde tucked the package under her arm and left the bakery. She smiled as she headed back home. Even before she left the house, she knew that her plan would work, and she would get at least one loaf for free. It turned out that she got three. Now she had plenty for the entire week. Well, the Jews were scared. It would suit her just fine to keep them that way.

However, Hilde didn't go to the Jewish sector to get her cheese. She stole the cheese from her neighbor's pantry while babysitting their child two nights before. She hid it in her dresser drawer because she didn't want to share it with her parents. Luckily, they were not home very often. When the neighbor came over and asked about it, she denied ever having seen it, and the neighbor left. She was happy to share it all with Gretchen.

"Actually, yes. I'm very hungry," Gretchen admitted.

The girls sat at the table and ate. "This bread is delicious," Gretchen said. "I've never had bread like this."

"It's an egg bread. I'm not sure what it's called but I made it," Hilde lied. She couldn't tell her the truth.

"You'll make some fellow a very good wife one day," Gretchen said.

"I hope it's Hann Meier." Hilde smiled.

"I think he has been seeing Thea. Have you heard that too?"

"He might have been seeing Thea, but I'll bet when he hears that she's half Jewish, he'll run."

"Do you really think she is?"

"Sure. I know it. Look at that bump on her nose. It looks like a Jew nose to me. And just look at her hair. Sometimes when her fake blonde color is growing out, you can see that her roots are very dark. Black, like Jew or Gypsy hair."

"Really? I've never seen that."

"That's because you're not looking. But I saw it. And besides, who but a Jew in our group would dare to steal my lipstick? Everyone knows Jews are thieves."

Gretchen shrugged. She didn't want to argue with her friend, but she felt sorry for Thea. In a matter of a month, Thea lost all her friends. She went from being the most popular girl in the Bund to being ostracized. Gretchen was pretty sure that when the gossip about Thea being half Jewish reached Hann, he would probably abandon Thea too. *Poor thing*, Gretchen thought. *A few malicious words can ruin a person. This fear is what the führer has brought to Germany. Suspicion, hatred, anger, and fear. No, I really don't care for Adolf Hitler at all.*

The girls finished eating, and Hilde quickly cleaned up the kitchen.

"Now, come with me. I want you to see the dresses."

Gretchen followed Hilde into her room. Hilde had laid both frocks out on her bed. Gretchen's eyes lit up when she saw the dresses.

"Oh, Hilde, they're both so pretty."

"Which one do you like?"

"Yellow, I think."

"All right. Try it on," Hilde giggled. As expected, the dress was a little too big, but when belted it fit nicely. "Do you like it?" Hilde asked.

"Of course. Are you sure I can borrow it? I will be afraid to eat or drink anything. I don't want to spill on it."

"You can keep it. It's too small for me anyway."

"Oh, Hilde, you are such a good friend." Gretchen hugged Hilde, and Hilde swelled with happiness. Gretchen was the first real friend she ever had. She felt almost like Gretchen was her sister.

CHAPTER TWENTY-SIX

The dance was held in the school gymnasium, where the odor of sweat mixed with bleach lingered in the air. The wood floor was polished to a spit shine; the tables were covered with white linen, and Nazi flags and pictures of the führer hung on the walls.

"Look," Hilde whispered to Gretchen as they walked by the refreshment table displaying cake and punch. "There is cake. I can't believe they have enough cake for all these people. It's hard enough to get sugar to bake a small cake."

"I know; I see. Of course, there's plenty of cake. It's the führer's birthday," Gretchen said trying not to sound sarcastic.

A few couples were moving slowly on the dance floor while a band of three young men played dance music. Most of the girls were on one side of the room and the boys on the other. Nervous female laughter rang out over the music, and a couple waltzed by Gretchen and Hilde.

Hilde tugged at Gretchen's sleeve. "Look over there. It's Hann Meier. He's here alone. Doesn't he look handsome?"

"Yes, he is handsome, but I don't want you to get hurt, Hilde. He's alone, but he is probably looking for Thea."

"You don't think he's heard all the talk about her?"

"I don't know," Gretchen said. Then not being able to stop

herself, she added, "I feel kind of sorry for her."

"Oh, please. She's a liar and a Jew. And furthermore, she's a thief. I bet he's here alone looking to meet someone new. He's probably fed up with her reputation. He would be a fool to keep seeing her now. Everyone would call him a Jew-lover."

'I noticed that Thea wasn't here tonight, but I thought it was because she was kicked out of the group," Gretchen said.

"You're right. She wasn't allowed to come because she's a half Jew.

Gretchen didn't want to argue with her best friend, so she said nothing. She just nodded and poured herself a cup of punch.

"I am going to go over and talk to him," Hilde said.

"Wait a few minutes, and he might come over here. Let him ask you to dance."

"I don't want to wait until he decides to ask someone else. I want to get to him first before it's too late."

Gretchen nodded, but she was afraid her friend was setting herself up for rejection.

"How do I look?" Hilde asked.

"Fine. You look fine," Gretchen said, thinking that the dress was a little tight on Hilde. Even though she was just a teenager, Hilde looked matronly, more like one of the older teachers than one of the young girls. Gretchen couldn't figure out what to do to make Hilde more attractive, so she said nothing.

Hilde squared her shoulders, winked at Gretchen and then turned and walked over to Hann. *Oh my, I hope he will dance with her. Her feelings will be hurt if he rejects her. Yet she is so bold. I have to give her credit for that. I wouldn't have the courage to approach a handsome, popular boy. If he didn't approach me first, we would never meet.*

Hilde and Hann were talking. Hilde's hands were moving quickly as she spoke, and she was laughing loud enough for Gretchen to hear across the room. Gretchen watched Hilde and Hann, thinking Hilde looked almost cartoonish. But then a tall, slender boy with blond hair walked over to Gretchen, interrupting her thoughts and introduced himself.

"Hello, I'm Norbert," he said. He was very handsome, impeccably clean with clothes that looked expensive. His features were as perfect as if he were a statue chiseled out of marble. His chin and cheekbones were strong, and his pale hair was full.

"I'm Gretchen."

"Would you like to dance?" he asked.

"Yes, but I am not a very good dancer," she stammered. "I don't dance much, I am afraid."

"Well, we will just have to fix that, won't we? A girl as pretty as you should dance every day even if it's in front of the mirror in your own home."

She put her cup of punch down on the table, and he took her hand leading her out to the dance floor.

Norbert moved Gretchen across the floor so gracefully that she could almost make believe that she was a wonderful dancer. After the music stopped, he followed her to retrieve her cup of punch and then led her to a seat on the other side of the room.

Sitting down beside her, he said, "So tell me a little about yourself."

"What would you like to know?"

"Anything? Everything?"

She laughed. "Everything? I'm afraid that the dance won't last long enough for me to tell you *everything*."

He laughed too. "Then we will just have to see each other again, won't we?"

Gretchen found him charming. They talked about their schools, their teachers, and their families. She learned that Norbert came from a wealthy family. He made it clear without bragging that he did not want for anything. He explained that his family was not aristocratic; in fact, they were not even educated. They'd been fortunate in that his father's restaurants had become local hangouts for some of the top men in the SS. And at the same time, he made Gretchen feel like the prettiest, most desirable girl in the room. He made her feel that everything she said was important to him. His eyes were fixed on hers as she spoke. Not once did he look at any of the other girls as they sat side by side. His knee brushed hers, and she felt a spark of sexual desire pass through her body. She never felt tingles in the places where she was feeling them now. It was as if electricity was shooting through her body, and every nerve was responding.

They danced again and again, and before Gretchen realized it, the time had come to go home.

"I really would like to see you again. My father owns three restaurants with lovely outdoor beer gardens. They are scattered throughout Berlin. I would like to take you to dinner one night. Would you have dinner with me?"

"I would." She smiled.

"Well, then, how about next Friday?"

"Yes, that would be fine."

"Give me your address, and I will come to your home to pick you up. Would seven be too early?"

"No, it would be fine," Gretchen said smiling.

"May I walk you home?"

"I'm afraid not. I came with a girlfriend, and I have to find her, so we can walk home together."

"Everyone is leaving; shall I wait with you until you find her?"

"No, I'm all right, really. I will find her. Go on home. I'll see you Friday."

After Norbert left, Gretchen searched for Hilde but couldn't find her anywhere.

CHAPTER TWENTY-SEVEN

Gretchen was worried about Hilde, and at the same time she was sick to her stomach from all the sugar in the cake and punch. With the sugar being so expensive and not a necessity, she rarely ate so many sweet things. Her belly ached and cramped as she wretched in the bathroom stall, feeling the bile rise in her throat. *I should have never separated from Hilde. Never.* After she was done throwing up the punch and cake, she leaned against the wall and tried to regain her composure. She knew she would have to go to the leaders of the group and tell them that Hilde was missing. Her heart pounded. Anything could have happened to Hilde, anything at all. Gretchen shivered. She cleared her throat and walked to the sink where she splashed cold water on her face.

"Gretchen, is that you?" It was Hilde's voice coming from one of the bathroom stalls.

"Are you all right?" Gretchen asked.

"No, I am not."

"Are you ill?"

"Hann rejected me flat out," she said, opening the stall door. "All he cared about was Thea. That was all he wanted to talk about. Thea this and Thea that. Would you believe he said he was hoping she would show up at the dance? I mean, is he stupid? Of course she would not be allowed to come to the dance, being a Jew and all. But listen to this. He said that Thea's father walked out on her mother because of the gossip about her having an affair with the Jew doctor," Hilde said. Hilde's face was red and tearstained. "Everyone knows about it. Hann told me first then Judith told me. Her mutti and Thea's mutti are best friends, or at least they were. Now, Judith's mutti won't have anything to do with Thea's family. They are tainted by Jew blood. They have a bad reputation. Hann didn't know she had been kicked out of the Bund, so I told him. He didn't believe any of the gossip, but I told him that I saw everything with my own eyes, and it's all true. I told him how I saw Thea's mother and the Jew doctor naked and having intercourse. I told him to look at the bump in Thea's nose the next time he saw her. I was sure that he would turn his back on Thea once he realized the absolute truth, but he didn't. Would you believe that he started to cry?"

"Oh no," Gretchen said.

"So I tried to offer him some comfort, if you know what I mean."

"Comfort?"

"Yes, you know . . . the stuff that happens between a man and a woman."

"You mean you kissed him?"

"No, silly. Boys don't care about kisses. I mean sex. I've done it before. Haven't you?"

"No. Never," Gretchen admitted.

"It usually softens fellows up. They go crazy for it. But not Hann. He didn't want to do anything with me. I even told him I'd put it in my mouth."

"Hilde! That's disgusting."

"They love it. But not Hann. He just shook his head and said no.

127

Would you believe it? He was all broken up over Thea. He said he was going right to Thea's flat to see if she was all right. I couldn't believe it. I am starting to think he is a Jew-lover too, just like Thea and her mother," Hilde said choking on her tears.

"Let's get you home and into bed. You'll feel better in the morning."

"I'll feel better after I tell everyone that Hann is nothing but a Jew-lover."

"Don't do that, Hilde . . ."

CHAPTER TWENTY-EIGHT

Hilde never said anything about Hann to anyone, yet she refused to give up on him. Instead, she tried to seduce him by bringing cookies to his house. To get the sugar, she intimidated the Jewish baker by threatening to say he raped her. The Jews would do anything to keep her from calling the Gestapo. Their fear of arrest was her good fortune.

Hann made it clear that he was devastated to lose Thea, but Hilde was quite certain that if she could just get him into her bed, he would forget Thea and become her boyfriend. Hilde could be relentless when she wanted something. In her mind, it was one of her best traits. She learned early on that if she cried loud enough, her parents would give her whatever she asked. Not because they loved her—she doubted seriously that they did—they were far too consumed with their own lives. No, they gave in because they couldn't bear to listen to her scream. Although she wasn't screaming at Hann, she wasn't going to let him go either. He was gentle but firm as he insisted he just wasn't interested in her. As time went on, Hann began to withdraw. He stopped answering the door when Hilde dropped in on him unexpectedly. She told herself that no one was home, but in truth, she knew he was avoiding her. Sometimes Hilde waited outside Hann's flat to walk to work with him. But when she tried walking beside him, he walked so fast that she almost had to jog in order to keep pace. Even worse, he didn't make conversation with her at all. If she asked him a question, he gave her a one-word answer. She knew he was trying to push her away, but she wanted him too much to give up. She ignored his signals and kept trying to penetrate his hard exterior.

Hilde had met several of the other boys who were in Hann's Hitler Youth group. She knew some of them from childhood and some from previous Bund events. Anytime she saw one of them, she asked about Hann. They all said he rarely showed up for his Hitler Youth meetings anymore. He made the excuse he was too busy working. His close friends swore he had also stopped going out to drink with them. One friend said he often saw Hann walking home alone. "He's been keeping to himself." The boy shrugged. "Don't know why."

Hilde didn't know why either, but she constantly speculated. She wondered if Hann had confronted Thea, and if so, what happened between them.

Hilde soon discovered the truth. Thea's father had, in fact, believed the rumors and left her mother. No one could blame him; no one wanted the stigma of a wife who was even faintly rumored to be sexually involved with a Jew. Thea and her mother moved quietly out of Berlin without telling anyone they were leaving or where they were going. Gretchen didn't know if it was because Thea and her mother couldn't afford to keep their flat without the father's income and were forced to move in with relatives somewhere, or perhaps they were just running away from all the gossip. Either way, Hilde won. Thea was gone. When Hilde talked to Gretchen about her victory over Thea, Gretchen felt awful.

"She had Hann in her clutches, and he was too good for her," Hilde said. "Well, she's gone now, isn't she? No one knows where she is, and that's for the best."

"It's kind of sad. I hope she's all right," Gretchen murmured.

"Oh, please! I hated Thea even before we found out she was a Jew. She was always pretending to be so perfect. Everyone was always saying she was so pretty. She was good at cooking, good at sports. Well, I'll tell you what she was not good at. She was not good at hiding her true identity."

Gretchen didn't feel comfortable asking Hilde to tell her the truth, but she secretly wondered if the rumors that Hilde had started about Thea were really based in fact. She wasn't sure how Hilde would react if she thought Gretchen doubted her truthfulness. Even though Gretchen and Hilde were friends, sometimes Gretchen was secretly a little afraid of her. If Hilde could ruin Thea, what could she do to Gretchen if she became angry with her? Gretchen didn't want to find out.

Even though Gretchen felt sorry for Thea and her mother, she was too filled with joy to stay unhappy for very long. Gretchen had begun seeing Norbert on a weekly basis. Sometimes he took her to one of his father's restaurants where they enjoyed lunch or dinner together. Other times, they walked through the park and the Berlin Zoo holding hands. Norbert was the first boy she had strong feelings for; she decided she was falling in love.

Norbert gave Gretchen her first kiss, and they spent hours hugging and fumbling with each other, whispering how much they cared for one another. They stayed up long after Gretchen's father went to bed, necking and coming as close as they could to intercourse without actually making love.

Hilde and Gretchen both graduated that spring. Gretchen had hoped to go to on to the university to further her education, but there was just not enough money. She and her father needed her salary to make ends meet. So, she began working more hours at the factory.

When summer arrived, the heat penetrated every corner of the factory where Hilde and Gretchen worked. Both of the girls had sweat stains in the armpits of their dresses by 8 a.m. each morning. The overwhelming heat made the days long. By the time afternoon came, they were both tired. Hilde and Gretchen took their lunch break together every day. Sometimes they sat outside while Gretchen divided up their food. Most days one of the girls brought bread and the other brought cold, boiled potatoes.

"I brought carrots today," Gretchen said, adding some to Hilde's plate.

"Oh good. I am starving."

"I know; I'm always hungry," Gretchen said. "Have you ever wondered what it would be like to eat until you were absolutely full?"

"I have wondered often. Which brings me to another question," Hilde said, her mouth stuffed with bread. "Are you going to the BDM camp this summer? I bet we'll get plenty to eat there. Good food too. Maybe meat of some kind. Think of it . . . sausage or chicken."

"I forgot about the Bund summer camp," Gretchen said honestly. "I've been so busy."

"I think it will be a lot of fun. And the best part of it all is that there is no charge. It's free, and from what I hear, they will be providing everything you could possibly want. I'm sure we'll play a lot of outdoor sports games, and there will be activities like swimming. I know how much you enjoy sports."

"Yes, I always have." Gretchen smiled.

"I know. Far more than I do." Hilde laughed. "That's because you're good at sports. I'm not nearly as good as you. In fact, I have to admit, I'm pretty bad. But that doesn't matter. What I am trying to say is that we will really enjoy the camp. I think you should come. We can have several weeks together without our parents. My folks aren't around much, but for you, it would be wonderful. You wouldn't have to take care of the house or cook for your dad. It would be a nice break."

"I know. It would be a lot of fun, and I would love to go, but that would mean leaving Norbert for several weeks. I don't want to leave him. We've become so close."

"Isn't he going? I am hoping Hann will go. I know he's been isolating himself since Thea left Berlin, but a holiday might be just what he needs to get back into the swing of things."

"Norbert can't go. He has to help his parents with the restaurants. They need him."

"Well, if Norbert can't come, there will still be plenty of other boys at the camp and no parents to keep a watchful eye." Hilde winked.

"It really sounds like fun. But I don't think I can go."

"There will be cookouts with the boys . . ."

"Yes. I think you should go. You will have a good time, but I want to stay home and be with Norbert."

"I realize this. I know you like him, but don't pass up this wonderful opportunity. Who knows when you will have another chance to take a holiday? Especially one that is completely paid for. We're about to graduate school. Soon we will be expected to join the workforce full time, and then we won't have time for much else. And besides, a holiday like this would be far too expensive for either of us if the government wasn't paying."

"I agree with you. You're right. But Hilde, I think I might be falling in love. I want to stay with Norbert. Can you understand?"

Hilde's face fell, and for a few moments, Gretchen just stared at her friend. She was suddenly sorry that she told Hilde how happy she was with Norbert. Gretchen knew that Hilde was terribly disappointed by Hann, and it made her bitter. Although Gretchen tried to put

Hilde's potential for cruelty out of her mind, she knew the truth. Hilde could be vicious. She saw Hilde's ugly side firsthand with Thea. Gretchen wondered if telling Hilde about her relationship with Norbert sparked the evil flame of jealousy in her, because as she looked into Hilde's eyes, she saw things she didn't like. A shiver ran up the back of her neck, and she felt her body shudder slightly.

"You really think you're in love? I mean, you think you might marry him?" Hilde asked, practically spitting the words out as if they were vile to her taste.

"Oh, I don't know," Gretchen said, realizing she'd said too much and trying to make things sound less serious.

"Do you think you might?"

Gretchen shrugged. "I have no idea. But I can't go to the camp anyway because my father needs the extra money that I earn. So I will have to work through the summer," Gretchen lied.

"Oh, all right. I know how that is. My parents are always nagging me for my pay. I'm really sorry you have to work the whole summer," Hilde said. The fact that Gretchen was going to have to work instead of going to camp seemed to satisfy her.

Gretchen saw Hilde's face relax, and she knew that Hilde liked the idea of Gretchen working all summer much more than she liked the idea of Gretchen falling in love.

After work, Hilde and Gretchen walked home together. As soon as they separated at the corner to go to their own homes, Gretchen breathed a sigh of relief. She was glad Hilde was going away for the summer. If she could, she would sever the friendship. The expression on Hilde's face when she told her she thought she was in love frightened her. However, Gretchen dared not break the friendship. Although Hilde had the potential to be a dangerous friend, she was an even more formidable enemy.

CHAPTER TWENTY-NINE

Summer 1934

At least once a week, Esther would sneak out of the flat she shared with her husband. She could only get away when her husband went into town to buy supplies to keep his business running. But as soon as he was gone, she practically ran the entire mile to Rebecca's house. How she loved to visit with her old friend. They laughed like children. As soon as Esther saw Rebecca, her face lit up like the golden sun. Somehow, poor Esther had ended up married to a man just like her father. Esther's husband, Daniel, had a tendency to drink too much, which sparked his terrible and irrational temper. Daniel struck Esther for the least little thing. If she burned a meal, he beat her. If he felt the house was not clean enough, he slapped her across the face. At first, Esther tried to hide her terrible marriage from Rebecca, but when Rebecca saw the bruises and asked about them, Esther finally told the truth. She admitted that her husband was an alcoholic, and not only that, he was a mean and vicious drunk. Then filled with despair, and being a lesbian, Esther knew she could never be happy in the arms of any man.

Rebecca didn't know what to say to Esther. It broke Rebecca's heart to see her friend suffering. She was so distraught about Esther that the next time she went to visit her parents she told them everything that was going on with Esther, except she did not tell them that Esther was a lesbian. But instead of showing sympathy for Rebecca's oldest and dearest friend, Rebecca's parents just glanced at each other. Then her mother cleared her throat and gently put her hand on Rebecca's shoulder and said, "Your father and I have discussed your friendship with Esther. We know that you and her have known each other for a very long time, but lately, when we see Esther at the market, she looks unkempt. Poor Esther comes from a less-than-perfect family. Her father is a drunk, and her mother is always a mess. Her mother walks around the neighborhood with her head uncovered, wearing a dirty dress. They are unrefined people."

"Mother! But Esther is my friend," Rebecca said.

"Esther is your childhood friend; I know this. But now it seems you have outgrown her. You are now an important woman. You are married to the son of a very well-respected rebbe. And Esther? Well, let's just say she has become a bad influence. People talk, you know, Rebecca. They will assume that because you spend time with Esther, you must be just like her. She doesn't mean to hurt you, I know, but believe me, if you are seen with her it will bring you down to her station in life. The best thing for you to do is to find new friends. I'm sure Eli has friends who are married. Make friends with their wives. You could also look for girls who live near you who have babies. Perhaps their luck will rub off on you, huh? And maybe you'll give me some nachas, some joy? Yes, maybe you'll make your old mother smile when you come and tell me that you are pregnant finally?" Rebecca's mother said, gently pinching Rebecca's cheek. She was trying to lighten the blow of what she just said.

Rebecca stared directly at her mother with her eyes blazing and shook her head. She was annoyed, but she would never argue with either of her parents. She would never dare to disrespect someone older than her, but especially not her parents. When she realized how brazen she was being by looking at her mother with such open rage, she looked away. Her parents didn't care about Esther. They always said they were sorry to see anyone suffer. But the truth was they never really and truly cared about anyone who wasn't a part of their family.

Rebecca knew her parents were proud of her husband. They felt she had made a very advantageous match, and they didn't want any interference from an old childhood friend. It hurt Rebecca to know her family could be so cold and calculating, but she knew they were always looking out for her best interests.

It also bothered her that, lately, all her parents and in-laws could talk about was how much they longed for a grandchild. Nothing else seemed to matter to them. It mattered to her too, and it wasn't that she didn't want a baby. She did. Rebecca believed that every woman wanted a child of her own, even though she was secretly terrified of being pregnant and giving birth. Yet she would have put her fears aside had she been able to conceive.

However, she was too ashamed to tell anyone that most nights Eli fell asleep without ever coming to her bed. He would come home from the yeshiva, wash, eat, and climb into his own bed. In minutes, he would be snoring softly. It made Rebecca feel inadequate. Perhaps she was not pretty enough? Perhaps she was not obedient enough? Perhaps she was not a good enough cook, or her housekeeping skills left something to be desired? She didn't know, but each day she tried harder to please her husband. And it seemed the harder she tried, the more distant he became.

She thought of asking him to come to her bed to give her a child. However, she couldn't bring herself to do so; she couldn't find the words to say. All she could do was wait until he chose to come to her bed. Most Friday nights, he would make a concerted effort to have intercourse because it was a mitzvah for a couple to become pregnant on the Sabbath. But quite often, even on Friday nights, he was unable to sustain an erection. After clumsily trying for several frustrating minutes, he would return to his own bed without a word.

She longed to comfort him, yet all she could do was lay there in the darkness with silent tears running down her cheeks and onto her pillow. Rebecca resigned herself to the fact that she was destined for a lonely life. She had no one she could speak freely with except Esther. Eli wasn't a bad husband—he never struck her or spoke rudely to her. His speech was always mild, and his voice was always soft. He was kind enough to her, but she found it strange that they were married a year now and still hardly spoke to each other. They never had full conversations, and their sexual unions were still awkward and uncomfortable. The worst part was that Rebecca knew Eli did not desire her. It made her feel worthless. After all, she grew up believing that a woman's purpose in life was to get married and serve her husband. She was raised to be a good wife and mother. It was most important for a good Jewish wife to make her husband happy. His food should be delicious, his home kosher, his clothes clean. He should find her attractive enough to want to give her children. Rebecca could easily see that her husband was dissatisfied with her, and to prove it, she had no children. Rebecca had failed.

No matter what her parents said about Esther, she refused to abandon her friend. Esther had already told Rebecca that she had no one else in the world. Rebecca cherished the friendship too. She felt unloved by her husband and like she'd failed her family. The only person she could rely on completely was Esther.

"My husband is a monster," Esther said. "He doesn't allow me to make friends. I am living like a sexual slave. If I do something he doesn't want me to do, he beats me. You're all I have, Rebecca."

"Your husband doesn't know you come here to see me?" Rebecca asked.

"No. He would never allow it. He doesn't even let me go to the shul. If I take too long at the market, he gets angry. And when he gets angry, he is impossible. Last night, he threw a shoe at me because I was taking too long to wash the dishes after dinner," Esther said, pulling up the sleeve of her dress to reveal a dark purple bruise on her skinny upper arm.

"Oh, Esther! I wish there were something I could do for you," Rebecca said.

"I know you wish you could stop him. But believe me, you do plenty for me just by being my friend. I can't tell you how much I look forward to coming here to see you when Daniel goes into town to buy what he needs for the store."

"Yes, and I am always glad to see you too, my dear old friend."

That day, when Esther left, Rebecca felt strange. The door closed, but she could still hear Esther's footsteps as she descended the stairs to the street. Rebecca looked out the window and watched Esther walk to the corner. Esther was so skinny and small that from the window, she looked like a child dressed in her mother's clothes. Her old dress was too big for her. Rebecca thought about the wrinkles that had formed around Esther's eyes and the misery she saw in them. *She only looks like a child from far away. But when I look at her face, I can see that she has aged. My poor friend. It breaks my heart to think of how much she has suffered in her life.* Rebecca watched through the window until Esther disappeared, then an overwhelming sadness came over her. She wanted to just put her head in her hands and cry. *This is not the way our lives were supposed to be. We were supposed to be married and happy.* Rebecca felt the tears begin to form behind her eyes. *My marriage is far from perfect. I know my husband isn't pleased with me, but at least he is gentle, and here, in the rebbe's house, I am treated with kindness. What more can a girl want out of life? Things could be a lot worse. Look at Esther. She suffers every day. She suffered as a child because of her terrible father. Now she suffers from her terrible husband.* Rebecca put her hands on her heart and began to pray. *Dear Hashem, please help my friend Esther. Please protect her and keep her safe.* Rebecca took a deep breath, then she went into the kitchen to scrub the floor. If she couldn't keep her husband happy at least her mother-in-law was always grateful for her help around the house.

Later that week, Rebecca was returning from shopping at the fish monger where she'd bought a piece of white fish for her mother-in-law. She was carrying the bloodstained package wrapped in white paper when she saw her mother walking down the road toward her home.

"Mama? Are you coming to visit me?" Rebecca called out. She was glad to see her.

"Yes, I brought you a fresh challah I baked yesterday," her mother said. But as she got closer Rebecca could see, in her mother's eyes, that something was wrong.

"Mama? Is something the matter? Is Papa all right?" Rebecca was worried. It was not like her mother to look so grim.

"Yes, your father is fine. But I need to talk to you."

"What is it?" Rebecca said as she opened the door to her house. "Come on inside and sit down," Rebecca said as her mother sat on the sofa, placing the challah, wrapped in a kitchen towel, on the coffee table in front of her. Rebecca was still holding the fish as she sat beside her mother.

"It's your friend, Esther"

"Esther?" Rebecca cocked her head.

"Yes." Rebecca's mother took her daughter's hands. "Something terrible has happened."

Rebecca looked into her mother's eyes. "To Esther?"

"I don't know how to say this, but she murdered her husband with a knife, then she killed herself."

Rebecca's mouth fell open. She turned white. Her body was shaking. "Are you sure?"

"Yes. I am sure. It's a terrible shame."

"Esther is dead?" Rebecca said in disbelief

Her mother nodded. "I'm sorry."

Rebecca could not speak. The fish, wrapped in white paper, fell from her trembling fingers, landing with a thud on the floor. She put her head in her hands. Her mother moved closer to her and tried to hug her, but Rebecca pulled away. "I'm sorry, Mama. But I need time alone," she said coldly. *If only I could have helped her. If only my parents had been willing to try to help her when I told them about how her husband was treating her. All they cared about was my reputation and the shanda it would be for a rebbe's daughter-in-law to have a friend with such problems. No one understood what a good friend she was and how much she meant to me.* Rebecca thought. *But it doesn't matter now. She's gone. My poor, dear friend, my poor, dear Esther. At least you won't have to suffer anymore.*

"Rebecca, let me make you some tea," her mother said. "You're so pale, you look like you have been possessed by a dybbuk. Pew, pew, pew, God forbid."

Rebecca glared at her mother. "I don't want anything. I'm going for a walk," she said, leaving her mother sitting in the living room.

There was nothing more to say. Rebecca's mother felt the tears forming in her eyes. She watched through the window as Rebecca ran down the street. Then she left the rebbe's house feeling guilty for having failed her daughter.

When they were children Rebecca and Esther had sometimes gone to sit on a bench that was under a tree by a small pond. It wasn't far from the rebbe's house, and although Rebecca had not been sure where she was going when she ran out, she found that her heart led her there. She sat down on the bench and looked out over the water. Then she wept.

When Eli returned home from the yeshiva he saw the package on the floor. He picked it up and opened it to find the fish inside. *Something has to be wrong. Rebecca would never have left this on the floor,* he thought. First he went to look for her in the bedroom, but she wasn't there. Then he searched the house. But when he didn't find her, he went outside and began to walk. He walked the entire Jewish sector before he came upon her sitting on the bench, her face stained with tears.

"Rebecca, what is it?" Eli asked.

"My best friend is dead, Eli. She was not the kind of girl your family would have wanted me to have as a best friend. She was a girl from a troubled family. I am not ashamed of her. I should never have allowed my parents to make me ashamed of her. Her name was Esther, and she was the closest and dearest person to me. She loved me, Eli. She loved me even though I couldn't love her the way she wanted me to. But her heart was so big and so good that she loved without needing anything from me." Rebecca was weeping. In between deep, heartfelt sobs she continued, "Her husband was beating her. She killed him, and then she killed herself. I knew he was treating her badly. I should have done something to help her. I told my parents, but they didn't want to bring shame on your family . . ."

He looked at her, his eyes as deep and dark as a black full moon.

"Shh, it's all right," he said. " I don't care about the scandal. I am so sorry for your pain. I wish I had known all this. I would have tried to help." Then he sat down beside her and took her into his arms. "You can always tell me anything, Rebecca."

She leaned her head on his shoulder, and he held her as she wept.

On a Friday night, two weeks after Esther died, Rebbe Kaetzel came home from services feeling tired. It was unlike him not to be social during the Sabbath dinner, but on this night, after he finished saying the prayers, he was out of breath and dizzy. He told his family he was feeling light-headed and had to lie down. Rebecca, his kind, quiet, and obedient daughter-in-law, brought his meal to him in his room.

What a joy this girl Rebecca was! How he kvelled, his heart filling with pride and happiness when he thought of the beautiful, young wife he found for his only son. She was everything he had hoped she would be. Eli seemed content, if not completely happy, but then, of course, Eli was never happy, not completely. The rebbe understood his difficult son better than most fathers would have. He was aware that his Eli had a restless spirit. His boy was searching for something. The rebbe knew that Eli felt discontent with the world he grew up in. Eli wasn't sure what he wanted; all he knew was that he was in search of a better way of life. Although Eli thought he was hiding his forbidden books from his father, the rebbe saw everything. He was well aware that Eli secretly read books that were not to be read by Hasidic Jews. But the rebbe remembered that when he was a boy, he too was restless—a seeker in search of something better. Throughout all of his searching, he came to know in his heart that there was no better life than the one he was born into. The rebbe never regretted his thirst for knowledge, but what he did regret was that, in his quest, he hurt his father by arguing with him about the old ways. And now Eli hurt him the same way. Even though Eli never told him, or argued with him, the rebbe knew that Eli was restless and questioned his faith. The rebbe's own restlessness was why he waited so long to marry and have children. The rebbe had waited until later in life, and then there had only been time enough for one son, his precious Eli.

Sometimes the rebbe wished he had married earlier. If Eli had been born when the rebbe was younger, he would have had more patience to deal with the active mind of his ever-questioning son. Sometimes he worried about Eli. However, the old man had confidence in God's ability to lead Eli in the right direction. After all, God had led him back from his wanderings to his rightful place as a Jew, so he trusted that God would do the same for Eli. In God's time. Because Rebbe Kaetzel's faith was strong, he gave his son a long leash.

The following morning was Saturday. The old rebbe sat among the men in the shul, as he had done since he was thirteen, after his bar mitzvah. The men began davening, and he joined them in swaying back and forth, feeling the power of prayer fill his soul as it always did.

For several minutes, no one noticed anything strange—they were too enraptured in prayer. But when everyone stood up to recite a prayer, Eli glanced over and saw that his father was not standing. Instead, he sat still, quietly slumped over. A lightning bolt of fear shot through Eli. All around him, men were praying, but he could not hear the prayers. A thunderous voice filled Eli's head, reiterating what he already knew. His papa was gone. He didn't cry out for help. This was a personal matter between Eli and the father who had given him life and tried to share his wisdom.

Eli leaned over and looked directly into his father's face. *Papa, you look so at peace. Where are you? Can you see me now?* Eli knelt between the seats in the shul and took his father's lifeless body in his arms. Eli held his father close and wept. He knew that in a single instant on this not-so-unusual day, his life was changed forever. From that moment on, he was on his own. Never again would he argue with his father, and

144

never again would he draw on his papa's wisdom to make decisions. *Alone. Completely and utterly alone.* Eli's shoulders shook as he wept. *I've failed him in so many ways. I've never been good enough to be the son of a great rebbe. I have always known it. But not my papa! He refused to believe I wasn't worthy. No matter what I did, my papa always believed in me. And now it's too late for me to find a way to prove to him that I can be the son he always wanted. Why do I always try to fix things after it's too late? Why is it that I am never contented? I am uncomfortable in my own skin. I really do appreciate the gifts God has bestowed upon me, but I am always in search of something more. What is wrong with me? What is it? Oh, Papa, it was too soon for you to go. I wasn't ready. I still have so many questions for you. I have so many doubts. I need your advice, your leadership. I know that I wasn't the son you wanted me to be, but what you never knew was that deep down in my heart, I really always admired you. It was just that I couldn't see myself capable of growing up and leading our people. You were strong, Papa, and now you are gone. You will never know how much I learned from you. You will never know how much I loved you.*

Eli saw the other men notice him and his father on the floor. Several men rushed over to Eli, and someone called an ambulance. Eli's mother and wife both came running down the stairs from the women's section in the balcony, but it was too late. There was no need to rush because there was nothing to be done. The old rebbe had left the earth while in prayer. Within the next few days there would be a burial then the family would sit Shiva. Eli would do what was expected of him. He would gather nine other men and together they would say the Kaddish, the prayers for the dead. The family would mourn, and then life would have to go on.

But how? Eli wondered. *How am I going to go on without my father? People will come to me for advice now, expecting me to know how to advise them. How will I ever do that? I don't have my father's wisdom, and I don't have a brother or anyone else to consult. I was raised to be the next rebbe, but I am not ready.*

Rebecca tried to help Eli up from the floor, but he shook her off, not wanting to look as weak as he felt. Immediately, he saw the hurt look on her face, and he was sorry. He knew he should apologize, but he couldn't. The words wouldn't come. *I hardly know my wife.* It was difficult for him to talk to this pretty, young woman he married. He wished she would yell at him: tell him off even. Tell him how angry she was that he pushed her away when she was trying to help him. He would be impressed if she would just challenge him. But he knew she would not. And because of that, he often thought of that outspoken, sassy, and adorable, little, forbidden shiksa, Gretchen Schmidt.

CHAPTER THIRTY

September 1935 Nuremberg

After the loss of WWI and the signing of the Treaty of Versailles, Germany was a broken land. She fell into a great depression with high unemployment. Every material thing necessary for life was rationed. Jobs were scarce. Hunger squeezed the Germans with an iron fist. All this left the German people shrouded in hopelessness.

When Adolf Hitler was appointed chancellor in 1933, assuring the German people that a new dawn of prosperity was on the horizon for their beloved fatherland, many people rallied in support. Hitler gave emotional speeches that filled his followers with hope and a guarantee of a Third Reich that would last for a thousand years. In short, he promised to restore Germany to her rightful place in the world.

But this bright promise came with a price. At first, many believed that the hatred the führer spewed toward Jews, Gypsies, Jehovah's Witnesses, and others whom he found undesirable, was merely talk. So many people said nothing would come of it. However, a few were alarmed. They weren't sure how bad things would be, but they knew a dark cloud was falling upon the land. Perhaps some were able to see that the treacherous reign of the Third Reich would end in the deaths of ninety million people: six million of whom were Jews.

On the fifteenth of September in the year 1935, in a town called Nuremberg, the Nazi Party held its annual rally. On this crisp autumn day, the red-and-black flags with the swastika insignia blew proudly in the soft, gentle breeze. A crowd gathered, bursting with excitement and anticipation. Pictures of the beloved führer hung on the walls of the buildings. Everyone was filled with hope for the promise of a new and better Germany.

At this meeting, the Nuremberg laws were adopted. Henceforth, German Jews were no longer German citizens. Jews weren't defined by their religious beliefs, but by their blood. If a German had at least three Jewish grandparents, he was considered a Jew. Even if his grandparents had converted, he was still considered Jewish.

Jews were excluded from politics. Many lost their jobs, and they were not allowed to marry or have sexual relations with anyone of German blood. Any contact between a Jewish person and a German citizen was considered racial infamy and a criminal offense. Jews Unwelcome signs hung in most public places. The only exception was during the 1936 Olympic Games when Hitler removed the signs to hide his hatred of Jews from the world. At least for a short time. However, even though the signs were removed, no German Jewish athletes were permitted to participate in the Olympic Games.

The Jews were losing their rights, but very slowly. So slowly that many people refused to pay attention. Jews and Gentiles alike. They ignored what was blatantly happening right in front of their faces. They went on with their lives as best they could, hoping it would all just go away. But it didn't, and they should have been alarmed.

Summer 1937

The relationship between Norbert and Gretchen grew deeper. They saw each other at least four times a week, often dining at each other's homes. Sometimes they went out to restaurants or took long walks through the park or the Berlin Zoo. They were young and full of passion. As soon as they found themselves alone, even in public places, Norbert passionately pushed Gretchen against a tree or the side of a building and stole a kiss. On afternoons when Gretchen's father worked late and Gretchen and Norbert were not working, Norbert came over, and the couple spent hours wrapped in each other's arms necking, petting.

One such afternoon, Gretchen and Norbert each took off work so they could be alone. They lay on the sofa, Gretchen with her head on Norbert's chest.

"I love your teeth," Norbert said.

"You what?"

"I love your teeth. They look like pearls."

"Pearls are round, Norbert."

He laughed. "I thought it sounded good. I heard an American actor say it in a movie when I was a child."

She laughed. "So, my teeth don't look like pearls?"

"I don't know. They're white and pretty."

"My teeth, Norbert? This is all you have to compliment me with?" She giggled and began tickling him.

"Don't, please . . ." he begged, laughing.

"My teeth?" she said again. Now they were both laughing.

"All right. All right. It was a stupid comment. I was trying to sound sophisticated."

She stopped tickling him, but they were both breathing heavily from laughing so hard.

Norbert took Gretchen's hands in his.

"Seriously. Do you know how I feel about you?" Norbert said, clearing his throat. "I think you do know."

"No, I don't . . . tell me." Gretchen smiled and winked at him.

"You little minx. You are teasing me again."

"Yes, maybe I am. But I want to hear you say it. Tell me how you feel."

"You aren't going to make this easy for me, are you?" Norbert asked.

"No, I am not. I am going to make you work very hard." She squeezed his hand. "Tell me, or I'll start tickling you again."

"Very well, then. I couldn't take another tickling round." He nodded. "So I guess I'll have to fess up."

She giggled. "Go on. I am listening."

"Gretchen Schmidt," he said, looking down at the floor then slowly raising his head and staring into her eyes. "I think I am in love with you."

"You think so, or you know?"

"I know."

"Then say it."

"Say what?"

"Come on, Norbert. Say it if you mean it," she said glaring at him in mock anger.

"I love you," he said. His voice was hoarse.

"I love you too."

"I want to marry you . . . if you'll have me."

"Marry you?"

"Yes. We'll have a good life together. My father is wealthy. You won't want for anything. And don't worry. We will help your father financially. I promise. He will be family, then."

"Marry you?" she repeated then sucked in her breath.

"You said you love me."

"I do. But marriage is so life changing."

"It is, isn't it? We won't have to find time to be alone together. We'll be together every night. You'll share my home, my name, my bed. I love you, Gretchen. Please, say yes."

"Yes," she said. "Yes."

"You will marry me?"

"I will," she said. Norbert leaned over and kissed Gretchen gently.

"I have a ring for you. It was my grandmother's."

"Oh!" Gretchen gasped as he placed the gold ring, with the small stone, on her finger.

"You're my fiancée now."

"Yes, we are engaged. Oh my gosh, we are, aren't we?" She giggled.

"We are! WE ARE! Now all we have to do is tell our parents."

"Let's not think about that just yet," she said, pulling him closer and kissing him.

"I'm sure it will all go just fine. Your father likes me well enough, doesn't he? I know that my folks adore you."

"Shhhh . . . you're ruining the mood," she said, kissing him and placing his hand on her breast. "I want you to make love to me."

It was her first time, but she wasn't afraid. She was ready to become a woman.

CHAPTER THIRTY-ONE

Over the next two weeks, Norbert and Gretchen spent endless hours discussing their wedding plans and carefully mapping out their future as husband and wife. One night, after Gretchen's father went to bed, they were sitting in Gretchen's living room when Norbert declared, "I want eight children at least. More is preferable. And I want them to be seven boys and one girl."

Gretchen laughed sarcastically. "Oh? Then why don't you give birth to them? Besides, silly, we can't determine what sex they'll be."

"Sure we can; just look at me. I'm a strong, virile male. We'll have boys. Besides, we owe it to our country to have plenty of Aryan children. And with a mother like you, well, they'll be beautiful. And having a handsome father like me wouldn't hurt either," Norbert joked.

"Eight, Norbert? Really?"

"Why not? Besides, the more little monsters we have, the more likely it will be that you'll get an award from the Nazi Party for being an ideal Aryan wife. You know how much they stress having plenty of kids. Now wouldn't you want that?" You'll be the envy of all your friends."

"Sometimes you're ridiculous. How are we ever going to manage with so many little ones? They'll run me ragged."

He jumped up and took her into his arms. "I wish we were married, so we could start having them right now." He giggled, caressing her breast. She giggled too.

She touched his face. "Eight?" she murmured, but before she could say another word, his lips were on hers.

Every time they got together, they tried to find a place to be alone where they could make love and then lay in bed, excitedly sharing their dreams. Gretchen enjoyed going over details for the wedding, but Norbert was more concerned with getting things underway. He wanted to announce their engagement to their families as soon as possible. Secretly, Gretchen was a little worried about her father's reaction. She knew he would want her to be happy, but she also knew that if he had his choice for a son-in-law, he would not have picked Norbert. He liked him well enough, and Norbert did come from a nice family. But Norbert was not an intellectual; he was a working-class man and a strong Nazi Party member. Neither of those traits appealed to her father. He never said a word, but Gretchen could tell by the way he looked at Norbert that he found him too crass, uneducated, and lower class. Although Gretchen knew her father would say he approved, she also knew he would be secretly disappointed: this put a slight damper on her giddiness. However, she knew it was inevitable that she and Norbert must tell their parents if they were ever going to get beyond the dreaming stage.

"Let's get this going, and tell them all. What do you say?" he said, gently caressing her arm.

"Yes, I suppose you're right. I love getting lost in the magic of it all—the flowers, the food, the cake. But you're the practical one," she said, winking at him and trying to send all of her worries to the back of her mind.

"Well, someone has to be practical, right?"

"Yes, you're right. I agree with you. And I'm glad you are practical, so we will do what we must do. We will tell them," Gretchen said.

"Are you free tomorrow after work?"

"Of course."

"Then, if it's all right with you, as soon as you finish work we will go and see my parents together."

Gretchen didn't mind going to talk to the Krauses. She knew they liked her, and she had no doubt they would be happy for the upcoming marriage.

The following day, Norbert met Gretchen at her home after he finished work at his family's restaurant. They walked to his flat together. As they walked, he told her his new plans.

"Once we are married you can work at one of my family's restaurants too if you would like."

"Sure. I would love to."

"We'll talk to them about it after the wedding."

Neither of them anticipated any problems with Norbert's family. Gretchen had been to dinner several times at Norbert's home, and she got along well with his parents. And although Gretchen was secretly worried about her father, Norbert was not. He believed that Professor Schmidt liked him. He often dined at Gretchen's home and wondered if the professor might have preferred an intellectual like himself for Gretchen. Even so, he was pretty sure that Professor Schmidt would accept the marriage because he knew that Norbert and Gretchen were happy.

Norbert's mother was a heavyset woman with a ruddy complexion. Although she was missing two teeth, she still had a hearty smile. When Norbert and Gretchen arrived, she immediately took an extra plate down from the cabinet.

"You'll stay for dinner, Gretchen?"

"Yes, of course. But we have something to tell you," Gretchen said, turning to Norbert and taking his hand.

"Mama," Norbert said, "Gretchen and I are getting married."

"Oh, what news!" Norbert's mother began crying and laughing all at once. Her large belly shook as she blotted the tears from her cheeks with a kitchen rag. "I'm so happy," she said. "My boy is getting married and to such a lovely girl." She embraced Gretchen.

Norbert's father, Gunther Krause, overheard the conversation. "What's this? You two are getting married?"

"Yes, Father," Norbert said. Gunther patted Norbert on the shoulder then he shook his son's hand. "I couldn't be happier," he said, then he embraced Gretchen. "You have chosen a wonderful girl for your wife. Now, the real question is, what does she see in you?"

"Father!"

"You know I am just joking," Norbert's father said. "You're our son. We love you, and, of course, we think you're quite the catch, but we love your little Gretchen too."

"Thank you for the encouraging words, Father."

"And furthermore, I don't know if you have made any plans for the wedding yet, but if not, you are certainly welcome to the family's nicest beer hall. After all, Gretchen will be our daughter soon."

"That's so generous of you, Herr Krause," Gretchen said, a single tear of joy running down her cheek.

Gretchen was excited and happy. But now, she must tell her father. She didn't share her feelings with Norbert, but she was secretly anxious about her father's response. He wouldn't deny her if she wanted to marry Norbert; she was certain of that. But Gretchen felt sick to her stomach when she thought about the look on his face. She and her father were very close. After Gretchen's mother died, her father devoted his life to his daughter. He never dated or showed any interest in getting married again. And because of this bond between them, Gretchen could easily read her father's feelings in his face. Even when she was a little girl, if she saw disappointment on his face, she would regret any actions that had caused it. He never had to spank her. All he ever had to do was give her that look of disappointment, and she would immediately change her behavior. What was she going to do now?

The following day, Norbert came to Gretchen's home right after his work, and the couple then waited for Gretchen's father to come home from the university. As soon as he walked in the door, Gretchen brought him a beer and told him to sit down on the sofa.

"What's all this?" her father asked, holding the beer in his hand as a mask of worry came over his face.

He thinks I'm pregnant, Gretchen thought. *This just keeps getting worse.* "We, Norbert and I, have something to tell you."

"No, that's not exactly right," Norbert said. "I have something to ask you."

"Go on." Gretchen's father stared at both of them with a look of concern in his eyes.

"I would like to ask for your permission to marry your daughter, sir," Norbert said.

Karl Schmidt almost spilled his beer. "My, my."

He shook his head then mustered a smile. For a moment, he didn't speak. Then he cocked his head and looked first at Norbert and then at Gretchen. "Is this what you want, Gretchen?"

"It is, Father. It is."

"Then, of course, by all means, you have my permission." Her father nodded and put the beer down on the table without taking a single sip.

"Thank you, Father."

"Thank you, sir. But we not only want your permission, sir. We would very much like to have your blessing."

"My blessing?" Karl Schmidt said, practically choking on the words. "Yes, of course, of course, you have my blessing."

"Father?" Gretchen said in a small voice looking away because she didn't want to see the disappointment in his eyes. She wondered if he was not only disappointed in her choice of husband but also feeling a little heartbroken knowing that she would soon belong to another man. She would no longer be her father's little girl, running to him carrying a bunch of wildflowers as she did when she was a child.

She turned to face him, and the sadness in his eyes almost made her say she would cancel the wedding. But she couldn't because she wanted to marry Norbert. It was time for her life to begin. Gretchen was ready to be a grown-up, to have a husband and children of her own. Her father would always have a special place in her heart, but it *was* time.

"Yes, Gretchen," he said.

"May I wear my mother's wedding dress? I would like to honor her."

It was as if the world stopped moving. The room was eerily silent.

Her father's face fell. He looked away from Gretchen. He couldn't let her see his eyes lest she read his thoughts. *Aidie's dress.* It had been a long time since he had last pictured Aidie in that dress. And suddenly, all the pain of losing his wife when she was so young came back. He felt it, like a sword piercing his chest, driving right through his heart. His hand automatically went to his heart. *Gretchen looks so much like her mother. How am I going to find the strength to bear the pain of*

157

seeing her in that dress? It is going to bring back such memories, memories that cut deep.

He wanted to run outside into the fresh air, but instead, he forced himself to look into his beloved daughter's eyes. And as he did, in his mind he could hear his Aidie's voice. *Of course, she should wear my dress, Karl. She is my child, my daughter, our daughter . . .*

"Yes," he said, clearing his throat. "Yes, of course, you will wear your mother's dress."

"And we have good news, Professor. My father wants us to have the ceremony at the nicest of his restaurants. Has Gretchen told you that my parents own beautiful restaurants?"

"No, she hasn't told me. But that is very generous of your father."

"He is doing quite well. So many of the high-ranking officials in the Nazi Party frequent his business. It has given him a good reputation and plenty of customers. I have been working at the factory part time until I finish school, but once I graduate my father says that there is plenty of business, and I would be of much better use working for him full time. Perhaps, if she wants to, Gretchen could work there too. But I'd prefer she stay home and be a wife and mother."

"Very good." That was all Karl could bring himself to say.

"I am not telling you all this to brag." Norbert smiled. "I am telling you so that you know that your daughter will not have to worry about money. She and I will be very comfortable."

Karl nodded. "What more could I ask for?" he said and smiled wryly.

Planning a wedding was expensive. Norbert and Gretchen were forced to compromise on what to serve their guests. Norbert's father had connections with many high-ranking party officials that ate and drank at his restaurants, so he was able to acquire some extra food and beer for the wedding.

Even flowers were thought to be a waste of money, but Norbert insisted they splurge so Gretchen could carry a bouquet of sunflowers. "I love sunflowers. They are so filled with hope," Norbert said. "And besides, they are the official flower of the Nazi Party."

Fall 1937

Hilde returned from the Bund summer camp, disenchanted and sick with rage. She hoped that Hann would come, but he never showed up. The camp itself was not disappointing; it was everything the BDM promised. There were plenty of sports, swimming, races, and cookouts. The boys and girls slept in separate barracks, but they spent a lot of time together. It was quite easy to slip out at night and meet with the boys. One of the group leaders brought a guitar, and many evenings before bed, the boys and girls sat outside under a star-filled sky and sang songs of patriotism and devotion to their wonderful führer and their precious fatherland.

Hilde had a keen eye, and because she watched things closely, she knew that many of the girls took advantage of the leniency and snuck out after lights out to meet with the boys. She eavesdropped as they shared their sexual experiences with their friends, and she recorded the information in her brain. It was knowledge, and knowledge gave her power. If she ever needed it, she knew plenty about all the girls she went to camp with. She always listened when others shared secrets. It seemed that no one ever noticed her. Sometimes she felt invisible, and Hilde knew why. She never told anyone, but the story was branded into her mind when she was just a child, and she carried it with her like a cancer eating at her soul.

When Hilde was only eight years old, her mother came into her room in a drunken stupor and said, "Hilde, do you realize that people don't even know you're in the room? Would you like to know why that is?"

"Yes, Mother," the small, frightened eight-year-old answered.

"Well, I'll tell you why. It's because there is nothing special about you. You are plain, fat, and dumpy, just like me." Her mother let out a laugh. "And let's face it. You are borderline ugly. All you have to do is look in the mirror to know I am speaking the truth. And my poor, little Hilde, no one wants to look at an ugly girl."

"Am I ugly, Mama?"

"You certainly are! Can't you see that? Just look at yourself in the mirror. I was an ugly child too. It's a hard life you're in for. Especially when you get to be a teenager and start to think about marriage. Nobody loves an ugly girl. Look how your father treats me. The good-for-nothing bastard."

"Do you think anyone will ever love me?"

"I love you, Hilde. That's why I am telling you this. But don't look for love from boys. A girl like you would do well as a nun. I should have been a nun." She let out a cackle and almost fell. She sat down on the edge of Hilde's bed. "But, of course, we aren't Catholic, so I am afraid even the convent wouldn't want the likes of you or me."

"So what will happen to me, Mother?"

"Who knows? Look at me. That will give you a pretty damn good idea of your future." Hilde's mother broke out in a fit of laughter. It was at that moment that Hilde realized she hated her mother. She had

160

terrible thoughts of poisoning her mother's bottle of schnapps.

Hilde didn't sleep that night. She lay in bed asking God to make her pretty. But when she woke in the morning and looked in the mirror, nothing had changed. She got up and quietly got ready for school. Her mother was locked in her room asleep, and she knew that she dared not wake her. If she woke her mother, she would be in a terrible mood.

In the very beginning, when she first heard her parents fighting, Hilde felt sorry for her mother. But after her mother told her that she was ugly, Hilde began making up stories to her fellow classmates about her mother. She told them that her mother was an alcoholic and a prostitute. When she saw the pity in their eyes it made her feel as if they cared about her.

One night she heard her parents arguing. Her father was telling her mother that he wanted a divorce.

"How can you do this to me? How can you do this to Hilde? We need you. At least help us financially. You have never been faithful, but how can you leave us without enough money to live?" her mother asked. "This family is your responsibility. And you are willing to walk out on us for some girl because she is young and beautiful?"

"I'm sorry. I know that I am hurting you. I don't mean to, but the fact is I want a divorce," he repeated in a cold tone.

"Get out of here. I can't stand to look at you anymore," her mother screamed.

Hilde heard the front door close, and then she heard her mother weeping.

Hilde trembled in the corner of her room until she heard the front door slam again, and she knew that her mother had left the house. Then she took the one doll she owned off the shelf, the only toy her father had ever given her, and as hard as she could, she smashed her fist into the doll's pretty face. She did it again and again. "Take this, Mother. And this . . ." Hilde said. Her fist and palm were both bleeding, and the doll no longer had a face.

Hilde didn't go to school that day. Instead, she wrapped her hand as best as she could with a kitchen rag and lay in her bed thinking. Oh, how Hilde loathed her mother! She despised her cruelty, and even more, she hated her mother's honesty because deep in Hilde's heart, the words her mother said rang true. Hilde wholeheartedly believed she would have to try harder than the others with their pretty blonde curls, to get anyone to love her. If it was even possible.

She was just a child when her mother branded her as an unfortunate, so Hilde came to believe she was ugly, and that anyone who looked at her saw a hideous child. It made her furious.

Why was she not cute like the other little girls? Why had God chosen to give her a face and body that repelled even her own mother? She looked in the mirror and confirmed her mother's harsh words. She wept alone in her bed knowing for certain that no one would ever call her adorable or smile when she sang a song or said something clever. No, not Hilde.

Hilde's mother cut her deeper with her words than any physical injury could have done, leaving a gaping wound in her soul. So at the tender age of eight, Hilde decided she no longer believed in any sort of a god. For months before making that decision, she prayed. Every night, she would beg God to make her beautiful when she awakened. She was very specific. "Dear God, please, I am begging you to give me long, curly hair and a lovely, angelic face. Please make me slender like the other girls in school. Please, God, I beg you. Please don't make me live my life as I am."

Every morning, Hilde rushed to the mirror, but to her disappointment, she saw the same, sad, overweight, and unloved child. So, to cope with her overwhelming unhappiness, her childish mind sought refuge by creating two fantasy worlds that had their basis in fairy tales. In one of these worlds, Hilde was already a grown-up. But despite her mother's prediction, she had not grown up to be ugly. In fact, she was a great beauty. She was a Valkyrie who sat upon a white horse with a mane of pure golden strands. She rode bravely into impossible battles, but no matter how difficult the battle, she never lost. Hilde saw herself as this magnificent Norse woman with wild, blonde hair flowing behind her and absolute power: the power to raise one finger and decide who would live and who would die. But most of all, in her fantasy world, Hilde had grown into a woman with the power to destroy anyone who hurt her or made her feel inadequate. She was no longer the helpless victim who cowered when her mother came looking for her.

Many nights, as she slept, she dreamed of herself as this Valkyrie woman. In this reoccurring dream, her mother was on her knees as Hilde rode forth on her horse. She took her sword from its sheath and cut her mother's head off with one swipe, yelling, "That's what you get, you bitch, for lying and saying I am ugly. I am not. I am beautiful." As her mother's head rolled down a mountain, Hilde galloped away.

In the other fantasy world, Hilde saw herself as a magical creature: graceful, and sleek. A mermaidlike thing that lived on land and could become small and invisible at will. Because her childhood was harsh and filled with disappointment, young Hilde moved between these two fantasy worlds, only entering reality when it was forced upon her. And that was rarely.

When her father returned to collect his things and she heard her parents fighting, she became invisible. When her mother criticized her relentlessly, she became invisible. In the beginning, the Valkyrie fantasy didn't work against her parents. She was too afraid of them. But it worked when she found helpless insects or stray animals. She took them into the basement of her tenement building and tortured them. Then when she was ten years old, her mother insisted that she earn a little extra money. Hilde found a babysitting job helping a young mother with her two small children. When she was alone with the children, Hilde became the Valkyrie. When either of the children cried, she slapped both of them hard. She enjoyed seeing the fear in their eyes. It made her feel even more powerful than when she tortured small animals. They were too young to understand what she was saying, but she told the children that they were ugly and worthless. She was careful not to leave any scars. She hid every trace of her cruelty. Sometimes she pinched them hard and made them cry. However, the mother began to realize that something wasn't right when her two children started crying as soon as they saw Hilde. So she pretended to go to the market leaving Hilde with the children, but left a small opening in the living room drapes. It was tiny, but she was able to see inside. As the poor mother expected, she caught Hilde slapping her children. Horrified, she fired her. Hilde cried and begged her not to tell her mother. Perhaps the young mother was afraid of Hilde because she never said a word, but she never allowed Hilde anywhere near her home again.

Of the two fantasy worlds, Hilde favored the Valkyries. But most of the time, invisibility served her better. So when the other girls her age were winning trophies or being praised at school, instead of crying, Hilde became invisible. As time went by and she grew into a teenager, she began to blend the two fantasy worlds. Most often, she retreated into the world of invisibility. But once she was away from the hurtful situation, she would replay it in her mind, changing the outcome. The ugly, insignificant girl who was invisible was replaced

164

by the magnificent Valkyrie. She would replay each painful moment like a movie in her head until she was satisfied with the outcome.

And this was how Hilde coped with her horrific childhood and lonely teenage years. She also found another, more practical use for her mask of invisibility. When she was playing invisible, she was very quiet and unobtrusive. It was easy to go unnoticed. She would watch and listen and mentally record other people's interactions. No one noticed she was listening as they revealed their secrets and mistakes to their friends. She held these secrets like piles of currency deep in the recesses of her sick mind.

If she ever needed a favor, she got what she wanted by threatening to expose them. Every time she blackmailed someone, they gave her whatever she wanted to keep her quiet. By the time she was seventeen and she went away to the Bund camp, spying on others was already a well-honed skill. Hilde was very good at what she did; she never let on what she was up to. Instead, she gained the trust of the other girls by smiling a lot and always seeming agreeable. She never voiced an opinion of her own. Instead, she blended in with the crowd, agreeing with all the popular opinions. She was especially adamant about everything the Nazi Party taught them—not that she really gave a damn about the party, but because she was at a summer camp sponsored by the Bund. She wanted to fit in, and Hilde knew exactly how to do that. She listened carefully to whatever she was told and then reworded and repeated it as if it were her own idea. Goebbels said the Jews were ruining Germany, so she made it clear to everyone that she felt the Jews were ruining Germany. She giggled and said she thought the führer was as handsome as a Nordic god. All the girls agreed, and Hilde was a part of the group.

When the girls were getting dressed for dances, she made sure to tell the others how pretty they looked, whether she thought so or not.

She laughed with them and catered to them. But most importantly, she made sure that no one saw her as the threat she really was. If anyone confided in her, she pretended to be sensitive and caring, when in fact she was laying the foundation for future blackmail.

Hilde was confident she had secured herself a place among the girls. In the past, it always gave her a sense of comfort and control to know everyone's secrets. She felt smug having so much ammunition, so much power.

But not this time. She had gone to the camp to see Hann, and he wasn't there. Consequently, she couldn't find anything to make her happy. Her heart was aching because she hoped that, somehow, in the summer sun and the fresh air, among the beautiful trees, she could win his love.

Her disappointment overshadowed everything else in her life. That night when she saw him at the dance to celebrate the führer's birthday, Hilde had boldly told him how she felt about him. It was very hard for her. She was uncomfortable telling him her feelings, but she wanted him so badly that she was willing to do anything to win him. She even offered him her body in the hope of enticing him. Hann was kind but gently refused. Nothing she said turned his head that terrible night at the dance. And as she watched him walk away from her, she heard her mother's voice in her head saying, "Ugly, repulsive child! What did you expect?" Her entire body shook, but she had to hide her feelings from the others, so she ran to the bathroom. And that was where Gretchen found her.

She assured Gretchen she was fine as they walked home that night. But once they separated, she walked to the park alone. It was late in the evening and certainly not safe, but she didn't care. If something happened to her, it didn't matter anyway. No one loved her, and she was quite sure no one ever would.

She saw a piece of broken glass from a beer bottle lying on the ground. Hilde picked it up and began slicing her arm. Not too deeply, but just deep enough for her to feel it. Lines of crimson formed on her skin. The pain of the cutting helped take her focus off the more intense pain of not being loved. She fell asleep under a tree. When the sun rose, she got up and began to walk home. The blood was dry, but that didn't matter either. She knew that no one at home would be waiting for her. Or if by chance her mother were home, she wouldn't even notice the cuts.

Hilde kicked a rock and wished she could just give up on Hann—maybe even give up on life. But she couldn't. *After all, what did I expect? I am always being let down. This was another letdown. I can't give up this easily. I just have to try harder. Girls like me have to fight for what they want. I am, after all, a Valkyrie. I am strong. I can have anything I want.*

Tears fell down her cheeks. But instead of letting Hann go and searching for a boy who would like her just as she was, Hilde went to camp looking for him. Again she faced disappointment. Still, she wasn't ready to accept defeat. As she was riding home from camp on the bus, she decided that as soon as she returned to Berlin, she would go to Hann's house to see him.

The day after Hilde returned from camp, she put on her nicest dress and carefully applied her red lipstick. Even before she went to visit Gretchen, Hilde walked to Hann's flat. She steadied herself before knocking on the door and eyed her reflection in the front window. She wanted to be sure she looked her best. Hilde shook her head with dismay at the girl she saw in the reflection. *How unattractive I am. Perhaps I should just commit suicide.*

Tears welled up behind her eyes. Disappointed at her image, she wished she could somehow be reborn as Thea. However, that was not possible. *I am a Valkyrie. That girl reflected in the window isn't real. The real woman who I am is a great beauty.* Before Hilde could find the courage to knock on the door, she had to envision herself as the Nordic warrior. She saw it vividly in her mind's eye—her long, golden hair, her white frock. Anyone who saw this woman would have to say she was stunning. Secure in the fantasy, Hilde knocked on the door. A few minutes later, a woman answered wearing a crisp red-and-white housedress. Her hair was pulled neatly into a tight bun without any stray hairs.

"Can I help you?" she asked, opening the door.

"I'm looking for Hann."

"I'm his mother. Who are you?"

"Hilde. I am a friend. I belong to the Bund that is affiliated with his Hitler Youth group."

"I see. Well, he's not here. I'm sorry."

"When do you expect him?"

"He moved a few months ago. He got a job and left Berlin."

"Moved?" Hilde was genuinely shocked. "To where?"

"Hilde? I don't recall him mentioning your name."

"Oh, that's because we have not been close friends. But I've known him for a long time."

"Oh? Well, he moved. His uncle had a friend who was able to help him secure a good job working on the autobahn."

"Where?"

"Frankfurt."

"Frankfurt?" Hilde could hardly hide the disappointment in her voice. "Can I write to him at least?"

Hann's mother studied Hilde. Not finding anything at all threatening about this poor girl who seemed to have a crush on her son, she shrugged. "I suppose. Come in. Let me give you his address."

Hilde walked inside the immaculate apartment. Not a single item was out of place. The house smelled like fresh-baked bread, and it made Hilde's stomach groan with hunger. She grimaced, hoping that Frau Meier didn't hear her stomach begging for a piece of the bread. She would die of embarrassment if she heard it.

"Here is his address," Frau Meier smiled.

"I bet you miss him."

"Yes, very much. But I am so glad he has such a good job."

"Well, thank you," Hilde said, putting the paper into her handbag as she walked to the door.

"You're quite welcome," Frau Meier said, closing the door.

Hilde gripped her handbag with the precious information inside and walked slowly to the street. Hann was gone. He'd left Berlin. It was going to be more difficult to reach him now.

I know I should give up, but I'll try just one more time. I'll write to him. He probably won't answer, but he's everything I want, and I went through so much to get rid of Thea so that he and I could be together. How can I let him go this easily?

Hilde watched her shoes as they hit the pavement. She was heartbroken. Her plan to get rid of Thea was successful, and it had given her such hope. But in the end, she had not won Hann's love. After all that effort, she was alone. *You ugly, repulsive, worthless cow. Did you really believe that a man like Hann would want a pig like you?* She heard her mother's voice echoing in her head. She put both hands over her ears, and inside her head, she screamed. It was a silent scream, the sound of a tortured animal that only Hilde could hear.

Don't despair.

It was the voice of the Valkyrie. *You are a beautiful Nordic warrior. You will not be whole until you kill that horrible witch who claims to be your mother. In truth, she is not your mother. Your mother is a beautiful, loving, powerful woman. She is a Valkyrie like you. This woman who claims to be your mother is an imposter. Kill her, Hilde. Kill her, and the curse she had put upon you will be gone.*

Hilde began to think of ways she might kill her mother and not be caught. The plans frightened her, but at the same time, she found them comforting. She began to devise a way to rid herself of the mother she hated who had broken her self-esteem. *Easy, Hilde, it will be easy. There is a bottle of rat poison under the sink; put the poison in her schnapps. She'll be dead by morning.*

The idea appealed to Hilde. When she got home, Hilde checked to see if there were any schnapps left. There was nothing in the cupboard. Her alcoholic mother had finished it all. So, that same afternoon, Hilde took money out of her savings and bought her mother a bottle of schnapps. *This will be my last gift to you, you bitch.* She poured off enough of the alcohol to accommodate the contents of the bottle of poison. She left the schnapps on the counter. Her mother might return tonight or tomorrow, but it was certain that as soon as her mother came home, she would see the bottle and drink it. Then Hilde would be rid of her for good.

It took three days for Hilde's mother to return. Hilde did not know where her mother went when she was gone for extended periods of time. But she heard the door open, and she knew her mother was home. For a single second, fear gripped Hilde's heart, and she almost ran out of her bedroom and grabbed the bottle before her mother drank it. She heard her mother's high heels clicking on the floor. Her heart beat to the rhythm of the footsteps.

I have only a few seconds left to stop this plan of murder, she thought, as she stared at herself in the mirror. But her feet were frozen.

"Hilde, where the hell are you?" her mother called out. "Get me some breakfast right now, you disgusting pig. Damn it, Hilde, if you were better looking, I'd have you out on the streets selling your body, like I do. It's easy money, and you could take half the burden off me. But you're too ugly. That's why you have to slave away in that factory. What man would spend money for a night with a girl who looks like you? Damn it! What is taking you so long to come in here and make me something to eat? I've been working all damn night, and I'm hungry."

Hilde stared at herself in the mirror. She couldn't move. She saw her face growing smaller, and then it disappeared, replaced by the face of the beautiful Nordic warrior, the Valkyrie. She smiled, and the Valkyrie smiled back at her. *Go to her, and cook for her. Don't let on that you know she is an imposter. Feed her and then give her the special bottle that we have prepared for her. This will be the last time she will ever call us ugly names. Once she is dead, from this day forward, you and I will be one, and you will never need to be invisible again.*

Hilde walked into the kitchen and took out the bread and the last egg in the pantry.

"What the hell took you so long? Were you sleeping, you lazy cow?" Hilde's mother asked.

Hilde didn't answer. *Choke on it*, she thought as she took down a plate. With her head down, she began to prepare her mother's breakfast.

Once her mother had eaten, Hilde handed her the bottle of schnapps. "I bought this for you. I wanted to give you something to show you how much I appreciate how hard you work to take care of us," Hilde said.

"Well, wasn't that nice of you?" her mother said. "But it's open?"

Hilde trembled. *Does she suspect?* "I had a swig. I'm sorry."

Her mother nodded. She opened the bottle, and Hilde watched with horror and fascination as the woman who raised her took a long swig of the poisoned alcohol. "Tastes funny," her mother muttered, but she took another long drink. And then her face turned gray and claylike. She grabbed her throat, and Hilde's mother fell to the ground.

For several minutes, Hilde sat on the kitchen chair staring at her mother writhing in pain. She was overcome with a myriad of emotions: fear, relief, hate, and love.

And then it was over.

Her mother was no longer moving. To be sure her mother was dead, Hilde waited for a full hour before she headed to Gretchen's house. She would pretend that she hadn't been at home when her mother died. She took the bottle of schnapps with her in a brown paper bag and put the bottle of poison on the counter. Then she walked the opposite way from Gretchen's house for several streets. When she got to an unpopulated area, she poured out the poisoned alcohol and walked for several more blocks before throwing the empty bottle into a trash can.

CHAPTER THIRTY-TWO

Gretchen was cleaning the kitchen when Hilde arrived. As soon as she saw her old friend, she put her arms around her and giggled. "How was camp? Did you have fun? I missed you."

"It was all right. Hann wasn't there. I went because of him, you know."

"Yes, I know. I'm so sorry, Hilde. But there are a lot of other boys . . ."

"Not for me."

"You just feel that way right now, but as time passes you'll get over Hann. You'll see," Gretchen said, brushing the hair out of Hilde's eyes. "Let me make us a pot of coffee, and we can sit and talk for a while. What do you say?"

"I'd like that. Too bad we don't have anything to go with it," Hilde said.

"I know. I'd love a piece of strudel."

"Me too."

Gretchen put a pot of water on the stove to boil then she sat down next to her friend at the table.

"Are you still seeing Norbert?" Hilde asked.

"Yes . . . actually . . ." Gretchen suddenly felt uncomfortable telling Hilde how happy she and Norbert were. She knew that Hilde was hurt over Hann, and it would just add salt to her wound to learn that she was getting married. But she couldn't lie. Hilde would have to know sooner or later. She might as well tell her the truth now.

"It's been a long time," Hilde said.

"Yes," Gretchen said hesitating. "Hilde, there's something I have to tell you."

"Of course, you're my best friend. You know you can tell me anything."

"Norbert and I are getting married."

"Married?"

"Yes. And of course, you will be at the wedding."

"Yes, of course," Hilde said.

Gretchen poured two cups of the ersatz coffee and sat down again.

"Hilde . . . nothing will change with us. I promise."

"I don't believe that. You'll be a married woman. You won't have time for me."

"Yes, I will. I'll always make time for you. And before you know it, you'll meet someone too. And no matter what happens, you and I will always be best friends."

"Of course we will," Hilde said. "But I am going to get going. I have to go to the market."

CHAPTER THIRTY-THREE

Hilde didn't feel like going to the market or to the Jewish sector of town to force the shop owners to give her goods. She was too depressed. She walked to the park and sat on the bench to think things through. Gretchen was getting married. *I'll really be all alone now. I haven't heard from my father in years, my mother is dead, and my best friend is abandoning me. Hann doesn't want me. I'll be the last single girl in town. An old maid. I am a girl too ugly to find a husband just like my mother said. If Gretchen didn't have Norbert, she and I would be friends forever. We would always have each other. Maybe we could even share an apartment because I am going to have to move now that my mother won't be helping with the rent. I'll have to find something much smaller and less expensive. Norbert is really becoming a problem. He's going to spoil my friendship with Gretchen, and she's the only real friend I ever had. I'll just have to think of a way to get rid of him.*

CHAPTER THIRTY-FOUR

Hilde knew she would have to go home and take care of the mess with her mother. *It shouldn't be that hard.*

She left the park. She wanted to be seen entering the house. When she walked in, she screamed as if she saw her mother lying dead for the first time. Her upstairs neighbor came running down and knocked on the door.

"Hilde? Hilde?"

"It's my mother," Hilde cried, opening the door. "Look!" Hilde indicated to her mother's lifeless body on the floor.

"Oh my! You must go to the police. Do you think she was murdered?"

"I don't know what happened," Hilde said. "But I am going to the police station right now."

Hilde ran to the police station. As soon as she opened the door she began yelling, "Help me; please, help me." Her face was beet red, and she was out of breath from running. She appeared terribly distraught.

An officer raced over to her. "What is it?"

"My mother is on laying on the floor in our apartment. I think she is dead. Help me, please."

"What happened?" the officer asked.

"I went to visit my friend, and when I got home, I found my mother on the floor with an empty bottle of rat poison. I don't know if she was trying to commit suicide or if she thought it was her bottle of schnapps and drank it by mistake. Oh, how terrible for her. My poor mutti. I am so ashamed to tell you, but I know that I must tell you. You see, my mutti was an alcoholic. Oh God, please, you must help me. I am so afraid that my mother is dead." Hilde began weeping.

"You poor child. We'll send an officer over right away."

Hilde screamed and cried when her mother was pronounced dead. She sobbed with her head in her hands as the body was carried away. But once the door closed and Hilde was alone, she smiled. It was over. Her mother would never say those terrible things to her again.

The investigation into Hilde's mother's death went as smoothly as Hilde planned. "Poor Hilde," the neighbors said. "She is distraught over losing her mother. But the truth is, her mother wasn't much of a mother at all. Since the father left, that woman was always running after him and trying to win him back, never taking any time to care for her child."

And no one ever suspected.

CHAPTER THIRTY-FIVE

Professor Karl Schmidt was preparing to leave his classroom one afternoon. He had just finished his last class of the day, and he was ready to go home and relax. He packed his books and some student papers he planned to read that night, into his small Magritte. He grabbed his hat from the coat rack and took a last look around the room to be sure nothing was left lying around. Satisfied that his classroom was in order, Schmidt turned off the lights and locked the door. His heels clattered as he walked down the long hall.

He pushed open the heavy door and walked outside and down the steps to the walkway that led off campus. The weather was getting warm; soon it would be summer. If the present temperature was any indication of what was to be expected, then it was going to be a hot one.

He was just about to leave the campus when an old friend and colleague, Dr. Felix Gellerman, approached him. He'd known Felix since he started teaching at the university. He met Gellerman in the teacher's lounge his first week there. Gellerman was considerably older than Karl, but Karl liked him right away. Gellerman was funny and a bit cynical, but also kind and generous in helping Karl find his way around.

"Karl, how are you?" Gellerman asked. He was a short, round, ball of a man with thinning black hair and a lazy eye.

"Felix, I haven't seen you in quite a while."

"Yes, I know. We must keep missing each other," Gellerman said. His face was deeply lined with a map of wrinkles and his eyes dark with worry. His quick humor seemed to be gone, and Karl couldn't help but wonder why.

Gellerman said, "You won't be seeing much of me in the future, I'm afraid."

"Schedule changes?" Karl hoped that was all it was. Perhaps Gellerman had opted to teach night classes. But from the look on his face, he doubted it. Karl hoped no one was ill.

"No, no schedule at all, I'm rather sorry to say." Gellerman gave him a sad and wry smile. "It seems the university has no need of my services anymore. I have been let go."

"What happened? I don't mean to pry, and you can feel free to tell me it's none of my business, but I have to ask. What was the reason?"

Felix frowned. "It's because of the new laws. The Nuremberg Laws. You see, Karl, my old friend, I am a Jew. I don't know if you knew that."

"I don't know if I ever thought much about it, Felix."

"Yes, well, Germany is now thinking a great deal about it, I am afraid. Being a Jew is not safe here anymore."

"But this is absurd. I don't believe it! You are a very knowledgeable professor. You're an asset to this institution, and I find it difficult to understand why the university would to let you go for no good reason," Karl said, shaking his head in disbelief. "This is clearly wrong. And it's upsetting."

"It's not as simple as that. I am afraid we Jews are quickly losing

179

our rights as German citizens, and quite frankly, I am very worried about the state of things here in Germany. I am afraid that things are going to get much worse."

"I can't understand. How could it possibly be worse than this? When a good man is losing his job for no reason at all?"

"Who knows? But the climate in this country, right now, is very unfriendly for my people."

"So what will you do for work now? Do you plan to teach at a Jewish university?"

"No, I am looking further ahead than that, although I am uncertain of what is to come. I feel very uneasy, Karl. Very uneasy, indeed. I am going to move my family out of Germany. I have a brother who lives in Holland. He says he can get me work teaching there."

"But you know that we have many Jewish professors on our faculty. Are they planning on firing all of them?"

"Many have been fired already. And yes, I believe they are."

"This is just not right, Felix. I should probably go to the head of the faculty about this."

Felix nodded. "You're a good person, Schmidt. I've always admired you. But this is bigger than both of us. I don't think it will help. In my opinion, you, being a pure German, should keep your head down. And if you stay quiet, you'll be safe. You've told me before you are a single father. I know that you need this job. The last thing you want is to be ostracized because of me."

"Well, we'll see."

"Be smart, Karl. Stay quiet."

Karl nodded. "Best of luck to you wherever life takes you, my friend," Karl said. He felt terrible about the treatment of his Jewish colleagues. But at the same time, he was relieved not to have to take a stand. Although he wanted to help, and he knew it was the right thing to do, he was glad that his friend had, in a way, given him permission to remain silent.

"And to you, Karl."

CHAPTER THIRTY-SIX

Karl Schmidt couldn't sleep that night. He lay in bed, twisting his fingers in the quilt that his wife had made for them when they were first married. How he missed her! She was such a bright light in his life. After she died, all he had left was his precious daughter and his career as a professor, which he loved.

His mind drifted to Gretchen. She looked so much like his wife, Aidie. She had the same expressions too. Funny how she could have the same facial expressions as her mother even though she had never seen her. A warm glow of love filled his heart when he thought about his daughter. She was full of intellectual curiosity. Her desire for knowledge and her love of sports came from him, and that made him proud. But her good looks, those she got from her mother.

Karl always enjoyed sports, and he kept himself in good shape even though he was approaching forty. Every morning, he got up and walked a mile and then ran home. On Wednesday nights, he played soccer at the park with a few of the other men from the neighborhood. He taught Gretchen how to play soccer too, and she had played with a group of friends since she was ten. But that was before she joined the BDM. Now, between the BDM, work, and school, she hardly had time to breathe. He didn't care for the friends she made in the BDM, especially that girl Hilde who came over all the time. He didn't like her. She gave him a bad feeling, but he wasn't sure why.

Karl still mourned the loss of his beloved wife, his Aidie, who died giving birth to Gretchen. It had taken a lot for him to love his daughter and accept his role as a father. When Gretchen was first born, he could hardly look at her. He blamed her for taking away the one woman he loved. He was alone with a baby, and he was in trouble. He didn't think he could raise Gretchen. He wanted his sister, Margrit, and her husband, Gunther, to take his baby girl home with them.

Karl couldn't even bear the sight of the tiny infant as she lay in her little cradle in the hospital. He left the hospital and went to a public phone and called Margrit, his sister.

"I just don't want her, Margrit. I don't feel any love for her at all. She is the reason that my Aidie is gone," he said. His voice cracked, and he felt sick to his stomach. "If you don't want the child, I am going to give her up for adoption. I don't care who takes her, or what happens to her. I'll put her in a home for orphans."

"Please don't do anything, Karl. Wait for me. I'm on my way. I'll be there before you take the baby home from the hospital. Just don't do anything rash. Please, all I ask is that you wait for me."

Margrit left her husband, Gunther, in Munich and traveled all night by train. Karl was glad to see his sister. He thought she came to take Gretchen home with her.

For the first two weeks of Gretchen's life, Margrit took care of Gretchen by herself. Karl never set foot in the nursery that he and Aidie had so lovingly put together. Margrit cared for Gretchen and prepared food for Karl, which he hardly ate. She washed his clothes and cleaned his house, but he didn't bathe or go out at all. Margrit contacted Karl's job and explained the situation, and the university excused him from his duties for three weeks.

Karl hardly even saw Margrit. He spent most of his time hiding in his room, thinking. He drank excessively, which fed into his melancholy. As the days passed, his thoughts drifted back to the first time he saw Aidie. She was a fellow student at the university. He was on his way to the library when she ran up to him, soaked but radiant, and asked him where she could find the cafeteria. His breath caught in his throat as he looked at her. Even drenched to the bone, Aidie was the prettiest girl he'd ever seen. He had always been an introvert; her speaking to him left him tongue-tied. He was so overcome by her that he could hardly find the words to explain something as simple as how to get to the cafeteria. As the rain came down harder, he tried to give her the directions. "You turn right at that building over there. You see the one with the red brick?"

"Which one? There are two with red brick."

"That one." He pointed. "The one over there. Walk about twenty feet and you will find yourself at the assembly hall. Then turn to the left, and then make another sharp left, and go into that building. Once you are inside, just head straight down the stairs."

"Oh my goodness! I don't think I'll ever find it. Are you on your way to class?" she asked.

"No. I don't have a class now. I was going to the library. I can walk you to the cafeteria, if you would like," he stammered.

She smiled. "Yes, that would be so helpful. Thank you."

A flash of lightning filled the sky.

"The rain is getting heavier," she said. "Come on; let's get inside." She took his arm, and they ran, Karl leading the way. By the time they arrived at the cafeteria, they were both soaking wet and laughing.

"For goodness sake! The water is dripping off my eyelashes," he said.

"Mine too. Will you join me for lunch?" Aidie asked.

"Yes, I would like that," Karl said, forgetting all about the library. They had lunch together. Aidie kept the conversation going, and by the time they finished, they had set a date to see each other again the following evening. So it began.

Karl was in awe of this beautiful, high-spirited girl. He couldn't believe a girl like that was actually paying attention to him. She was vivacious, intelligent, and gorgeous. He saw himself as a withdrawn intellectual. Within six months, they were engaged. Neither family was wealthy, so they had a small wedding. Aidie insisted on dropping out of school and getting a job to support the two of them while Karl finished his schooling. The plan was that as soon he started working, Aidie would return to her studies and earn her degree. It was a financial struggle for the couple to survive on Aidie's meager salary but they managed.

"We live mostly on love," Aidie always said, laughing and messing his hair whenever he complained that the apartment where they lived had rats or that they hardly had enough food. It was easy for her to lift his spirits. Just a smile from her lips, and he could see the light at the end of their struggles.

Karl graduated. As soon as he was hired at the university in Berlin, they got a nicer flat just a few streets away from the campus, so he could walk to work. The flat was small, but the building was well maintained and very clean. Aidie registered for school, but before the semester began, she was pregnant. Karl was afraid she would be disappointed, as the pregnancy meant she would have to forfeit her education. But she wasn't unhappy. In fact, she was ecstatic. Her joy was contagious, and before Karl knew it, he was excited about having a child.

During her pregnancy, he tried to make Aidie feel as wonderful as she made him feel. He brought her chocolates and flowers, both of which were frivolities they could hardly afford. But she was worth it. He worshiped her.

All seemed perfect and ideal until the baby came two weeks early. Aidie labored for fourteen hours until she was exhausted, but the child refused to turn. Then the unthinkable happened. The doctor told Karl that he had to cut Aidie open and take the baby out, or the mother and child would die. Karl was distraught, but when the doctor told Aidie, she was not concerned for her own well-being.

As Aidie was wheeled into surgery, she begged the doctor, "Promise me that no matter what happens to me in surgery, you will put my baby's life first. Save her life before you save mine."

In his mind, Karl screamed out, "No! No!"

But before he could find words to express himself, his wife and the doctor were gone behind the metal door of the surgical theater. Karl wrung his hands for two hours before the doctor returned. The doctor had kept his promise to Aidie. The child was fine. But Aidie . . . Aidie was gone.

Karl felt the room spin, and then everything went dark. He leaned against the wall in the hospital, then he passed out, sliding down to the floor. It was the beginning of a nightmare Karl never thought would end. He was consumed by misery.

Two weeks after Margrit and Karl brought the tiny bundle home, Margrit finally decided to confront Karl. One night after Margrit put little Gretchen to bed, she called Karl into the living room.

He was in his room, lying facedown on his bed, sick from too much alcohol. He groaned at the sound of Margrit's voice. *The last thing I need right now is to talk.* He wanted to be left alone, to drown in his drunken stupor in the darkness of the bedroom he once shared with his beloved Aidie. If he could, he'd put himself into a casket and be buried with his memories sealed inside forever.

But Margrit refused to give up. She was relentless. She came to his bedroom door and knocked. "Karl, please. Come out. I need to speak to you now."

He didn't answer, hoping she would think he was asleep and go away.

"Karl! I mean it. If you don't come out right now, I am going to pack my things and leave here. I am going home. Do you hear me, Karl?"

She won't stop until I give in, Karl thought. He got up from the bed knowing his clothes were dirty and disheveled, and his hair was uncombed. He didn't have the strength to make himself presentable. It was all he could do to walk out to the living room and sit down on the sofa.

"I need to talk to you," Margrit said as she poured them each a cup of tea. She set both cups on the used coffee table Karl and Aidie found at a rummage sale. She sat across from him and took his hand.

"I know you're hurting. I understand how you feel. But this little girl didn't kill Aidie. She is just an innocent child. Your child, Karl. Your child and Aidie's child. And she is so helpless, Karl. She needs you so much." A single tear ran down Margrit's cheek. Quickly, she wiped it away with the back of her hand. "Karl . . . please . . ."

"I can't look at her."

"You have to look at her. She's yours . . . and she's Aidie's. Would Aidie have wanted you to turn your back on her?"

"No." He shrugged. "But how can I ever go on without my wife? I always played like I was the strong one, but the truth is, it was Aidie who was my rock. She was my strength, and she was my weakness too. Oh, Margrit, I loved her so much. She was too good for me.

Much too good for me. This is my fault. If I had been more careful, she wouldn't have gotten pregnant, and she'd still be here today." Tears ran down his cheeks.

"Karl, don't think that way. Aidie wanted this baby. She wanted her so much. Every time I called and Aidie and I talked, she told me how happy she was to be pregnant."

"What did I do wrong? How did I anger God so much that he would take my wife? My only love. My reason for living. Why, Margrit? Why?"

"I don't know, Karl. I wish I had an answer, but I don't." She squeezed his arm. He raised his head and looked into her eyes, and she said, "However, what I do know is that all you have left of your Aidie is that tiny baby in the crib. And as she grows up, you'll see your Aidie in your daughter. Once you see Aidie in your child, you'll know that Aidie isn't gone—not completely."

Karl's shoulders slumped. It was as if all the fight went out of him. He was no longer angry—just terribly sad. He fell into his sister's arms and wept. She held him like a child, and she didn't say another word. Then, when he was spent, he swallowed hard and looked into his sister's eyes.

"Come. Let's go to the baby's room," he said in a small voice. "I am ready to look at my child."

It was the first time he allowed himself to actually see Gretchen. A strange feeling came over him as he looked into the crib to see the tiny figure wrapped in a blanket. His heartbeat quickened, and a fierce desire to shield his child from pain and danger came over him. Gretchen was asleep, but as Karl stared into the crib, she opened her eyes. It was dusk outside, and he could see her clearly, so clearly that she was finally a real living person in his mind. She was his child, his and Aidie's little girl. Her eyes were shaped like Aidie's; her lips curved like Aidie's. Tears began to fall down his cheeks once again. He could hardly believe how much this small infant reminded him of his beloved wife. He reached out and touched her tiny foot, marveling as he counted the five toes. A wave of love came over him. Karl Schmidt hardly recognized himself. He was a different man. He finally allowed himself to realize that he loved his daughter.

Margrit squeezed her brother's shoulder.

"Look at her," Karl said, turning to Margrit. "She's beautiful, isn't she?"

"She is very beautiful," Margrit said smiling as a sigh of relief escaped her.

Gently, Karl touched the baby's hand, and immediately, Gretchen responded by grabbing his finger. It was at that moment he knew he would love this little girl, and she would be his reason for living. He would love her with his whole heart, and he would raise her alone. Never would he remarry. Instead, he would do the best he could on his own. In his mind, he could hear Aidie saying, *I am so glad you can see how much you do love her, Karl. You were a wonderful husband; I know you will be a wonderful father too.*

Karl knew from that moment on he would give Gretchen everything he had, including all his knowledge. As he looked at his daughter, he remembered the conversations he had with Aidie about all they planned to teach their child. Now he would fulfill those dreams alone. But he would fulfill them.

"How am I to manage once you go home?" Karl asked Margrit. "I will have to go back to work."

"I'll help you hire a nanny to watch the baby while you are at work. Don't worry, Karl. It will be all right."

He nodded, knowing that he was now ready to be a father. He decided then and there that Gretchen would learn right from wrong.

She would grow up with a solid sense of ethics and a strong character. Gretchen would be a woman of substance. A woman to be admired.

And as she grew, Gretchen had proven to be all that her parents hoped she would be. She was a good-hearted girl, and even as a young child, Karl was proud to say that she showed the promise of having integrity.

But since Hitler had become chancellor, it was very hard on Karl to know that Gretchen was growing up in an angry and hostile world. Every day, he watched his beloved country descending into hell under the direction of a hatemonger. And now all the hatred had come home to him. He could no longer ignore it. It had found its way into his precious university.

He couldn't stop thinking about the fact they were firing the Jewish professors. He knew several of his other colleagues would be happy when they heard the news. And they had their reasons. He could name a few he knew who were threatened by the intelligence of at least one of the Jewish professors. He had heard others spouting messages from Hitler's speeches. It was easy to see they had fallen into a Jew-hating cesspool that was drowning the country. Some of them were good teachers and good people, but they were lost in the propaganda being fed to them daily.

Karl was not in agreement with any of the Nazi propaganda. He'd always been one to think for himself, and he wasn't about to change now. He enjoyed working beside the quick-thinking Jews he had worked with over the years. He found their intellect challenging, and he thought they were an asset to the school. He firmly believed the firing of valuable professors was a mistake. But even though he thought the treatment of his Jewish colleagues was despicable, he was not one to speak up. He'd never been a man to call attention to himself. And not only that, he had to be extra careful because of

190

Gretchen. He was all she had in the world, her only living parent. If he got into trouble, what would happen to her? And even worse, if he were to be labeled a Jew lover would the authorities take their dislike for him out on his daughter? Karl shivered at that thought. No, he decided; he would not say anything. This matter with the Jews did not concern him or Gretchen. It was sad, but it was not worth the possibility of punishment. He would keep his head down and keep his unpopular opinion to himself.

Karl turned over in his bed, the same bed he had once shared with Aidie, and gazed out the window at the moon. It was only a small sliver of light in a blackened, starless sky. Unable to sleep, he stared out into the darkness. Then, in the shadow of the moonlight, he saw a spider building a web on the outside of the window. The web stretched from the pane of glass to the leaves on a tree branch several feet away. In the minuscule light, he could see the intricate pattern of the web. The spider was working fast. Karl had never been afraid of insects, and this one was outside, so in his mind, he knew there was nothing to fear. Yet a shiver of dread ran down his spine.

He got out of bed and took a bottle of brandy out of his dresser drawer. He kept it there for nights when he was haunted by the pain of his memories. But tonight, it wasn't Aidie's memory or her death at such a young age that was tearing his insides up. It was fear. Karl was afraid. He couldn't put his finger on exactly what it was that was terrifying him. He took a swig from the bottle of brandy, and the hot, sweet liquid warmed his throat. Then he lay back down and watched the spider weave. Sometime in the wee hours of the morning, Karl drifted off to sleep. He slept only a short time because a strange dream awakened him.

In his dream, a giant bird of prey with a white head and a black body swept down and began fighting with the spider. In the dream, the spider was larger than in reality. It was enormous and black, with a red violin on its back. Even so, the insect was no match for the giant eagle—a large and fierce creature with long talons. Within minutes, the eagle devoured the spider.

Karl heard the bird scream as it took the spider from her web. It wasn't that Karl cared much for spiders, but seeing the entire web torn to shreds unnerved him. The vision was so real that it jarred Karl awake. His sheets were twisted around his sweating body. He looked outside the window—the spider was still there, spinning and spinning.

CHAPTER THIRTY-SEVEN

Losing her husband plunged Chenya Kaetzel into a depression. Her days were clouded with grief. She, the daughter of a rebbe, married a rebbe and spent her entire life as the rebbetzin. And from this, she derived her identity. Most of her time was spent in charity work, helping those less fortunate in any way she could. Women came to her for advice, and she advised them to the best of her knowledge. But most of the time, she sent them to talk to the rebbe.

Some women might have resented living in their husband's shadow, but not Chenya. She adored Asher and never lost her awe of his brilliant intellect. He died so unexpectedly that it still didn't seem real to her.

The morning of his death, she prepared breakfast for him and Eli. When he finished, he stood up and thanked her for the lovely meal, as he always did. Then she watched him wrap his tefillin around his shoulders, her eyes filled with love. He looked her way, and she smiled at him. Running his hand over his beard, he returned that smile in the special way he had of looking at her. It made her feel loved and cherished, the way every wife should feel. The way she wished that Eli would make Rebecca feel.

Oh, how Chenya wished she could go back to that morning! She knew he wasn't feeling well the night before, but she had no idea he was seriously ill. He seemed fine as he left for the shul. If she had only known, she would have begged him to see a doctor. She asked him, "Are you feeling better, Asher?"

"Yes, my beloved," he said. "I am feeling just fine."

Then he and Eli left for the shul. There was nothing unusual about that morning. Nothing at all. Chenya believed her husband when he said he was feeling better, and she had no reason to doubt him. He never lied to her.

She quickly cleaned up the kitchen and went to pray at the shul. But that day was unlike any other, and was the worst day of her life. Her beloved Asher was never to return to their home alive. Chenya tried to comfort herself by remembering that it was Hashem's will, and she must accept Hashem's will. But still, her heart ached for her beloved.

She often went out walking alone, far away from the eyes of her family and friends and wept. She would find a quiet place and sit down under a tree. Then, as she remembered the day she met her precious Asher, she let her tears flow. Asher was a kind and gentle husband, many times treating her more like a papa than a partner, but she adored him from the day she first saw him. And even now, she could remember how her young heart skipped a beat when she walked toward him on that summer day wearing her modest wedding gown.

Oh, Asher, you have left me too soon. Much too soon.

Chenya knew that her son was destined to follow in his father's footsteps. But so far, Eli was not as wise or as able as his father had been. Although she was a quiet woman, Chenya knew everything that went on in her home. She thought her son might be questioning his religion and his faith, and she didn't know how to help him. As the

194

next rebbe, he was supposed to be the one to counsel and mentor others. But so far, he did not think himself capable, so he had not taken on any responsibility. Chenya could see Eli was kind to his beautiful wife—as kind as he could be—but he found her uninteresting.

But Chenya could see things in Rebecca that Eli had missed. She was sure Rebecca was smarter than she let on. Chenya wished Eli would allow Rebecca to guide him. She was sure Rebecca could help him more than he realized. Still, she could not say anything to her son or her daughter-in-law. She didn't want to be an interfering mother-in-law, so she just watched and waited, hoping that Eli would see Rebecca's potential on his own.

Eli could see his poor mother wasting away. She'd grown so thin and frail since his father's passing, but there was nothing he could do to stop it. Rebecca was like an angel. She made Chenya's favorite soup, and quite often, when her mother-in-law refused to come to the table, Rebecca brought the soup to her room. She spent hours trying to coax Chenya to eat. Chenya told Eli that she couldn't have loved Rebecca more if she were her own daughter. For this, Eli felt both guilty and grateful. He loved Rebecca, but not in the way a man should love his wife. He loved her the way a man loved a sister.

Every Friday night, he fulfilled his duties as a husband and performed the mitzvah of creation. But Rebecca did not conceive, and although the act itself was not unpleasant, it was not wonderful either. Eli often thought of his father and how much his father would have been disappointed in him as a son. When he thought of his papa, he tried harder to be the man his father would have wanted him to be, but no matter what he did, it seemed he was always restless and bored—in search of something he couldn't explain in words. He knew he dared not try to talk to his elders at the shul because he was sure they would never understand.

Winter of 1937

The frigid winter winds blew into Berlin with a vengeance. Rebecca had plenty of free time, so she took a job teaching children at the shul. She got up early and prepared breakfast for her husband and mother-in-law. She sat beside her mother-in-law to make sure she ate. Sometimes, Chenya refused to eat until Rebecca put the spoon of hot cereal into her mouth. It was warm and soft, and Rebecca would speak kind words until Chenya would swallow. Once she fed the old woman, she got dressed and ate something quickly then went off to work. As Rebecca walked to the shul, she thought about the children. She enjoyed them; they were full of life, and enthusiasm, and dreams. Often Rebecca wondered what had happened to her dreams. She'd grown old in her heart, even though she was still a young woman. Eli was a handsome man; he was a good man too. But he was distant, and no matter how hard she tried, she could not reach him. Her mother-in-law was weak and hardly left the bed these days. Rebecca knew that the sadness of losing her mate was slowly sucking the life force out of Chenya.

Rebecca wished she could do something for her mother-in-law, something that would at least bring her some joy. The only thing she could think of was to conceive. If she were pregnant, her mother-in-law might find a reason to live, knowing a grandchild was on the way. But even though she and Eli tried, she did not conceive. To make matters worse, lately, Rebecca found herself smiling at the milkman's son when she went to pick up the milk and cheese that Eli enjoyed each morning.

His name was Shmul, and although he wasn't as handsome as Eli, he was far more attentive. And she was so lonely. She was so starved for a kind word or a tender touch that when she walked into the milkman's small store in the center of town and Shmul's eyes lit up, it sparked something inside of her. Rebecca could feel the desire emanating from Shmul like heat from a fire. It shamed her that she liked the way he made her feel. In fact, if she had a girlfriend she could trust, she would have sent her to the milkman to pick up her milk and cheese rather than face Shmul and the feelings he stirred insider her.

By marrying Eli, she was destined to be a rebbetzin. She could never trust anyone enough to tell them her sinful thoughts. A rebbetzin should be above such things. So she would lower her eyes when she saw Shmul and try to avoid looking at him. But then, something would make her look up, and when their eyes met, she smiled against her will.

Oh, Rebecca! You must be careful! Sin is as close as your own hand.

She asked Shmul's papa for a pound of cheese. As he wrapped the yellow cheese in brown paper, she could feel Shmul's eyes on her.

On one crisp winter day when the sky was ice blue, Rebecca sat in her classroom, waiting for the children to return from their afternoon meal break. She was organizing her desk when Eli came into the classroom. Rebecca looked up, surprised to see her husband. "Eli? What brings you here?"

"Mama is very sick. I went home for lunch, and she was wheezing very loudly. I went into her bedroom, and she was lying in bed. Her face is very pale, and from the sounds she is making, I am sure she is having trouble breathing. I didn't know what to do, so I came here to you. We need to do something," he said, his voice edgy with panic.

"All right. I'm coming. Let me tell Marta that I am leaving, so she can take care of my class."

He nodded. Rebecca explained the situation to Marta, then she quickly put on her winter coat and scarf. She turned to Eli.

"Let's go home," she said. "Avigale is at day school. I'll have one of the neighbors go and bring her home."

He nodded. "Yes, that's a good idea. My sister should be at home with us." Rebecca could see how frightened he was. Sometimes he reminded her of a child. She swallowed hard. She knew how much her in-laws adored their only son, their only child. Since Eli's birth, they had pampered Eli to the point of paralysis. She heard them say they gave him everything he ever asked for. And she had learned by living with him, that he was used to being cared for by others. He couldn't make decisions on his own. Although her in-laws meant well, and Rebecca had come to love them both, she also slightly resented the fact they had not forced Eli to be a man and grow up.

Eli and Rebecca walked side by side as quickly as they could without falling on the icy, snow-covered sidewalk. Rebecca hated the silence. She longed to say something, but when she looked at Eli, he did not return her gaze. He kept his eyes cast down at the ground. *I wish I knew how to comfort him, but he is so far away, so consumed with his own thoughts that I don't know how to reach him. I am so afraid she is dying, and poor Eli is so lost without his father's guidance. Now he is losing his mother too. He needs me, but he doesn't realize it. And no matter what I do, he won't let me in.*

CHAPTER THIRTY-EIGHT

Chenya loved her daughter-in-law, but she cherished her son. Since the day he was born, she doted on him. Now that she was very ill, her son was her major concern.

As she lay on the bed she had shared with her husband since she was just a shy girl of fourteen, she gripped the quilt firmly in her hands. It was so hard for her to accept that she would never see her beloved Asher in this life again. How gentle and kind her husband was during their years together. How understanding of her fears and her needs. Chenya fell in love with him the first moment she saw him, and that was on the day she was married. She peeked under her veil as she walked down the aisle beside her father, nervous about her future. Asher Kaetzel, a boy of seventeen, stood waiting for her in front of the rabbi. He was tall and handsome.

A smile came over Chenya's face as she thought how skinny Asher was when they were married, but then how fat he got on her cooking. They had enjoyed a good marriage. They had cried together when she miscarried her first child. He had not criticized or blamed her; they both shared the same pain. Their home was also filled with laughter, like the time she accidentally burnt the brand-new sheitel that she bought from the kosher wigmaker on the Shabbat candles. She was so afraid Asher would be mad, but once they put out the fire and she was all right, he started laughing. Then she joined him, and before they knew it, they were both laughing so hard they had a hard time stopping.

But their greatest shared joy was the birth of their two wonderful children. First their son and then their daughter. How proud her Asher was of his family! And how happy it made her to see the pride in his face. Tears formed behind her eyes at the bittersweet memory. *Such pride my husband took in everything we had together: our wonderful children, our beautiful but modest home, and my cooking. Whenever he invited guests to our home, he would say, "My Chenya can cook, I tell you. Come, you'll taste her food and never be satisfied with anything less again." Oh, Asher, I know the truth. I am dying. I will miss my boy and his wonderful wife, but I am going home to spend eternity beside my husband, my Asher. My poor Eli. He is so confused. The only consolation I have is that I am leaving him with a good wife, a girl I can trust to take care of my son when I am gone. Asher and I loved our precious boychik. Yes, Eli was the light of our lives from the day he was born. Avigale was a joy, but Eli, he was something special.* Her wrinkled eyelids closed as she remembered the day of Eli's bris, his circumcision. *Asher gently took her arm and led her to their bedroom where she was to stay during the procedure, surrounded by her two sisters. She sat down on this very same bed, trembling, knowing that in the other room the moshel was cutting her child. Asher knew that it was unwise for a mother to be in the same room as her son when he was being circumcised. And Asher was right because Chenya almost fainted when she heard Eli let out a small cry. Oh, Asher, we have so many memories between us. I have missed you so much since you left me. I am ready to come to you; I am ready to come home.*

CHAPTER THIRTY-NINE

Chenya was already gone when Eli and Rebecca arrived at the house. Her limp, lifeless body looked peaceful on the bed. Eli knelt beside his mother and wept. Rebecca tried to put her hand on her husband's shoulder, but she could feel him stiffen up. She tried to massage his shoulder gently, but he did not yield to her at all. No words came to her. All she could do was watch Eli's body slumped in misery.

Oh, Eli, I know you are hurting. I don't know how to help you. I don't know what to do.

"I am an orphan now," was all he said, and he didn't look directly at Rebecca when he spoke. Still keeping his eyes cast down, he stood up.

"I must go to the shul so that I can make arrangements for my mother's funeral and the shiva to follow."

Rebecca nodded, feeling abandoned but trying to be understanding. *Eli has just lost his mother. I will be here for him even if he chooses to shut me out.*

Eli closed the door to the house gently, but Rebecca knew he was gone. Tomorrow she would go to her parents' home and tell them of her mother-in-law's passing. They would come to her aid. She had no doubt that her mother would help with the shiva.

She would go on pretending she was happy. Neither of her parents would ever know how miserable she was with Eli: how sad and alone she felt in her marriage. And it was because she loved them that she would never tell them. Instead, she tried to be grateful for her blessings, so she said a silent prayer, thanking Hashem that her parents were still alive.

Yousef and Eli remained good friends through the years.

But Yousef was a different man once he married. He raced home every afternoon to spend time with his wife. Eli sensed a contentment in Yousef that he envied. As a young man, Yousef had terrible skin problems. He often broke out in pimples, but since his marriage, his skin was clear, and his eyes were alert and joyful. He was focused during Torah studies, and his mood was always bright. *This is what my father wished for me. This is how it should be between a man and his wife. But it is not this way for Rebecca and me. Something is missing.*

Eli swallowed hard and rubbed his head as he walked over to Yousef.

"I need to speak with you," Eli said.

Yousef nodded, stood up, and followed Eli out of the prayer room and into the lobby.

"Nu? What is it?" Yousef asked, looking into Eli's eyes.

"My mother passed away this morning."

"Oy, Eli, I am so sorry."

Eli nodded. "Thank you. Will you help me arrange the funeral? I am sure my in-laws will help with the shiva."

"Of course, of course. And my wife will help with the shiva too," Yousef said, patting Eli's shoulder. "Don't you worry about anything, my dear friend."

CHAPTER FORTY

Rebecca did her best to comfort her husband during the shiva, but he spent most of his time with Yousef. Yousef's wife, Ruth, was a bright girl with a huge smile, and Rebecca felt the warmth emanating from her. Ruth offered her help in every aspect of the shiva. But even though she liked Ruth, she couldn't help but feel a sting of envy when she saw the way Yousef and his wife looked at each other. They acted properly, but when they thought no one was looking, they would smile a knowing smile at each other. Rebecca read a million things into that smile. To her, it represented everything that was lacking in her marriage.

Wouldn't it be wonderful if Eli and I had a relationship like that? But for some reason, we just can't seem to get close to each other. We more or less go through the motions of being husband and wife. I don't feel comfortable enough to share my innermost feelings with him, and he never shares his with me. He treats me with respect but not affection. These two seem so at ease with each other. I can tell that when they are alone, they talk freely, not like Eli and me. I can't speak freely to my husband. I feel as if I must always keep my head bowed and do as he says. That's the way my parents told me I must behave once I was married. And now, Eli and I live together; he shares my bed and my body. I prepare his meals and we eat together. I go to the mikvah after my menses every month. I keep the

Sabbath and a good kosher home, and I am obedient. Anyone on the outside looking in would say we have a perfect marriage. But we have nothing beyond the surface.

Rebecca walked past a mirror and was reminded of the sadness in the house when she saw the mirror covered with a sheet. This was a tradition that always bothered her. It was meant for the mourners so they would not look into the mirror and see their grief, but she always found it unnerving.

Eli was sitting on a hard wooden box in his stocking feet as was expected of a family member of the deceased. Once again, as it was for his father's shiva, the lapel of his jacket was torn to show the world he was in mourning.

"Can I make you up a plate of food?" Rebecca asked.

"No, thank you, Rebecca," Eli said.

She nodded and walked away, feeling he didn't need her for anything. Rebecca didn't want to sit in the living room beside her husband. Being with him made her feel lonelier than being alone, so she went into the kitchen to straighten up. Even though there were many women at the house who were willing to take care of everything, Rebecca wanted to keep busy. She began wiping the counters and neatly rearranging the food that the visitors brought. As she set up the table, there was a knock on the back door. Rebecca was only a few feet away so she opened it. It was Shmul, carrying a big block of cheese wrapped in white paper.

"I brought this for you," he said. "I think it's your favorite. I mean, it's the one you always buy."

"Thank you. That was very kind of you," Rebecca said, putting the cheese on a plate. She placed it on the table then took a knife from the drawer and put it next to the cheese. The cheese wasn't her favorite. It was actually her mother-in-law's favorite, and Rebecca had always purchased it for her. But there was no point in telling Shmul that.

"Please, won't you have something to eat?" she asked.

"Yes, I will. Thank you." Shmul took a plate and began to fill it. Rebecca tried to leave the room, not wanting to be alone with him any longer than necessary. It wasn't proper.

"Rebecca?" he said. His voice was soft and gentle, and it made her long to be held and touched. Not in a sexual way, but in an affectionate way. Eli never touched her or held her. If Shmul even tried, she knew she would run out of the room because it was strictly forbidden. But something inside of her yearned for human touch.

"I have something to say to you," Shmul said. "I have been watching you every time you come into my father's store. I can't stop thinking about you. I think I am falling in love with you."

Rebecca felt her face burn with embarrassment. "You must not say such things. You must not think them either. I am the wife of the future rebbe. I am proud to be Eli's wife. I can never think of any other man in that way. Do you understand me?" Rebecca said firmly.

He nodded, but he looked as if he might cry. "I understand. You are a good girl: a frum girl. A girl any man would be lucky to have as his wife."

"I'm sorry, Shmul. I hope you find someone who makes you happy. You're a good man. You deserve to be happy," Rebecca said. She walked out of the room leaving Shmul alone. She quickly went into the bathroom and locked the door. Once she was alone, she began to cry. She wept for all that Eli wasn't. She wept for all that he didn't give her, and for all her broken dreams: all the dreams she had to give up because it was the right thing to do.

Avigale, Eli's younger sister, sat quietly next to him on a wooden box in her stocking feet. She had been jealous of Rebecca's relationship with her mother, so she was never close to Rebecca. Now she would have to live with her brother and sister-in-law, acting as parents to her, unless one of her other relatives offered her a place to stay. She always wanted to visit Holland, and she did have an aunt and uncle living there. She thought perhaps she could convince Eli to send her there. He was the head of the house with Papa gone, and now all decisions would have to be approved by him. Avigale decided to ask him after all the people who came to pay their respects left, and the family was alone.

Rebecca's parents arrived at the shiva. Her mother handed a cake to Rebecca.

"Thank you, Mother," Rebecca said, not meeting her mother's eyes. She knew if she saw the reflection of her own sadness in her mother's eyes she would break down, and she was trying so hard to stay strong for Eli's sake.

"How is my shana madel, my pretty girl?" her father asked. "You are so busy you hardly come to see us anymore."

It was true. Rebecca didn't go to see her parents because she was afraid they would ask how she and Eli were doing as a couple, or even worse, they might ask why she had not yet conceived.

"Oh, but I do come to see you, Papa. However, my poor mother-in-law was sick for a long time before she passed, and it was difficult for me to get away and leave her. Eli was in the shul every day, and his mother couldn't be left alone. She needed my help."

"Of course. Your mama and I understand, and you have always been such a good girl. My sweet child. But now you'll have time on your hands; you'll come and see us, yes?"

Rebecca turned away because she felt the tears forming behind her eyes.

"Of course, Father," Rebecca said, choking back the tears.

At sundown, Eli gathered ten men, a minyan, in order to say the

Kaddish, a special prayer for the dead, for his mother. Rebecca's father participated. The men stood alongside Eli and recited the familiar prayers.

Yisgadal v'yiskadash sh'mei rabbaw (Amen)
B'allmaw dee v'raw chir'usei,
v'yamlich malchusei,b'chayeichon, uv'yomeichon,
uv'chayei d'chol beis yisroel,
ba'agawlaw u'vizman kawriv, v'imru: Amen.
(Cong: Amen. Y'hei sh'mei rabbaw m'vawrach l'allam u'l'allmei
allmayaw)
Y'hei sh'mei rabbaw m'vawrach l'allam u'l'allmei allmayaw.
Yis'bawrach, v'yishtabach, v'yispaw'ar, v'yisromam, v'yis'nasei,
v'yis'hadar, v'yis'aleh, v'yis'halawl sh'mei d'kudshaw b'rich hu
(Cong. b'rich hu). L'aylaw min kol birchawsaw v'shirawsaw,
tush'b'chawsaw v'nechemawsaw, da'ami'rawn b'all'maw, v'imru: Amein

Meanwhile, Ruth and Rebecca cleaned the kitchen.

"Can I help you two?" Rebecca's mother offered.

"No, Mama. We are doing just fine," Rebecca said. "You should sit. You've been helping out all day. Sit and make yourself comfortable while you wait for Papa."

"Your papa and I are going to head back home once the men have finished the Kaddish."

Rebecca heard the last lines of the prayers, and she hugged her mother tightly. "Thank you for coming," she said, longing to say so much more, but holding back.

Y'hei shlawmaw rabbaw min sh'mayaw,v'chayim
awleinu v'al kol yisroel, v'imru: Amein
Oseh shawlom bim'ro'mawv, hu ya'aseh shawlom,
awleinu v'al kol yisroel v'imru: Amein

"Of course, we would come. There is no need for you to thank us, Rebecca. You are our daughter. Your husband's family is our mishpokha, our family too." Rebecca's mother touched Rebecca's cheek gently. "And please, try to come and see us. Your papa and I miss you."

Rebecca nodded. Tears fell down her cheeks. She couldn't hold them back.

Her mother wiped the tears from Rebecca's face the same way she did when she was a child. "Don't cry, meyn kind, my child. I know you are sad, but it hurts me to see you cry."

"I miss you and Papa," Rebecca said.

"Of course you do, but kaynahorah, you have a good life. And the evil eye should not fall on you." Rebecca's mother spit on the floor three times superstitiously. "You have a wonderful husband, such a smart boy, such an educated boy, and a lovely home."

"Yes, Mama." Rebecca choked out the words obediently. "You're right."

"So you'll come to see your papa and me next week. I'll make you a pot of my good chicken soup with matzo balls—not too soft—the way you like it. Yes? I remember. Of course, I remember. And you'll take some soup home for your handsome husband, yes?"

"Yes, Mama."

CHAPTER FORTY-ONE

Eli decided if Avigale wanted to stay with their aunt and uncle in Holland, it was all right with him. Their uncle was a prominent rabbi and would probably be able to find a good match for her. Eli promised Avigale he would make all the arrangements.

After Rebecca and Avigale went to bed, Eli sat outside alone looking at the moon. It was bitter cold, and it was only when he felt his eyelashes freezing that he knew he was crying. *Papa*, he said quietly to the moon and stars. *Papa, how am I going to follow in your footsteps? I can't advise anyone. I am so unsure of myself. I dare not tell any of the others at the shul or yeshiva lest they think me unworthy. But I need someone I can talk to, someone I can rely on to give me advice. But there is no one in the world who can guide me the way that you did. Rebecca is a good girl, but she is not a strong person. I know I should not expect this of a woman. Women are not to be consulted in this way, but I have no idea whom I can turn to. The only person I ever felt would be able to speak to me as an equal was the girl, Gretchen, whom I met long ago. I know that wherever you are, just hearing me say this girl's name has probably sent you into a fit of spitting on the floor. Of course, I know that you would never approve of me talking to her. First off, I am a married man, and to even think of spending time with a woman who is not my wife is a sin. And number two, to make matters worse, she is a shiksa. The fact that I am even thinking about her is wrong. And yet, I think about her all the time. I don't know why, Papa. Years have passed. I should have forgotten her long ago. I don't see her or talk to her. And it isn't as if I haven't tried to put her out of my mind. She's not nearly as beautiful as my wife. And yet . . .*

CHAPTER FORTY-TWO

Gretchen felt bad that every time Hilde wanted to visit her, she was busy. Either she was caught up in making wedding arrangements, or Karl was at her house. She saw the sadness in Hilde's eyes when she said she didn't have time to visit, and she knew that Hilde was feeling left behind. She thought it would be a nice gesture if she made an effort to see Hilde once in a while, but she was so busy that it never seemed like the right time.

Several months passed since Karl had spoken with the Jewish professor who had been fired from the university. Over that time the university had let go of all the Jewish faculty. And in consequence the other professors were overloaded with work. In the teachers lounge there were constant complaints about the workload. But no one mentioned the Jews or the law.

One afternoon Karl was in the teachers lounge. He was exhausted and becoming very unhappy with the increased workload he had been given. Several of the professors were talking. They were complaining about working ten-hour days. When one female colleague, Frances Hillman, said she could not understand why there was such a heavy increase in their work, Karl accidently let his innermost thoughts be vocalized. This was not like him. Not at all.

Perhaps it was because he was tired. Perhaps it was because these were his truest inner thoughts. Or perhaps it was his destiny to speak out. But Karl turned to glare at Professor Hillman. Then Karl said, "Don't you know why we are working like dogs? If you don't know, I'll tell you, Professor Hillman. It's because the university fired all the Jews. Now we're stuck doing all their work."

"We can't have Jews teaching Aryans. It's not right. They are inferior." Professor Hillman said. It was well known at the university that Hillman was a strong party member and a huge supporter of the Nazi doctrine. "Besides, it's the law."

"The law? The Nazi Party law? The Nazi lawmakers aren't here working like you and I, until they are completely exhausted, are they?" Karl said. Then he continued not giving the woman a chance to answer. "I have to go. I have another class in ten minutes." Karl walked out of the faculty lounge. An Aryan science professor who was Karl's best friend ran after him. When he caught up with Karl he whispered in his ear, "Be careful, Schmidt. You are looking for trouble. We are living in dangerous times. Take care of yourself and your daughter. I have nothing against the Jews, but I don't care enough about them to put my job or maybe even my life at risk. Do you understand what I am trying to tell you?" He patted Karl's back.

Karl nodded

A week later, Karl was called into the office of the University president.

"This is treason, Karl. Why would you say those things about the Nazi Party? And now, as much as I have liked you all these years that you have worked here, I have to let you go. Someone reported you to the party, and I have received strict orders that I must fire you. I am sorry."

"Who reported me? Was it Frances Hillman?" Karl asked.

Hillman was the female professor he argued with about the Jews, and he knew she was angry with him.

"I don't know who it was. The Gestapo didn't tell me, and I didn't ask. Karl, I am not looking for trouble. I don't want to know who is on what side and why. It's my job to keep the university going as an institution of higher learning under the laws of our fatherland. So I wouldn't tell you if I did know who turned you in. You have been flirting with danger for a long time. I begged you to stop when you came to see me last fall, but you persisted. And now you are out of a job. I am sorry. But I can't help you. I wash my hands of the whole damn thing."

There was nothing more to say. Karl knew he should have expected this. But even so, it came as a surprise. He always believed that somehow the educated people he worked with would see the truth and begin to fight with him against the Nazi hate propaganda they were being force-fed. *Many good people work at this university. It's just that they are afraid, and if I had any sense, I would be afraid too. Maybe I am. But I can't live with injustice. I never could.*

Karl walked slowly to his classroom, his head down, and cleaned out his desk. He turned off the lights in his classroom for the last time, and prepared to leave the hallowed halls he was once so proud to be a part of. He had no idea what he would do next. Although he had a little money saved, he would need to find a job as soon as possible. He had promised to help pay for Gretchen's wedding. Those extra expenses would deplete his savings in no time.

Karl walked to the bus slowly like a fractured marionette and no longer knew his purpose for being on earth. His limbs hung limply at his sides, his head bowed. He was on his way home from work two hours early, feeling his world had collapsed.

CHAPTER FORTY-THREE

Both Gretchen and Norbert were off work that day. They weren't expecting Gretchen's father for at least two and a half hours. Quickly, Gretchen put the kettle on the stove and started the soup for dinner. Then she and Norbert went into her bedroom. They quickly got undressed and climbed into her bed. This was a regular occurrence every Wednesday afternoon since their engagement. Gretchen insisted that Norbert not ejaculate inside her. Out of respect for her father, she told Norbert that she wanted to make sure she didn't get pregnant until after they were married. He agreed and was very careful.

At first, their sexual encounters were exciting, and Gretchen looked forward to them. But lately, they began to argue. The wedding was less than two months away, and there was still so much to do. Gretchen wanted Norbert to move in with her father because he was alone. But Norbert insisted they live with his parents because his family had a nicer home with more living space. The longer Gretchen and Norbert were together, the more demanding he became. Consumed with the excitement of the wedding and the idea of being married, she overlooked a lot of his faults. However, as Norbert grew comfortable with his fiancée, he became outspoken. It was growing more difficult to ignore the things she didn't like about him.

They finished making love, and Norbert reached for his cigarettes.

"I wish you would quit. I hate the smell of smoke. It stinks up the whole room," Gretchen said irritated.

"A good cigarette or cigar gives a man a feeling of well-being," Norbert said, lighting the cigarette.

"Well-being my foot," she said, shaking her head. "The smell is atrocious. And you cough constantly, so it can't be good for you."

"You're just not used to it. Your father is the only fellow I know who doesn't enjoy a good smoke."

"I am glad he doesn't."

"Come here and give me a kiss. You're adorable when you get angry," Norbert said.

"I can't. I have to check the soup."

"Oh, come on now, just a kiss."

She leaned over to kiss him, and as she did, she heard the key turn in the front door.

"My father! He's home. Get dressed quickly," Gretchen said. She got up and slammed the bedroom door and locked it. They rushed to put their clothes on.

"I can hear him in the other room. I hope he's not ill."

"He must be. Why else would he be home so early?" Norbert asked.

"I don't know, but straighten your shirt. You aren't buttoned correctly. Fix it. Hurry," Gretchen said as she pulled the blankets and quilt over the bed.

"Gretchen?" her father called out.

"Yes, Father. I'm home," she answered trying to sound calm but checking herself in the mirror to make sure she didn't look disheveled. She didn't want her father to know what she and Norbert had been doing. "Norbert is here with me. We were reading."

"Hurry, let's get out of the bedroom," Gretchen said, turning to Norbert and then checking herself one more time in the mirror, hoping she didn't look as if she had just been in bed with her fiancée.

Norbert and Gretchen walked into the living room. Karl was sitting on the sofa. He didn't look up. A wave of guilt and embarrassment at almost being caught in such a compromising position came over Gretchen. Her face was red with shame, and she couldn't look at her father directly.

"You're home early, Father. Are you feeling all right?" she asked as she headed straight to the kitchen to stir the soup.

"Yes. I am all right. But I had a rough day at work."

"What happened?" Gretchen said, suddenly forgetting her own feelings of embarrassment and returning to the living room.

CHAPTER FORTY-FOUR

Her father poured himself a full glass of whiskey and drank it quickly.

"Can I get you anything?" Gretchen asked him. But before her father could answer, there was a knock on the door.

"Who is it?" Gretchen asked.

"Gestapo, open up," a harsh voice said.

Gretchen was terrified. "Gestapo?" she said, looking from her father to Norbert.

"Open up, now."

Gretchen's hand trembled as she unlocked the door.

"There must be some mistake," she stammered.

Two Gestapo agents entered the room.

"Professor Schmidt?" the Gestapo agent said

Her father nodded, but his head was hanging down. But from where Gretchen stood, she could see his hands shaking.

"Father, what is going on here?"

Karl didn't answer; he just stared at her with the saddest expression she'd ever seen.

Then Gretchen continued, "There must be some mistake. My father is a good man. He would never do anything wrong.

"You want to know what your father did? Your father has broken the law. He is supporting Jews. From what I hear he's lost his job at the university for supporting Jews. What do you think of that, young lady?"

"Father?" Gretchen ran to her father and put her arms around him. She was so frightened she could hardly breathe.

"I complained about the workload being heavy, and I said that when the university fired the Jews . . ."

"Shut up, and lets go, Schmidt."

My poor gentle father. He is so scared. It hurts me to see him like this. And I am terrified of what will happen next. "Please, don't do this. Whatever he did, he didn't mean it," she said, grabbing the Gestapo agent's jacket. He shook her off, and she and fell to her knees begging, "Please, don't take him. Please."

"Move, Schmidt. Mach schnell." The Gestapo pushed Karl with the butt of his gun. Karl was shaking so badly that he fell forward hitting the floor with a thud.

Gretchen held tightly to her father until the Gestapo agent began to pull him away.

"Father!" Gretchen yelled. Tears were falling down her cheeks. Then she turned to the Gestapo agent. "Where are you taking him? Please, don't hurt him. Please, I beg you. Have mercy."

"We are taking him to headquarters for questioning."

"Father? What should I do?" Gretchen cried out, suddenly feeling like a frightened child.

"It will be all right. Just wait here." Karl tried to reassure her as the Gestapo agent shoved him out the door.

Gretchen bit her knuckles as she ran to the window to watch.

The two agents shoved Karl into the back of a black automobile. Gretchen saw her father hit his head as they forced him in, and she winced. The car drove off. Gretchen couldn't believe what had just happened. She stared out the window barely breathing and without speaking for several minutes. Norbert didn't say a word either. Then she turned and looked at Norbert. "Turn off the stove. The soup is boiling over," she said abruptly, tears of anger running down her cheeks.

Norbert went into the kitchen and turned off the stove.

"Your family must help my father. Your family knows plenty of high-ranking party members. They can help."

"They eat at our restaurant and drink at our beer hall, but I don't know if we know them well enough to ask for a favor like this. I am afraid to ask my parents. I am afraid to tell them what happened."

"Norbert, it's my father we are talking about. You have to help me."

"What was he thinking talking against the party? He brought this all on himself. Now you expect my family to put themselves in danger by asking someone in the party to help him?"

"Yes, I do. You are my future husband."

"I understand, but you're asking me to do something that would put all of us in danger, you, me, and my family."

"Damn you, Norbert. How can you be so selfish?"

"I'm not being selfish, Gretchen. I am being smart. Don't you see that your father is in trouble, and anyone who takes his side might as well consider themselves right there with him? I don't want any trouble with the government. And I know my parents don't either."

Gretchen walked over and stirred the soup. She watched the tiny pieces of potato swirl around and around. For several moments, she didn't speak. Then in a quiet voice, she said, "You should go home now, Norbert. I want to be alone."

He didn't argue. Norbert quickly put on his coat and scarf and walked out the door, closing it quietly.

CHAPTER FORTY-FIVE

The soup grew cold on the stove. Gretchen never went to bed that night. She sat at the window, staring out at the moon and the darkness. Terror filled her heart, and her hands trembled. It was well past midnight, and her father had not yet returned. Norbert had not come back either. Somehow, she thought Norbert would have returned. She thought he would go home and speak to his parents and then come back with a promise of help. But he didn't.

She was alone, shivering in the cold, dark apartment, alone with her thoughts and her fears. She knew how hard it must have been for her father to complain about his workload. It had taken all his courage to speak out. But right now, she was wishing he had kept quiet. Because if he had, he would be safe at home instead of being questioned at the police station. The very idea of her father under interrogation made her shiver. She was sure he was feeling alone and terrified. This could end very badly, but she couldn't bear to think of it.

Gretchen laid her head on her hands. She wished she could sleep. She had to be at work at 8 a.m. the next morning. How was she ever going to work an entire day without any sleep? How could she possibly go into the factory and work all day without knowing if her father was safe? *I'll call in sick. I can't go to work tomorrow, not until I see my father, and I know he's all right.*

Gretchen went upstairs to see Frau Bauer early the following morning. She was the only person in the building who had a phone in her apartment. Frau Bauer allowed Gretchen to use her phone, and Gretchen called the factory and said she was sick. Then she went back downstairs to her own flat. She still had not heard from Norbert or her father.

By noon, pure panic set in. She went back upstairs and asked to use the phone again. Frau Bauer looked annoyed, but she agreed.

"I'll pay you for the call," Gretchen said. "I have to telephone my Aunt Margrit."

Frau Bauer nodded. She stood around the corner and listened as Gretchen told her aunt that her father had been arrested.

"I'll come there to you. I'll leave tonight. Gunther is off work, so maybe he will come with me. Don't worry, Gretchen. You're not alone. We will be there to help you," Margrit said.

After Gretchen hung up the phone, she thanked Frau Bauer and left some money on the table. But she could see the suspicious look in Frau Bauer's eyes as she walked out the door of her flat. *People are scared. Norbert is scared too. I never thought he would be a coward like he is. He should be here with me, but he is nowhere to be found.*

Gretchen went back down to her flat. It was very cold outside, and with all that was happening she felt chilled deep inside her—deeper than she usually did. Glancing at the familiar rooms, she felt the heaviness of being alone. *What if my father never returns? I've heard that sometimes happens to people who are deemed enemies of this government. I can't imagine life without my father. His kind heart, and his calm intellect have guided me my entire lifetime. I don't know how to live without you, Father. Please be careful what you say to them. Please, Father; don't be self-righteous. You have nothing to prove. Oh, please God, I know I haven't believed in you, but if you're there, and if you really do exist, then I beg you to please guide him in what he says to them. He is so foolish and brave sometimes.*

Gretchen couldn't lie down on her bed, so she sat on the sofa and spread her quilt over her. It would probably be at least a day before her aunt arrived. And her father? There was no telling if or when he would return. The smell of the rancid soup filled the small flat. She stared out the window until her eyes closed.

She awoke to the rattling of the front door. At first, fear struck her like a bolt of lightning. *Perhaps the Gestapo has returned, and now they are coming for me?* But then her father limped into the apartment. He looked so much older than when he left only a day ago. He was bruised and beaten, and he appeared much smaller than his six feet. His hair was stuck to his forehead with dried blood. Gretchen gasped when she saw him.

"Father?" she choked out. "What have they done to you?"

He tried to smile, but there was a cut on his upper lip. "I'm all right, Gretchen."

"They beat you?"

"Yes, maybe a little."

"More than a little, Father." She felt the tears pool in her eyes, and she didn't have the strength to hold them back. "Here, sit down. Let me wash all this dried blood off your face," she said pulling out a kitchen chair. Obediently, he did as she asked.

Gretchen took a pot of water and warmed it on the stove, then she took a kitchen towel and wet it, wringing the extra water out. As gently as she could, she wiped her father's face and discovered the source of the dried blood. It was a terrifying gash on the top of his head. When Gretchen saw the wound, she gagged. Bile rose in her throat.

"It looks that bad?" Her father tried to make light of his wound, but she was looking directly at it, and she felt sick.

"You probably need stitches." She wondered if the gash was the result of hitting his head on the car door. "I don't think I should go to the hospital," he said. "Our government isn't very happy with me, I am afraid. It's probably best that I lay low until we can figure out our next move."

"What could that be?" Gretchen didn't understand.

"We may have to leave Germany," her father said, shaking his head. Then he continued, "I don't know. I don't know what to do, Gretchen. I am at a loss. I never thought that our brilliant country, a country as civilized and advanced as Germany, could turn out to be so barbaric."

She sunk onto the sofa. "Aunt Margrit is on her way here. I telephoned her last night."

"Why? Why did you do that?" He seemed angry.

"Because I was scared, Father. And I have been all alone here."

"Where is Norbert?"

"He went home yesterday."

"He left you alone?"

She nodded, turning away, but not before catching a glimpse of her father's eyes. Gretchen saw his loss of respect for Norbert, but she didn't know what to say. She felt the same way, and yet she couldn't discuss it with her father, not now. Her father stood up and limped slowly into his bedroom. "I want to clean myself up and take off these dirty clothes."

"When you have changed clothes I'll take the dirty ones and wash them," Gretchen said.

It was almost ten minutes before her father returned handing her his dirty pants and shirt, both torn and covered in blood.

Karl Schmidt sank onto the sofa. Gretchen glanced at him and saw his body shivering. She placed a blanket over him and leaned over and kissed his forehead, being careful not to touch the cut. "I'll make you a cup of hot tea," she said.

He nodded. "Thank you."

CHAPTER FORTY-SIX

The Gestapo could not come to someone's home in Hilde's neighborhood without her hearing about it. She had tentacles that extended all around her, sucking in any and all gossip. When she learned from Judith, a girl she knew from the Bund, what had happened to Gretchen's father, she listened intently to the story. She asked everyone she knew about it, from the butcher to the leader of her Bund group, and they all had plenty to share. Once she had enough information to piece the story together, Hilde had a plan. She quickly put on her most respectable-looking dress and went to Norbert's family's restaurant.

She had seen his father working there many times in the past and hoped to find him there today. Hilde sat down at the bar and ordered a beer. For a moment, she was afraid she might see Norbert, and she wasn't sure what she would say to him. She was relieved when he was nowhere in sight.

She heard loud male voices coming from the room behind the bar. "Is Herr Krause here today?" she asked the bartender.

"Yes, but he's in the back checking in a shipment. Can I help you?"

"No, it's personal. I need to see him."

"I see." The bartender shrugged. "I don't get involved with his personal business. I'll let him know there is someone here to see him. What's your name?"

"Hilde."

The bartender disappeared in the back room and several minutes passed. She thought Norbert's father would say he was too busy to see her, but she was wrong. Norbert's father walked out and went directly to her.

"Are you here looking for work?" he asked.

"No. I need to talk to you. It's about your son, Norbert."

Norbert's father's face grew serious. "Come with me," he said and led Hilde to the back room.

"Herr Krause," Hilde said, sitting down on a chair in the corner. "I am here because of Gretchen."

"Gretchen? Did she send you here to see me? Norbert has been distraught since the last time he saw her. He refuses to speak to his mother or me about her. I am very worried about him. Gretchen has not been at our house either. Did she break up with him?"

"You must promise me that you won't tell Norbert how you found out what I am about to tell you. He will be mad if he ever learned that I came to speak to you. But there is something that you must know."

"I promise I will never tell him. But you must tell me, please," Norbert's father said. "I am so worried about my son."

"Gretchen's father was arrested by the Gestapo. He has been acting out against the government. He is in real trouble. I am just sick about it. I have distanced myself from Gretchen because of it. You see, her father is a Jew-lover. He's been standing up for the Jews at the university where he works, and that is against the law. So for your sake and Norbert's too, this wedding must be stopped. I wouldn't have stuck my nose in your business, but I can't allow this to happen to Norbert. He was always kind to me. He has always treated me like a friend. I am sure he knows that he must not marry Gretchen, and that's why he is distraught. He probably realizes that if he marries her, you and your family will be dragged right into all this. So, just in case he changes his mind and decides to go back to Gretchen, I thought it was best to tell you."

"Yes, of course, you're right. I won't allow the wedding. I can't allow it."

"I didn't think you would."

CHAPTER FORTY-SEVEN

Margrit and her husband, Gunther, arrived at Gretchen's house early the following morning. Her blonde curls bounced as she came in, making her seem like a ray of sunlight in the dark, dismal flat.

She kissed Gretchen on both cheeks. "Where is your father?" she asked.

"I finally got him to lie down in bed. The police beat him up very badly."

"Oh dear, let me go in and have a look at him."

When Margrit returned, she sat down on the sofa next to Gretchen.

"Does he need stitches, Aunt Margrit?"

"I don't think so."

"Will he be all right?"

"Yes, he'll have a scar, but he'll be fine. The scar on his pride will be worse than the one on his head. Poor man. Your father has always been such a man of principle. He's always believed in the good in people. All the cruelty going on in our country right now is very hard for him to understand."

"I know. It's hard for me too."

"Of course, but your father must accept that things have taken a turn here in Germany. Either we go with the flow, or the new regime will crush us like ants."

"I am afraid for him. I am afraid it is too late for him. He has been very outspoken against the party."

"It will be fine," Margrit said. "Gunther is a high-ranking official in the party. He will tell your father what must be done. As long as Karl listens to him, it will be all right."

CHAPTER FORTY-EIGHT

The smell of cigarette smoke filled the small flat. Gretchen coughed and felt dizzy. She'd only seen her Onkel Gunther a handful of times that she could remember, but the most lasting memory of him was the odor of his cigarettes. For the second time since his arrival, he apologized for his smoking habit. But even as he did, he lit another one. He took a puff and then put the cigarette down in the ashtray.

"I know that our führer doesn't approve of smoking," Gunther said, picking up his cigarette and sucking the smoke into his lungs. "And I have been meaning to quit. I started to, right before we left home, didn't I, Margrit? But then, of course, all this mess with Karl. How could I quit? I am a nervous wreck."

Margrit didn't answer her husband's rhetorical question.

Gretchen didn't give a damn what the führer thought about her uncle's nasty habit. All she knew was that she hated it. It stunk and made it hard for her to breathe. Their flat was too small for all that smoke. But as much as she wanted to tell him he was stinking up the place, she held her tongue. After all, her aunt and uncle had traveled to help her father. So no matter how annoying her uncle was, she would restrain herself.

Karl Schmidt came into the room and sat down on the sofa. He studied his brother-in-law, Gunther. The man was overweight with a ruddy complexion, and fat, red fingers stained brown at the tips from smoking. He wanted to like the man for Margrit's sake, but the truth was he never liked Gunther.

"Why do you do these foolish things, Karl? Don't you realize that you are one man trying to fight a system that is far bigger than you? You are a fool. A goddamn fool." Gunther shook his head.

"Don't be so hard on him," Margrit said. "He has always been one to stand up for the unfortunate. That's just the way he is. My brother is not a fool; he's an idealist, Gunther."

"Same things. These are treacherous times. You need to take care of what you say and do. Look at you, Karl. They beat you to a pulp, and why? For what? For Jewish professors? Who are these Jews to you? Nobody! So what was the point?"

"Because someone must find the courage to stand up to the Nazis. And I was finally forced to do it. Oh, believe me, Gunther, I am no hero. And I have never been one to fight. In fact, I am not at all brave. All I wanted to do was protect Gretchen. So, I tried like hell to avoid taking a stand. But as they fired more of the Jewish professors, my workload grew. And before I knew it I was buried in work. I couldn't keep up. I was afraid I would lose my job. I had to speak out."

"So you stood up for the Jews because your workload became too much to bear?"

"At first, yes. But then I started to see that there were things happening all around me, which were bound to affect my daughter and I even more, as time went on. So, I realized something. No matter how much I tried to crawl under a rock and hide, I could not escape. I had to take a stand. The breakdown of a civilization doesn't begin with an earthquake of changes. It begins with the smallest crack in its foundation. And before you know it, that crack becomes a canyon. Yes, right now Germany is advanced in art, and culture, and science. No one could argue that she is not a civilized nation. However, since the Nazis came to power, we are facing a regime that could strip us of our humanity and turn us into savages. These Nazis have built their entire regime on hatred. And if you think that this snowball will stop gaining speed, strength, and momentum with the firing of a few Jewish professors and the forcing of Jewish students out of our schools, you can think again, Gunther. I promise you that it won't stop there. If we turn our heads and ignore this very tiny breach in our morality, that little crack in our respect for what is right and what is wrong will only grow bigger until the crack is a giant hole that will swallow us all. We will lose everything that makes us a respected nation, in the process."

"You really think that something as trivial as the firing of Jewish professors is a crack in Germany's foundation? I don't think so."

"Yes. Listen to me. I am trying to tell you something, Gunther. This is the beginning of something more horrible than we can even comprehend. Jews are no longer allowed to work for Aryans; we Germans are no longer allowed to buy from Jews. Any kind of romantic relationship between Jews and non-Jews is forbidden by law. Good God, man! Don't you see the foundation cracking? I can hear it in the back of my mind when I try to rest at night. I can hear the cracking. And mark my words, Gunther, I promise you that if everyone allows this madness to continue, and no one says a word, it will only grow and get bigger and bigger until . . ."

"Karl, please. Stop. I understand that you want to change things. But right now, you are walking on very thin ice. The police are watching you. You've openly made yourself an enemy of the Nazi

Party. This is a bigger mistake than you realize. I can see that the police have manhandled you, and still you talk like a childish fool. You are my wife's brother, and she loves you. So, of course, I am here to help you if I can. But in order for me to be of any assistance, you have to work with me, Karl. If you don't, the party will destroy you. It has destroyed more important men. Believe me."

"What is it you want him to do, Gunther?" Margrit said, standing up and putting her hand on Karl's shoulder. "Please Karl, you must listen to him."

"Your brother has no choice but to show his loyalty to Hitler and the Nazi Party and to do so in a very deliberate way. He must make a strong statement, and do it as quickly as possible. Are you a party member?" Gunther asked Karl, taking a puff of his cigarette.

"No," Karl answered. "How could I join such a terrible political group? I never felt comfortable with the Nazi Party. I never liked their ideals at all, and quite frankly, after what they did to me when they arrested me, I like them even less."

"Yes, well, it doesn't matter what you like and what you don't like. You had better join the party and quick," Gunther said, shaking his head as if he thought Karl was an idiot.

"Gunther, I told you. I never wanted to get in the middle of all this. But I was forced. I can't turn back now. I must stand by what I believe is right, even if it means that they will arrest me again. You have no idea how hard this is for a man like me. I hate fighting. I hate pain. I have always been a quiet man, keeping to myself. But I can't do that any longer. They've arrested me. They've beaten me. They've forced me to take a stand. And now, I have to see this thing through to the end."

"Really, Karl? Even at the risk of hurting your daughter?" Gunther asked. "Make no mistake, the party will assume she is just like you, and unless she is willing to stand against you, they will come after her too, and they will hurt her. If they even *think* you're a traitor, they will make both of your lives a living hell."

"Oh, Karl, think of Gretchen," Margrit said.

Karl stood up and put his hands on his temples and squeezed. He paced the floor for several moments without saying a word. He would do anything for his daughter. Anything at all. She was his reason for living. Now he glanced over at her sitting quietly in the corner of the sofa listening to this horrible conversation.

"Gretchen," Karl said. It was more of a statement than a question.

"Yes, Father?"

He had a million things he wanted to say to her. A million questions he wished he could ask her, but he knew that no matter what she said, her answers would not matter. Even if she said she would rather he stand up for what he knew was right regardless of the punishment, he would not. Because even though he would fight to the death if need be, he would never put her at risk, even if she wanted him to.

"Father?"

"Never mind," Karl said, shaking his head. He turned to Gunther. "What do I have to do next to prove my loyalty, to make them leave my daughter alone?"

"I am glad you are ready to listen to reason. In the end, you will be quite glad you did. Now the first thing you must do is join the party. Then show your loyalty by attending meetings. Make sure that you explain how wrong you were, and how you have begun to see the light."

Karl nodded, but he felt disgusted with himself.

"And then, since you're out of work, I think you should join the army."

"Are you serious?"

"Yes, of course, I am serious. You will receive a regular paycheck, which you will need now that you are not working. They will feed you and take care of you, so you can send your money to Gretchen. And if you play things right, it will appear as if you have had a serious change of heart."

"The army? Good lord, man. I am no soldier."

"They'll give you a desk job. They'll know that you don't have what it takes to be a real soldier. But you must make a grand gesture, and show them how loyal you are."

Karl looked at Gretchen, and she shook her head. "You don't have to do this for me, Father," she said in a small voice.

"Yes, I do," he answered.

CHAPTER FORTY-NINE

It had been over a week since Gretchen last saw Norbert. Ever since they first met, he came to her house after work at least three times a week. She tried to attribute his absence to his being busy helping his father open another beer garden. Norbert was good with a hammer and nail, so perhaps his father was working him hard. She wanted to believe that, but she knew something was wrong. She assumed that it was her father's trouble with the law. Norbert's family earned a nice living from the SS officers and Gestapo agents. Their popularity among the party members had given Norbert's family enough extra cash to open another location. To make matters worse, since Gretchen and Norbert got engaged, she hadn't taken the time to tend her friendship with Hilde. So now, when she needed someone to talk to, she didn't feel comfortable going to Hilde. When Hilde first returned from the Bund camp, she told Gretchen how upset she was that Hann had moved away. Gretchen had tried to be caring and sensitive, but it was impossible. She was too excited about her upcoming wedding, and she found herself talking about her own plans. After that, Hilde stopped coming to see her. When they passed each other at work, Hilde was polite but not as friendly as she'd been. It bothered Gretchen, but at the time, she'd been so caught up in the idea of getting married that she had not paid much attention to Hilde. Now she wished she had. Hilde was not perfect, by any means, but she and Gretchen were once close enough to talk about anything. And now, Gretchen had no one she felt she could turn to.

Aunt Margrit was sweet, and Gretchen knew she cared about her, but she always lived so far away that they never developed an authentic closeness. The truth of the matter was that once she was engaged, Norbert became her best friend. He monopolized all of her time. And somehow, she hadn't minded at all. There was the excitement of discovering sex for the first time, followed by the thrill of having a real boyfriend, a fiancée. Then there were all the wonderful plans for the wedding. She'd been swept away by the newness of it all. If she really thought things through, she knew that Norbert was wrong for her. She always knew. And she had never really loved him. Not really. Perhaps it was because he was nothing like Eli. But why was she thinking about Eli now?

Gretchen shrugged. It shouldn't surprise her that Norbert was acting strange. He never had her father's courage or intellect. He was always one to follow the crowd. Gretchen was angry with herself for pushing her friend aside. She had been avoiding Hilde. She'd been too busy with Norbert to spend any time with Hilde. And when Gretchen saw Hilde at work, she avoided her. That was because she knew Hilde would ask her why she couldn't find an afternoon once in a while to spend with her old friend. How could Gretchen explain that Norbert demanded her every free moment and all of her attention? And even harder to explain was that she willingly gave in to him because it was easier than arguing. Besides, she had been so caught up in excitement of the wedding that she was enjoying the time spent with Norbert even if he was all consuming. But now that Norbert seemed to have abandoned her, she felt alone.

Aunt Margrit came into the kitchen and put a pot of water on the stove to boil for tea.

"Your father and Gunther are going into town this afternoon."

"I know. Father is joining the army. I think it's a mistake."

"I can't say for sure, Gretchen. But I do know this; your father is in terrible trouble. Gunther will do his best to help him."

"I believe that. But my father is not a soldier. He's an intellectual, not a fighter."

"Well, we can only hope that Germany doesn't need her army."

"Yes, I agree with you. We can only hope."

"Gunther and I are leaving in the morning. He has to get back to work; he's taken too much time off already."

"Father and I will miss you," Gretchen said.

"I was hoping to meet your young man before I left. Norbert is his name, isn't it?"

"Yes, it's Norbert."

"So when is the wedding? I am going to come, of course. You know I wouldn't miss it for the world. But I am not sure that Gunther will be able to join me. I hope so, but he might not be able to take more time off."

"I understand. This trip was very unexpected for you. And believe me, I appreciate your coming to help us, Aunt Margrit."

"Of course! You are my precious, only niece, and your father is my only brother. I don't have any children, so you are like my own daughter. And even though we don't see each other very often, I always have you in my heart."

"I know that. I've always known it."

"I do wish I could have met Norbert before I left," Margrit said, touching Gretchen's hair.

"I know. I was hoping so too. But Norbert has been very busy. His family is opening another location for their business. They own restaurants with beer gardens. Norbert's been helping them. He's been working on the building."

Margrit nodded, but Gretchen could see in her aunt's eyes that she knew the truth. She, like Gretchen, suspected that Norbert was not around because of her father's problems with the law.

"Gretchen . . . if you need to talk, you know you can always call or write to me."

"Yes, I will do that, of course."

"And . . . well . . . I don't know how to say this. If, for some reason, you decide that you would like to come and stay with Gunther and me for a while, you are welcome."

"You mean if I decide to postpone my wedding, and when father goes off with the army?"

"Yes, exactly. I want you to know that our house is open to you."

"Thank you, Aunt Margrit. But I have a job here, and I am quite sure that everything with Norbert and I will be just fine."

"Of course, it will. But just remember, my door is always open."

CHAPTER FIFTY

Gretchen and her father walked Aunt Margrit and Uncle Gunther to the train station the following day. Gretchen hugged her aunt tightly and then her uncle a little less tightly.

A dusting of snow fell from the sky.

"Remember what I told you," Aunt Margrit whispered in Gretchen's ear as she and her husband boarded the train. "You can always come and stay with me."

Gretchen nodded. She and her father stood in silence as the train whistle blew. The train shook and sputtered and then came to life. Margrit waved through the window. Gretchen waved back. And then slowly, the train made its way down the track. Gretchen and her father waited until the train was almost invisible, then they began walking home. The snowflakes fell and hung for a brief second on Gretchen's eyelashes.

"When are you leaving for your army training, Father?"

"Right after the wedding," Karl said, clearing his throat.

They walked in silence for several minutes. "Father?"

"Yes?"

"I'm scared."

"I know. Me too. But you will have Norbert, and he will take care of

241

you."

"I haven't heard a word from him since your arrest."

"You haven't? Oh, sweetheart. I've been so caught up in my own problems that I haven't noticed. I'm so sorry. I caused all this. My problems have become yours."

"If Norbert is going to walk away from me because of what happened then he wouldn't have been a worthy husband anyway," Gretchen said.

"This world we live in has become so complex. If I knew that you would suffer because of my actions I wouldn't have done what I did."

"I love you, Father. No matter what you do, or where you go, I will always love you. You've always been here for me. You raised me all by yourself. I can just imagine how hard it must have been for you: a man without a wife. But you never let me down. You came to see me when I sang in the chorus at school. You never missed a performance. It meant so much to me. Oh Father, you have always been my hero."

"Gretchen, my precious child, you have always idolized me. You've imagined me as the hero. I wished I could be. Not as the coward that I really am. But I refuse to let you suffer anymore on my account. And that's why I must do what Uncle Gunther suggested," Karl said, his voice choked with emotion. Gretchen looked up at her father; she saw that he was crying.

CHAPTER FIFTY-ONE

Gretchen awoke the following morning with a heaviness in her heart. As she got ready for work, she thought about Norbert. She knew it was time to see him. No matter what happened, she must face the inevitable. She'd been hoping that Norbert would drop by her house, but he didn't. She gave him plenty of time to get over the initial shock of her father's arrest. Now too much time had passed for her to believe things were all right. She would have to go to his house and speak to him. It was time to find out where her future was headed.

While she was at work, she contemplated the upcoming meeting with Norbert. She longed for someone to talk to about her feelings. For the first time since she got engaged, Gretchen desperately needed a friend. So when lunchtime came, she sat down at the long lunch table next to Hilde.

"It's been a long time since you came to sit with me," Hilde said. "I gave up on you."

I deserved that. I have been a terrible friend, Gretchen thought.

"I know. I'm sorry, Hilde. I've been busy with work, and most days I take my lunch at my desk because I am trying to catch up," Gretchen said apologetically.

"Yes, I am quite sure you were. After all, you want to leave early, don't you? So you can be with your fiancée."

"Yes, that's true."

"To be with Norbert? Right?"

"Yes, to be with Norbert," Gretchen said.

Hilde grunted. "Well, I suppose that is how it is when you're in love, eh?" Hilde's tone was a little sarcastic, and it made Gretchen cringe. But she knew that she'd hurt Hilde, and any bad feelings Hilde had toward her were her own fault. If it were at all possible, she wanted to make things right with her old friend.

"Do you mind me sitting with you for lunch today?"

"I suppose it's all right with me," Hilde said.

"How have you been?"

"Fine, I suppose. How am I expected to feel when my best friend just stopped talking to me?"

"Hilde, I'm sorry."

"For what?" Hilde said a little too abruptly, and Gretchen could hear how hurt Hilde was in her tone. "You didn't have time for me anymore, did you?"

"I'm sorry for treating you the way I did. I was wrong. I got so caught up in my relationship with Norbert that I forgot what a good friend you were. You didn't deserve to be treated that way."

"No, Gretchen. I didn't."

"I am sorry if I hurt you."

"I didn't say you hurt me," Hilde said, wrapping her arms around her chest.

"I should never have behaved that way. You were always a good friend to me, and you deserved better."

Hilde shrugged. "It's getting late; I want to get back to my desk before the bell rings. I have to catch up on some work." She gathered her food into a cloth napkin and put it into her handbag.

"Do you really have to go?"

"Yes, I'm afraid so," Hilde said as she stood up.

"Hilde, before you go, I want to tell you that I value our friendship, and if you give me another chance, I promise I will never push you aside again."

Hilde stopped and sank back into her chair. "You really promise?"

"Yes, I promise. And I really am so sorry for what I did."

"I've missed you, Gretchen. The Bund camp was terrible. Hann never showed up, and without you there with me, I felt so alone. I had no one to talk to. Then I got home, and I was so excited to see you and tell you everything. I needed someone to share my feelings with. But you didn't want anything to do with me anymore. I was so hurt. I need you. You're my best friend."

"I know. You have always been a good friend to me, Hilde. You are my best friend too. I was so wrong to treat you the way I did. Can you forgive me?"

Hilde nodded. "I'm just glad you're back to normal, and I wish Hann would come back to Berlin."

"Have you talked to Hann?"

"I wrote to him. He doesn't answer my letters. I'm sure he's still upset over Thea."

"Still? You think so? It's been a long time."

"Yes. Well, he was quite taken with her. Although I can't see why."

"I shouldn't have ignored you for so long. I've missed you, Hilde. It's so good to talk to you again."

Hilde smiled. "I feel the same way."

"My father got arrested."

"I heard," Hilde said, looking away.

"Does everyone in town know?"

"Probably. Who cares? People talk. Gossip. That's because they have nothing better to do," Hilde said smiling.

"After my father's arrest, Norbert stopped coming to see me."

"But weren't you two engaged to be married?"

"Yes, we were. I don't know if we still are or not. I mean, we aren't officially broken up. So I don't know what to do."

"What about the wedding? Have you made wedding plans?"

"Yes, and now I just don't know what to do with him. I don't know if he still wants to marry me."

"How can you not know?"

"He hasn't talked to me at all. He stopped coming to see me. I am going to have to go to his house and talk to him. Hilde, I'm so scared to confront him. What if he breaks it off?"

"If he breaks it off with you, he wasn't worth marrying. You're a good girl, and you're a great catch. You're pure Aryan, beautiful, and very smart. He would be a fool to break up with you."

"But I think I will be heartsick if he does. I hate rejection."

"Everyone hates rejection. But if he's that stupid, you don't want him anyway. You deserve a man who recognizes your value."

"That's very sweet of you to say, Hilde."

"It's true. I know you better than anyone else. We've been friends a long time. I know that he would be lucky if you married him. He would be getting the perfect Aryan wife."

"You don't realize how much our conversation is helping me. You're giving me the courage to go and see him and to cope with whatever he might say," Gretchen said, thinking that she didn't remember Hilde being this kind and good of a friend.

Hilde patted Gretchen's hand. Gretchen smiled genuinely. *I'm glad to have my old friend back in my life. Hilde has her faults, but she is fiercely loyal.*

"Would you like some bread?" Hilde asked, taking the napkin out of her purse. "I baked this yesterday."

"Sure. Thanks. You always were an excellent cook and baker," Gretchen said as she put the bread into her mouth. "This is delicious. It melts in your mouth."

"Thanks," Hilde said, taking a piece of the small loaf and eating it. "Between us, Gretchen, your father is flirting with disaster. I wouldn't say this if I didn't care about you. But when he goes off defending Jews, it's a real mistake. It's unsafe. And to be quite frank, you may not realize this, but the Jews are very dangerous. They're liars and cheats, and God knows what else they do to good Aryan people. I know for sure that they are thieves."

"Oh, I don't know any Jews, but I'm sure you're right that my father was overstepping his boundaries. He is done with all that now, Hilde. He only did it because he worked with those professors for years. He wanted to help them. But he has made it clear to me and everyone else that he has since changed his mind," Gretchen said, choking on her words. On the outside, her father was looking as if he were an enthusiastic member of the Nazi Party. But on the inside, Gretchen knew her father's feelings about Hitler had not changed. Still, she dared not share any of this with Hilde. Hilde was a true Nazi and a firm hater of Jews. A girl like Hilde would never understand a man like Karl Schmidt. Gretchen saw her father back down, not because he was afraid of another arrest or beating, but because he wanted to protect her, his only child.

"Anyway, I have been thinking about taking some time off work. I could use a vacation from the day-to-day grind," Hilde said.

"Can you afford to?" Gretchen asked.

"I can if I have a baby for the fatherland."

"What do you mean? Are you pregnant?"

"No, I'm not pregnant. Not yet. What I mean is, I could go to a home for the Lebensborn and have a child for the fatherland. It's a

247

new program. Have you heard about it?"

"I haven't.

"It works like this. First, I get examined to determine that I am of pure Aryan blood, which, of course, I am. Then I go to parties where I meet men of pure racial blood, and I choose whom I want to have relations with. Then, while I am pregnant, I can stay at a home for the Lebensborn where they take excellent care of me. I'll have plenty of good food and medical care. If things don't work out with you and Norbert, you might want to do it too. If you have a few babies for our fatherland, you might even be given an award."

"I don't know how I would feel about giving my baby away," Gretchen said. "Anyway, my next move is to talk to Norbert and see where we stand."

"Would you think about it? Would you maybe consider going with me if you and Norbert decide to go your separate ways?"

"Going with you? You mean to the home for the Lebensborn?"

"Yes."

"Oh, I don't know. I really don't know," Gretchen stammered. "I mean, I couldn't imagine having a child and not knowing what happened to my baby as it grew up. I was raised without my mother, so often I wondered how things would have been if she lived. What would my child feel when he or she grew up and realized that I had given him or her away willingly, of my own free will? My mother died; she had no choice, so I forgave her for leaving me. But if she had just walked away from me without any reason at all? I don't know, Hilde. I'm sorry, but I don't think I could do that" Gretchen said. She didn't want to hurt Hilde's feelings, but the idea made her sick to her stomach.

"I never really thought about your situation. I mean, your not having your mother, growing up. I can see why this might be hard for

248

you. But remember this. You didn't have a mother raising you, so you glorified your mutti. I had my mother with me throughout my entire childhood. I don't have to wonder about her. I know she was a horrible person. When she died, I didn't even shed a tear. Because of the way she treated me, I don't glorify motherhood at all."

Gretchen didn't know what to say. She knew that Hilde's mother was an alcoholic, and she heard that the woman had committed suicide. To make matters worse, Hilde was the one who found her mother dead on the kitchen floor. Of course, Hilde was angry and bitter. How else could she feel? A few moments of silence followed, and then the bell rang.

"We'd both better get back to our desks," Gretchen said.

"Yes, it's that time."

"Hilde?"

"Yes?"

"Thank you for today. Let's spend more time together in the future. I didn't realize how much I've missed you."

"I'd like that," Hilde said.

CHAPTER FIFTY-TWO

As Gretchen walked to Norbert's house, she took notice of all the men on the streets wearing different forms of Nazi uniforms. She never paid much attention before, but now she looked at them with hatred burning in her heart. These people beat her father: her dear, gentle father. They took him from his home, and they beat him. Why? Because he couldn't bear to see an injustice done to one of his friends.

Everything she learned in the Bund suddenly made her sick to her stomach. She swore that, no matter what her father chose to do, even if he joined the army, she would fight this cruel and unforgiving regime in any way she could.

Norbert was sitting at the kitchen table eating a grilled sausage with sauerkraut and drinking a mug of beer when Gretchen arrived. The smell of good food filled the house. Yet even though Gretchen had not eaten in hours, she had no appetite. Her heart was racing. Norbert looked up at her, and she was sure she saw a million different emotions flash across his face. She couldn't read him completely. Did he still love her? If not, how could love disappear so quickly? She saw pity in his eyes. But what left her terrified was that he looked unhappy to see her.

"Gretchen," he said. His voice was just a note higher than usual, but Gretchen immediately detected the change in his tone. She knew he was distancing himself from her. In the past, when they were intimate, his voice would grow deeper and warmer. But when he was hiding something and pushing away from her, his tone was higher pitched.

"Hello, Norbert," she said.

For a second, which seemed like forever to Gretchen, he sat staring at her, still holding his knife and fork suspended in midair.

"Are you hungry?" he asked.

She shook her head. "Can I sit down?" she asked in a small voice.

He nodded, stammering, "Yes, of course. Please, sit."

She sat with her back rigid in the chair across from him. He carefully put the knife and fork down. His face was serious as he took a swig of the beer. "Would you like a drink?"

"No, thank you," Gretchen said, still wearing her coat and hat and feeling out of place and uncomfortable. "Norbert?"

"Yes?"

"I haven't seen you in a long time." The words stuck in her throat.

"I know. I'm sorry."

She thought about running out of the house before she heard what she knew he was about to say, but she couldn't. She had to push this as far as it must go. If he was breaking up with her, she must know and face the truth. Things could not continue with them both in limbo. They had wedding plans.

"Why?" she asked.

"Why, what?" he stammered.

"Why have you not come to see me?" The tears filled her eyes as she asked for an answer that she dreaded. She didn't want to believe what she knew to be true. She hated to face that this man whom she had once planned to marry was not the man she thought he was. And even though she knew she wasn't in love with him, and he wasn't the man for her, she felt terribly sad. In a very strange way, this breakup was the death of the certainty of a safe and steady future.

"Gretch. I . . ."

"You don't love me anymore?" she asked, wondering why this hurt so much when she knew she could never respect a man who could walk away from her because he didn't have the courage to fight for her.

"It's not that. Of course, I care for you. I can't just erase everything we shared, from my heart."

"Yes, Norbert. How well I know. After all, you were my first." A tear slid down her cheek.

"But . . ." He cleared his throat and took another swig of the beer. "I can't marry you."

"You're calling off the wedding?" She knew this was going to happen, but the shock of hearing him say it aloud made her feel ill.

"I have to. I'm sorry."

"Norbert? That's all you have to say?"

"I know. I know. I am hurting you. I don't want to hurt you. But . . ."

"But what?"

"But my parents. Their livelihood depends on members of the party. I can't marry you. My parents are against it, and I know they're right."

She felt like she might vomit. She stood up and turned to leave, but then she turned back and looked at him. "Were you going to tell me, Norbert?"

"I was avoiding telling you."

"I see."

"I said I am sorry. And God knows, I am."

"You're a coward."

He nodded. "Yes."

"I thought you were so much stronger. But you're weak. You can't stand on your own. You need your family's approval. That means you're not a man . . . not in my book."

He shrugged, but she could see that she'd hurt him, and if she stayed he might cry.

"I'm not strong, Gretchen. I can't fight the world the way you and your father seem to think that you can. Ideals are wonderful, but if you look back in history, many great idealists ended up dead at very young ages. I don't want to die. I want to live."

"Well then . . . may you live to a ripe old age, Norbert. And may you also be proud of who you are. Proud enough to tell your grandchildren that you did what you truly believed was right. Let them know how strong your character was, so they can be very proud to have you as their grandfather." Without looking at him, she turned and walked out the door.

CHAPTER FIFTY-THREE

Walking home with the cold wind on her face made Gretchen feel alone and lost. Tears fell down her cheeks and froze on her eyelashes.

What do I do now? My father will be off to army training in a month. My fiancée has broken off our engagement. I could always join Hilde. It's a nice idea to take a vacation. She and I could be grown-up Deutcher maidels having fun, no longer playing sports or helping German women with their children, but now as grown-ups we would be having babies for the Reich. I could do this and be admired for it by our neighbors. But let's face it; in my heart I know I can't. I don't believe in the Reich, and I could never give my child away. Norbert is right. I am a lot like my father. And I am not sorry that I am like him. I am proud to be like him. No. I am not sorry at all.

Gretchen was sobbing. She wiped the tears from her eyes and nose with her scarf. *It's almost funny, but I am thinking about Eli. How could it be that I think I have more in common with Eli than I do with Norbert? Eli was actually different from any man I've ever known. He was nothing like my father. He had principles, and he stood behind them no matter what the cost. Eli was intellectually stimulating and certainly well read. He was deep and soulful. I remember his dark eyes. I could have lost myself in those eyes. And it was always so apparent in everything he said that he cared about people. I remember how kind and sympathetic he was when we discussed my mother. I wonder what Eli is doing these days? I wonder if he ever thinks of me? Probably not. After all, he is living the life that he believes he was destined to live. If he had been different . . . If he had been willing . . . he and I would have probably been lovers. I wonder if he ever married the girl his father found for him? I suppose I will never know.*

CHAPTER FIFTY-FOUR

Summer 1937

Eli Kaetzel sat on a bench inside the yeshiva studying on a Friday afternoon. He was finishing up his reading of a book on the Torah, his eyes scanning the lines right to left when Yousef, who had just finished teaching a class, walked over to him.

"Eli! You're just the fellow I want to see!"

"Youssi!" Eli called Youssef by the affectionate nickname he used for him. As Eli looked up from his book.

"Shavua tov!" Yousef said.

"Shabbat shalom," Eli answered as they exchanged greetings and well wishes for the Sabbath that night. "Nu, so how are you?"

"Can't complain, can't complain. Listen, I would like to invite you and Rebecca to my son's bris next week. You'll come to our house?"

"Mazel tov! Of course, we'll be there."

"Ruthy and I will be so happy to have you," Yousef said, patting Eli's back.

"You enjoy being married, don't you?" Eli asked.

"I do very much enjoy it. I have never been happier. You? Do you enjoy it, Eli?"

"Of course, I do," Eli lied, feeling a little envious that Yousef was so happy in his life. And Yousef had a son. His newborn boy was the talk of everyone at the yeshiva. Meanwhile, Eli and Rebecca still could not conceive.

"Good, very good. I can't wait to tell Ruthy that you and Rebecca will be at our party. Anyway, I have to get going home now. Ruthy hates when I am late, especially on the Sabbath."

"I understand. Women spend all day cooking on the Sabbath; the least we can do is be on time for dinner," Eli said. Yousef smiled and stood up.

"So good Sabbath, and I will see you at the bris?"

"Good Sabbath. I am looking forward to it," Eli said.

Yousef walked away. Eli was angry with himself for feeling envious. It was wrong to feel that way, but every month like clockwork, Rebecca got her period. She waited until the bleeding stopped and then went to the mikvah. They were careful to follow every rule. He did not touch her at all, not even her hand when she was unclean with her menses. They never resumed sexual contact until she returned clean from the mikvah. But still, they had not been blessed with a child. Their relationship had not grown either. It was still strained, and they never seemed able to communicate comfortably with each other. Eli wondered if a baby would fix that. He couldn't say. But what he did know was that Rebecca never told him any of her feelings, and he never asked her.

So, their time together passed. She was a good, kind, and obedient wife. He was a gentle and considerate husband. Although they never discussed it, both of them knew something was missing.

It was a sweltering Friday afternoon. Because it was the Sabbath, Eli went home early. He put his book back on the shelf and walked outside the building. The grass, which had been so green in early spring, had now turned yellow and brown from the heat of the sun.

Even though it was the middle of summer, he wore his long, black coat, a white-cotton shirt, black pants, and a tall, black hat. A thin layer of sweat ran down his back.

"I should be hungry, but I'm not," he whispered aloud to himself. *I just realized that I was so engrossed in teaching my class that I forgot to eat this afternoon. Well, religious studies always had that effect on me. I don't always agree with everything I read, but I am always stimulated. In that way, I am like my father. I do love to learn. I am beginning to understand my papa when he used to say that he was glad he was born a Jew. I feel that way too. In spite of all the hatred of Jews, I wouldn't want to be anything else. Yet, even as much as I have grown, I am still not sure I am qualified to lead our people the way my father did.*

Eli walked through the gates leaving the campus behind. The air was muggy with humidity.

He didn't know why, but as he walked home he felt as if something in his life was missing. It was not only his fear that he lacked the ability to lead. It was something else as well. He was thinking about Gretchen, remembering how she'd made him feel. No one he'd ever met had affected him the way she did. And all the powerful emotions she'd brought out in him still lingered in his mind. Sometimes he had dreams of her and awoke filled with guilt.

On his way home he stopped by the old abandoned warehouse. He could not justify his actions, and yet, he did this occasionally. It gave him a bittersweet comfort to lose himself for a few moments in the memory of Gretchen. He entered the old building. The warehouse was dark and damp as always. Eli walked to the window and stared out, Then he took a deep breath and closed his eyes, losing himself in the moment.

That was why he didn't see her.

"Eli?" she said. "Is that really you, or am I imagining it?"

He heard a female voice whisper his name. The voice was familiar.

It made him tremble with fear and shiver with delight at the same time. Could it be? Was it possible?

"Gretchen?" he said, turning to look at her. "Is it really you? I didn't expect to find you here."

"I didn't expect to find you either. I came here because I couldn't stop thinking about you, and I wanted to be here where I saw you for the last time," she said.

"I couldn't stop thinking about you either. He walked toward her. She was even more beautiful than he remembered.

"How have you been?" she asked

"Fine," he stammered. "I'm doing fine."

"You look good."

"Oh . . ." He looked down at the ground embarrassed by the compliment. But his heart was beating with joy. *I can't believe it. Gretchen is standing right beside me. It's beyond a miracle. After all these years she still stirs my heart. But then again, she never stopped stirring my heart. Even when I didn't see her, she was never far from my thoughts.*

"I can't believe that you came here too." She shook her head in disbelief. Then she raised her head and gazed into his eyes. "I am so glad to see you. I need to talk to you. Something happened, and I need someone I can trust."

"What happened?" he said with concern.

"My father was arrested. Then he went away to the army. I was engaged. My fiancée broke it off. A lot happened . . ."

"You were engaged?" Eli asked then he continued. "But, now you're not?"

"No, I am not. He broke up with me because of my father's arrest," she said, then she continued, "You're married?"

He nodded.

"Oh."

"And I have to go home now. I'm late. I'm sorry."

"Yes, of course," she said.

He could hear the hurt in her voice. He knew he should walk away and go home, but instead, he turned to her and said, "There is no harm in talking. Perhaps we can meet again next week?"

"Where?" she asked

"Here, the warehouse."

"So, will you show up?" she asked.

"Yes. I will meet you," Eli said, unable to refuse, even though he knew he should.

"Monday afternoon? Four o'clock?"

"Yes."

"You'll be here?"

"I will."

CHAPTER FIFTY-FIVE

How can my feet feel as if they are weightless, and at the same time my mind and heart know that what I am planning to do is wrong, Eli thought as he headed toward the old, abandoned building. Every nerve ending in his body told him that he should turn, and go home to his righteous wife. And yet, his feet were attached to his heart, and they were practically running to meet Gretchen.

The warehouse was dark and smelled like the stagnating water that had seeped in through the holes in the roof. The walls were covered in mold, and the only light was the natural illumination that came through the cracked windows. There were no chairs, only a broken desk. Eli sat down on the edge of the desk for a moment but then immediately stood back up. His heart was pounding in his chest. Gretchen wasn't there. *Perhaps she's not coming. I should leave here now, and go home and pray for forgiveness.* He shivered. "Papa," he said aloud. "Help me. I am weak and unable to turn away from sin. You are not here, and I have no one else I can talk to about these feelings," he said, his voice echoing against the walls.

There was no answer, not from above or from any voice in his mind. Eli was alone. The decision to stay or to go was his and his alone. He walked toward the door preparing to leave as Gretchen walked in. Her eyes were like tiny candle flames lighting up the room.

"Eli, I'm sorry I'm late. I had work to finish before I could leave."

"I should get going home."

"Stay just a few minutes. I've been so looking forward to seeing you."

He looked down at the ground as a rat scampered across the toe of his black shoe. This girl was so bold and so outspoken. And although he couldn't understand why, he adored her. *I am a fool. I must be insane. I know this is wrong. But even so, I can't move. My feet should head home to Rebecca, but my heart holds them here, planted firmly on the ground of this old, decrepit building.* "My wife is a good woman," he blurted out.

"I am sure she is," Gretchen said. "And you are happily married?"

"Yes, of course, I am."

"Can I ask you, then. Why are you here?"

"Because you said you wanted to talk to me," he stammered.

"And you just couldn't say no? The only reason you came here today was because I wanted to speak to you?"

He turned away from her. "I have no answers. I don't know why I came. I am in anguish over my feelings. I wish I understood myself better. I shouldn't be here."

"But you are here, Eli. Maybe we should be friends. Maybe we can talk things out? Maybe we can help each other?"

"Talk about what? How can we possibly help each other?"

"We can discuss what is missing in our lives. I need a friend too, someone I can trust."

"My wife should be my best friend. She is perfect. She's beautiful, kind, frum, and very modest. Everything a man like me is looking for in a wife. You are a dangerous temptation." He put his hands on his temples and squeezed as if he could squeeze some sense into his confused mind.

"Frum? What does that mean?"

"Religious. Pure."

"I am not any of those things. But I can tell you what I am. I am a good friend."

"You are smart, and you are beautiful," he blurted out again. *What's wrong with me? Why am I saying these things?*

She blushed. "I'm also flattered. That was a nice thing to say."

He shrugged and then shook his head as if he were telling himself not to continue. "I should get going home."

"Eli, please don't go. I need to talk. I need someone to listen."

He looked at her, and the light from the window caught her hair illuminating her entire face, making her look ethereal and angelic.

"Remember, I told you my father was arrested, and my fiancée broke up with me."

"I remember."

"Can I talk to you about what happened?"

"Yes, yes, of course. It was selfish of me to forget the reason we came here in the first place. You came to me because you wanted to talk, and instead of helping you, I offered you a jumble of my own confusing emotions. I am sorry. Truly. Now, sit down, please." He indicated the broken desk. Eli tried to remain calm, but he was trembling.

"Can you sit beside me?"

"No, no it's forbidden. I'll stand. It's all right. I don't mind."

She smiled wryly. "Are you sure?"

"Yes, very sure. Now, please go on, and talk to me. Tell me what is weighing so heavily on your heart, Gretchen."

CHAPTER FIFTY-SIX

Later that night, Eli Kaetzel sat across from his wife at the dinner table. He felt guilty for having broken the rule of being alone with a woman. Rebecca was lovely, radiant, but his heart yearned for Gretchen. Although he lusted for her that afternoon as she told him all of her problems, Eli fought the desire to sin and did not even touch her hand. Instead, he listened as she bared her soul. When she wept, he longed to take her in his arms and comfort her, but he resisted. He offered words of advice and encouragement. They spent over an hour together, but when it was time to leave, he didn't want to go.

When she suggested they meet again, he was both thrilled and terrified. But no matter, he agreed to see her again. And now, as he sat across from Rebecca, his thoughts drifted to his next meeting with Gretchen. They agreed to meet at the warehouse the following Monday. He wished he could tell Yousef about this dilemma, but he knew he dared not. Yousef would certainly tell him to stop seeing Gretchen immediately. And truth be told, he didn't want to stop.

Rebecca was lovely with the white scarf covering her head and her eyes the color of blue topaz. She sat smiling at her husband, waiting to fulfill his every need, but they hardly spoke. She kept her head bowed, wishing they shared more. Sometimes she felt as if she would die from loneliness. Although they had intercourse regularly because they wanted desperately to have a child, she felt as if she were starved for affection, starved for the loving touch of another human being.

Eli never reached for her hand or caressed her shoulder. The longing for human contact drove her into a depression. But even so, she remained a good girl, an obedient girl, and never asked him for anything. She spent her time with the sisterhood at the shul, helping the poor and needy.

Acts of kindness helped her pass her days. She cooked and wrapped up an entire meal for a family where the wife had fallen ill. She cared for children while their widowed mothers were at work. Rebecca kneaded and then carefully braided her challah for Eli's Sabbath dinner. Each week, she took a loaf to the home of a bedridden elderly woman. Sometimes she stayed and cleaned the woman's small apartment. Being the wife of the rebbe, she believed she had social obligations, but she would have gladly extended her kindness even if Eli weren't destined to be a rebbe. Since she was a child, Rebecca loved to care for others, and she enjoyed giving. She needed no thanks; doing mitzvahs was thanks enough.

However, she would have loved to come home in the evening and discuss her day with Eli. She longed to tell him what she did when they were apart. She would have relished hearing about his days at the yeshiva. But Eli never asked, "What did you do today?" He just seemed too caught up with his studies to care. He never told her how he spent his time away from her.

Before she wed, Rebecca believed that once she was married, she would never feel alone again. However, since her wedding day, she felt more alone than she ever had. She missed her friend Esther every day. At least when Esther was alive, she had her visits to look forward to.

Esther was always there to talk to and laugh with. She knew that no matter what life handed her, she could always confide in Esther. Now with her best friend gone she had no one.

Rebecca never discussed her marriage with her parents. She didn't want to worry them. They were turning gray, growing older. Every time she went to see them, her papa would smile and touch her cheek and say, "My sweet daughter! You've come to see us!"

"Yes, Papa. I brought you and Mama challah."

"Oy, how beautiful you are. What nachas, what joy you bring us. I feel such peace in this old heart because I know that you made such a good match in Eli. Your mama and I rest easy because we know that you have someone good and kind to take care of you after your mother and I are gone. Eli makes you happy, mine kind?"

"Yes, Papa," she lied each time. "Very happy."

"Pretty soon you'll be coming to tell us that you will be giving us a grandchild? Oy, such nachas that will be."

"Eli and I hope so, Papa."

She knew her father, who was almost fifteen years older than her mother, was getting old simply because he repeated the same words every time she went to see him. Each time he said those words, she had to turn away, so he wouldn't see the tears fall on her cheeks. *One day, my parents will be gone. I won't be able to come here and see them forever.* Instead of telling them the truth about her and Eli, she cherished the moments they shared and hid her pain.

CHAPTER FIFTY-SEVEN

On the day Gretchen was to meet with Eli, she ran all the way home from work. She quickly changed into a clean dress and carefully combed her hair. It was rare that she set her stick-straight hair in pin curls, but she did the previous night, all because she was going to meet Eli. *I must be crazy. He's a married man. He belongs to someone else. I have never been one to compete with other women. I wonder if I find this attraction to him so damn exciting because it's illegal? Maybe I am just fighting back? Perhaps I just refuse to allow the Nazi Party to dictate how I live and who I associate with? That would be pure madness, especially after what happened to my father. But I have to admit there is something about Eli that I find terribly appealing. I just can't figure out what exactly it is. Perhaps it's because he is so shy and a little afraid of me? I do find that rather endearing. I feel wild and exciting, in control, like a tigress, when I am with him. And he finds me enthralling. That look of fascination I see in his eyes drives me wild. It makes me feel so special. He's even gone so far as to say that I am different from any woman he has ever known.*

A knock on her front door interrupted Gretchen's thoughts. Her father had been gone for several months now, and she had grown used to living alone.

"Who is it?" she called out not wanting to answer the door but knowing she must. No one answered, and for a moment she felt a shot of fear run up her spine. Could it be the Gestapo? Did someone see her with Eli last week and report her? She shivered as she asked again, "Who is it?"

"It's me," Hilde said.

"Hilde!"

"Yes, it's me. Open up!"

Gretchen opened the door.

"You look nice," Hilde said.

"Thank you."

"What are you all dressed up for?"

"Oh, nothing."

"Come on, tell me. Do you have a date?" Hilde asked smiling.

Think fast. Gretchen thought. Then she said, "Well, I was kind of keeping it a secret, but it's not a date or anything like that."

"What are you rambling on about? Just tell me already. I hate suspense."

"I'm just going to buy some flour."

"Dressed like that? And with your hair curled too?"

"I have been sort of flirting with the shopkeeper's son. He joined the army, you know."

"Yes, I saw him last week in town wearing his uniform. He looked quite handsome."

"I thought so too. And, well . . ." Gretchen smiled. "I did find him terribly attractive, and he is going away soon. So I figured maybe he and I might have a little fun before he left. Since he's leaving soon, there would be no messy ties. If you know what I mean."

"Of course I do." Hilde laughed. "I'll get going. You have fun. And by the way, why don't we have dinner together tomorrow night? Since you're all alone here, I'll come over. I'll bring some food. If you don't have any other plans?"

"No, I don't have any other plans. Dinner with you tomorrow night sounds perfect. What time were you thinking?"

"Seven?"

"Perfect. I'll see you then."

Gretchen waited until she was sure that Hilde had gone, then she grabbed her handbag and ran out the door. Just to make sure no one was following, she glanced behind her. She raced the half mile to the warehouse where she was scheduled to meet Eli, arriving twenty minutes late.

"You're late again," Eli said. Gretchen detected a touch of annoyance in his voice. Then his shoulders slumped, and he looked into her eyes. His voice softened. "I'm sorry. That was rude. It's just that, well . . ." He hesitated. "It's just that I was afraid you weren't coming and . . ."

"It's all right. I understand. I'm sorry for being late" she said. "I had a visitor. I had to make up a plausible story about where I was going, or she would have wanted to join me."

"What did you tell her?"

"A lie. I had to."

"Lying is wrong," he said more to himself than to her.

"Well, if you and I are going to keep meeting like this we'd better get used to it."

"I don't like the way that sounds at all." He shook his head.

"Eli, sometimes you have to lie. It's just a part of life."

"I understand. We are both doing a lot of lying. I am lying to my wife by being here."

"Yes, but if she knew it would hurt her feelings."

"It would. Maybe I should stop coming."

"That would hurt my feelings."

"So?" He smiled, throwing his hands up in the air. Then his voice softened. "We have a dilemma."

"Yes, we do." She smiled, and she knew by the look on his face that he was no longer angry with her.

They met every Monday through the summer, and when they were together, they discussed everything. They had long talks about Jesus and about stories from the Talmud. Gretchen told Eli about her family, including Margrit and Gunther. Eli explained how his father had been a respected and revered rebbe. He also shared his secret fear that he would never be good enough to fill his father's shoes. Gretchen asked Eli about his wife. "What is your wife like?"

"She's kind. She's good. But to be quite honest with you, I know you better than I know her. She's very shy and reserved."

"Don't you two talk?"

"Not much."

"But why?"

"I don't know. I don't know what to say to her. What to ask her."

"Talk to her the way you talk to me," Gretchen said.

"I can't."

There were several moments of silence.

"You've told me more than once that she's very beautiful."

"She is."

"What does she look like?"

"Light blonde hair. Bright blue eyes. A very sweet smile."

Gretchen folded her arms across her chest. "Do you love her?"

"I don't know. Does it matter?"

"Of course, it matters. You're married to her, aren't you?"

"Yes, but love has nothing to do with marriage."

"How do you figure? It has everything to do with marriage."

"Not for me. Not for us."

"I don't understand."

"It's quite simple. For us, my people, marriage is about having and raising children. A good wife is a frum and faithful wife. She is a good mother. She knows how to keep kosher."

"Kosher?"

"Yes, it's the way we keep our homes, our food."

Gretchen smiled at him. "I don't think I will ever grow tired of listening to you. Every time we meet, I learn something new about you or about your strange and fascinating culture. You're so different from anyone I know."

By August they were both sharing the edge of the broken desk. He was careful not to sit too close to her. He did not allow his leg to accidentally touch hers.

CHAPTER FIFTY-EIGHT

Hilde and Gretchen had dinner together at least once a week, always at Gretchen's house. Regardless of their meager salaries, somehow Hilde was always able to bring extra food. One evening, Hilde arrived with an apple cake and three eggs.

"What a lovely cake! Did you bake it?"

"I got it as a gift from Axel."

"Who's Axel?" Gretchen said, giving Hilde a sly smile.

"A boy I've been dating. He's the reason I haven't gone off to have a baby for the fatherland. I don't want to be away from him."

"You never told me you were dating anyone. How long have you been seeing each other?"

"About four months. He's in the Wehrmacht. I wouldn't exactly call him handsome, but he does have a promising future."

"Well, I am truly happy for you."

"He is going for special training. I think he hopes to be recruited for the SS."

"SS?"

"Yes. He has mentioned that he would love to be a personal bodyguard to Hitler. And he could very well get the job because he has friends in high positions."

"Oh my goodness." Gretchen felt flushed and dizzy. She sat down quickly.

"I'm so proud to be seen with him. He looks so powerful in his uniform. Sometimes I just stare at him. Then I secretly wonder what a man like him would see in a girl like me."

"Why would you say such a thing?" Gretchen asked, but she was finding it hard to concentrate. *One of Hitler's bodyguards? If Hilde only knew about Eli.* Gretchen shivered.

"Are you all right?"

"Yes, I'm fine. Sorry, I got my period today, and I sometimes get hot and cold flashes," Gretchen lied.

"Your whole body trembled," Hilde said, her voice filled with genuine concern.

"That happens sometimes when I get my period."

"Maybe you should see a doctor."

"I'm all right. I promise." Gretchen managed a smile.

"You look so pale."

"Do I? Like I said, my periods are hard on me. I get cramping, and the pain makes me pale, I guess."

"Well, please take care of yourself."

CHAPTER FIFTY-NINE

October 1938

Rebecca could sense something different in Eli. Not because Eli said anything to alert her—he wasn't that obvious. There were small changes in him that only Rebecca would detect: a look of contentment in his eyes, tenderness in his voice. Sometimes she would catch him looking at her, and there was sympathy in his gaze. He was often exceptionally kind and considerate of her feelings. Sometimes when he was getting dressed, she found him singing softly to himself. Lately, he always seemed to be in high spirits, regardless of what was going on. This was so unlike him that it made her wonder.

Eli had never been cruel to her; he'd just been uncaring. But now he made a special effort to be exceptionally kind. He would compliment her cooking and even carried his own plate to the sink one night. On a summer afternoon, he returned from the shul and surprised her with a gift of a pretty silk headscarf. She caught him smiling out the window in the middle of reading or studying. In fact, in the past several months he smiled far more than he ever had since she met him.

It was hard to imagine Eli having anything to do with another woman. He was so strict with himself that she found the idea hard to grasp. The very idea that Eli would break one of God's Commandments was unfathomable. Yet, she couldn't imagine what else could have made him so happy. She'd heard that Kabbalah could make a man happy, but Eli was not even close to forty years old, and he was forbidden to study Kabbalah until then.

It should have bothered her to think of Eli with another woman, but it didn't. It only made her wonder.

What is he like when he is with her? I doubt he would actually have intercourse with a woman who is not his wife. I can't imagine him doing such a forbidden thing. Besides, he's never really cared much for sex. But maybe he just feels that way about sex with me. Our sexual relations have always been stilted and obligatory. Every Friday night he makes an effort to do his duty and give me the child we both long for. Is it possible that my husband is a different man when he is with another woman? Or am I just imagining all this?

Rebecca was curious if Eli was up to something or if it was all in her imagination. She thought about following him when he went out, especially on Monday afternoons when he returned home very late from the shul. She could have done so easily. *I could wait outside the shul behind the side of the building and follow him to see where he goes. He might not go anywhere at all. He might just stay late at the shul. However, what if he does go somewhere? What if he is seeing someone? How will that make me feel? Right now, I am not upset because I am not sure if I am imagining all this or not. Is it perhaps better not to know?*

Rebecca loved the smell of autumn. She loved the colors in the blanket of fallen leaves that covered the ground. Sometimes, after she made sure her house was clean, she would sit outside under a tree and marvel at the beauty of Hashem's creations. Since she was a child, she could see the beauty in all things. Her mother had been frightened of insects. She, on the other hand, was fascinated by their tiny bodies and multiple limbs. Even if she found a spider in the house, she refused to kill it. If a mouse got inside she would do her best to catch the rodent in a box and then put it out in the grass or under a tree. All things had a right to live. Because of her kindness, her papa had always called her his "gentle little soul." And she supposed she was because she couldn't find it in her heart to hurt anything at all. She could see the workings of Hashem in every living creature. The ants walking in a line carrying bits of food amused her. The spider spinning her web fascinated her. Sitting outside and watching the workings of Hashem's creatures took away some of her loneliness: the birds overhead, the squirrels in the trees, the children playing. All these things eased the pain of her loneliness and filled her with hope that someday she and Eli would have a child. And once she had a child, it wouldn't matter if Eli didn't have time for her. She would devote her life to her baby.

CHAPTER SIXTY

Gretchen was waiting inside the abandoned building with a thick slice of pastry wrapped in a clean white cloth when Eli arrived.

"I brought you a slice of strudel," she said.

"Oh, that's so kind of you. But I can't," Eli said.

"No, please. It's all right. I have plenty."

"It's not that."

"Then what is it? Are you ill?"

"No, it's just that, well, it's not kosher."

"You're kidding me." She shook her head. "With food being so scarce?"

"I'm sorry."

"I don't know what to say."

"I'm sorry," he repeated.

She put the cake, which was wrapped in a clean white towel, into her handbag. "I don't know why it's not kosher."

"Does it matter? I can't take it. I hate to offend you. I never mean to offend you."

"We're so different. I sometimes feel like we should stop meeting here. There is no point in it. Not only are we different, but you're married. And me? I'm on the fast track to becoming an old maid. I suppose I should be out looking for a husband instead of meeting you here," Gretchen said in an angry, raised voice.

Eli sighed, taking a deep breath. His beard had started to grow in thick, and he ran his fingers through it. "Yes. You're right. It would be selfish of me to ask you to keep meeting me here."

"We are nothing but friends, Eli. You won't even touch my hand. You won't even sit here beside me. You would rather stand than risk your knee brushing against mine."

He shrugged.

"Tell me that meeting me here is important to you. Tell me that you have developed feelings for me. Tell me, Eli. Tell me or go, and I'll try to get on with my life. Right now, you are the main focus of everything I do. And what's so ridiculous about it is that there is really nothing between us." She got up and wrapped her arms around her chest. Then she walked to the broken window and gazed out at the unkempt, sunburned grass.

Several long, uncomfortable moments passed. A hawk outside the window let out a piercing cry. Gretchen shivered in spite of the perfect weather. She smiled wryly to herself. *It's usually too hot or too cold in here. Today the temperature is perfect.* Then in a very small voice, Eli said, "Hashem forgive me, but I do care for you."

She whipped around to look at him. He was sitting down on the edge of the broken desk. "You do?"

"Yes." He nodded, his head down, his hands on his temples, and his eyes glued to the ground.

She didn't say another word. She walked over to him and raised his head with her hand. At first, he flinched. Their eyes met, and he felt the longing to sin wash over him. Leaning down, she placed her lips on his. Eli knew he should draw away from her; it was the right thing to do, but he couldn't. His heart ached with desire, and his whole body trembled. He stood up, and he put her arms around him. For a

278

few moments, he didn't move. His arms lay at his side. Then he looked into her eyes. "I do care," he said. "More than you know, I care." Eli reached up and embraced Gretchen. The old passion that ran like a current between them reignited despite their intentions to be just friends. A sigh escaped her lips as she kissed him again. This time, he held her tightly and returned her kiss with a passion he knew would haunt him for the rest of his days.

CHAPTER SIXTY-ONE

Eli was shaken by his inability to control himself. He walked home quickly, feeling ashamed, fearing that God would punish him for what he'd done. How could he face Rebecca? Would she not see the lie in his eyes, the sin on his face? He stopped walking and sat down on a tree stump. His heart was heavy with guilt. He'd kissed a woman who was not his wife. Not only did he kiss her, but he felt a stirring in his loins he never felt before. *For Gretchen's sake, for Rebecca's too, I must not return to the warehouse next week. I must never return. I have nothing to offer poor Gretchen. I am a married man, and I owe it to my wife to be faithful. My father would be so ashamed of the man I have become. So ashamed. I wish I could pray, but I am too ashamed of what I've done to ask God for forgiveness. How could I? I should never have agreed to meet with Gretchen all these past months. Even though we did nothing but talk, I have been lying to myself. I've always known that feelings were developing between us. And today was the culmination of those feelings . . . today we sinned.*

The following Monday, Eli walked slowly home after the shul. His thoughts were on Gretchen. He knew she would be waiting at the warehouse. He could see her sitting on the broken desk looking down at her well-worn, low-heeled, brown shoes and gripping her matching handbag. The vision was so clear that it made him want to cry.

Gretchen would feel hurt and abandoned when he didn't come today. And hurting Gretchen was the last thing Eli ever wanted to do. Every nerve in his body was trembling with self-doubt. *I want to go to the warehouse. It's not too late. She'll still be there. Hurry and get there before she starts crying.* The thought of Gretchen crying tore at his heart, especially because he knew he was the reason for her unhappiness. *Isn't it better if I just leave her alone? What happens if I can't stop myself, and we dare to go further than a kiss? What then? What if she became pregnant? The laws of our country forbid it. The laws of my religion forbid it too. I have a wife whose feelings I must also consider. And I would cause poor Gretchen trouble and pain. I must be strong; I must stay away from her.*

Eli stood up. His shoulders ached as if he were carrying a weight on them. He sighed and shook his head. Life was confusing. Why couldn't he feel about Rebecca the way he felt about Gretchen? He had no answers, so he picked up his books and walked home. Eli opened the door to his apartment to find Rebecca cutting potatoes for latkes. Two apples with a dash of cinnamon were simmering in a small amount of water on the stove. The aroma of freshly made applesauce filled the small flat.

"Can I get you anything?" Rebecca asked him as soon as he took his coat off.

"No, thank you." He began walking toward the back of the apartment to hide in his study.

"Dinner will be ready soon. Are you hungry?" Rebecca called out to him.

"Yes. Very hungry," he said, trying to sound believable but feeling as if he'd just lost everything that mattered to him in the world.

"Are you all right, Eli?" Rebecca's voice was gentle and full of concern. "Are you ill?"

"No, I'm sorry. I'm just distracted. I have to prepare a lesson for my students for tomorrow."

"Are you sure you're all right?"

"Yes, of course," he said, trying to lift his voice so it sounded credible. "And it smells wonderful in here, like an apple orchard."

"One of the elderly women from the shul, who is bedridden, gave me some apples today. For the last six months or so, I have been dropping by her house every couple of days to check on her. Anyway, last week her son came by to visit her and brought apples from his orchard."

"Oh, very nice," Eli said, trying to sound interested. "He lives on an apple orchard, but his mother lives in Berlin?"

"Yes, his wife's family owns the orchard. When her father passed away, he moved there to help take care of the farming."

"So, you must know these people very well?"

"I suppose. Yes. I do. I've gotten to know them over the past year."

"There's so much I don't know about you," he said sighing. Then he added, "Well, let me know when dinner is ready. I have some work to do." Eli walked into his study and closed the door. Once he was alone, he sat down at his desk, dropped his head in his hands, and wept. Then, even though he was ashamed before God because he had sinned, he begged God for forgiveness.

CHAPTER SIXTY-TWO

Gretchen waited two hours before she finally gave up on Eli and accepted the fact that he was not coming to meet her. Her heart was broken, but she was angry too. There was no doubt in her mind why he had not come. He was in love with her. She was sure of it. And at the same time, she knew he was consumed with guilt. Gretchen knew she was in love with Eli, but she also accepted the fact he was married. She decided that as long as he was willing to admit he was in love with her, she could live with the situation.

Before she met Eli, she would never have thought she would be willing to have an affair with a married man. But now, everything had changed. What was it about this strange and quiet man with his soft eyes, long, curly sideburns, and tall, black hat that touched her like no other man? His religion was foreign; his way of dressing was odd. He was forbidden to her by law. And yet, Gretchen had never met any other man who had reminded her so much of her father. Of course, he hadn't shown up. How could she have believed he would? Once he realized he had feelings for her, he could not be in her presence without sinning in his mind. Before he said he cared, he could believe they were just friends talking over issues. However, she knew him well enough to know that he had probably not slept or eaten much since they kissed. He was probably praying for forgiveness like mad.

"Damn him for being married. Damn him for making me love him," she said aloud. But even though she voiced those angry curses, her tender heart blessed him with every beat.

November 1938

The temperature dropped suddenly, bringing the chill of winter to the Jewish sector of Berlin. It would get colder as the months passed, but it was clear that autumn was giving way to the season Eli most dreaded. The winter months always gave him a dark, lonely feeling. It was strong right now as he walked home from the yeshiva after a day of teaching. Thoughts of his parents passed through his mind as the cold wind seeped through his coat. Yousef's wife was pregnant for the second time. He was happy for them, but he and Rebecca remained childless, and he began to feel that God had turned his face away from their marriage. He wondered if the forbidden kiss he shared that October afternoon with Gretchen had anything to do with his falling out of Hashem's favor. Perhaps it didn't help, but he and Rebecca had not been able to conceive long before the kiss.

Eli tried not to think of the kiss, tried not to remember how his heart had raced, how he had longed to hold Gretchen in his arms forever. He wanted to protect her from danger, from hurt, and from shame, and the only way he believed he could do so was by leaving her alone. Perhaps she'd met someone else, a man from her own world. Perhaps she was thinking about marriage. The idea of Gretchen getting married should make him happy, because he wanted her to be happy. But it didn't. It hurt him more deeply than any cut he ever had.

After dinner, he went into his study leaving Rebecca alone in the kitchen. Over the years, she'd grown used to spending time alone. She carefully washed the dishes and the pots and pans. Then she sat down on the sofa and began to knit. The house was quiet, and the solitude that had become her best friend came over her. "Knit one, purl two," she whispered to herself, trying to remember the pattern for the blanket she was working on. "Knit two, purl one."

Rebecca heard a commotion coming from outside. People were screaming; some were cursing. "Dirty Jew. Kill the Jew!" a man's angry, loud voice said. "Put the knife in the Jew." A group of what sounded like drunken boys started singing: "Put the knife in the Jew! They slaughter Christian children. They slit their throats and make soup out of their blood." A man no older than twenty yelled out, "No, they use it for their matzo."

Rebecca moved the drape just an inch and peeked out the window. Just as she did, a group of angry young men smashed Otto Schmidt Fleischwaren's window. She'd gone to Schmidt's butcher shop just a day ago to buy bones for her soup. Otto Schmidt was a kind and generous man. Rebecca had only enough money for two bones, but he gave her three, and all of them were rich with marrow. Her hand went to her heart as she watched the same gang of thugs write Jude in black paint all over Otto's door. A heavyset man came running toward the thugs. He had thick arms and muscular calves. "Get out of here! Go away!" he was hollering. Rebecca recognized him as the cobbler who owned a store just a few feet away. He appeared to be strong and capable of putting up a good fight. But he was no match for a gang of ten strong, young men. They fell on him and began beating him with clubs. Rebecca gasped.

"Eli!" she yelled. But she needn't have called for him; he was already on his way into the living room.

"What's going on outside?"

"I don't know. It looks like a pogrom."

"A pogrom?"

"Look for yourself, but be careful. Don't let those crazy boys see you."

Eli turned and looked at his wife, then he peeked through the drapes. Mayhem filled the streets. The cobbler lay in a pool of blood on the sidewalk. A woman lay on the street with a lake of blood surrounding her head like a bright red halo. "Get in the bedroom. Get under the bed, and stay there."

"Don't go outside, Eli. Please, don't go out."

"I should go," he said, but there was a note of uncertainty in his voice. *I have been passive all my life. I've accepted whatever was handed to me as Hashem's will. But now, it seems that someone must lead my people. I am the son of the rebbe. Shouldn't I be the one to go out and lead them? But if I do go out there and demand that they fight back will I be of any help to anyone, or will I just end up dead? And even worse, will I get other people killed too. If I tell them to them to stand up and fight all the Jew haters will I just be putting nails in their coffins? Look at this mob; they have gone mad. They're hungry for blood.*

"No, Eli! Have you gone insane? Come with me, please, come and hide with me. You are a Hasidic man. Your clothing alone will make you a target. There's an angry mob out there. They won't listen to reason. They'll kill you because you look like everything they hate. They'll use you to make an example. Please, I beg you; I've never begged you for anything before."

He looked into her eyes. *Where am I going? What am I going to do if I go outside?*

"Please," she begged him again as the shul down the street burst into flames. Rebecca was weeping. She grabbed Eli's shirtsleeve, and he allowed her to lead him to the bedroom.

She got under the bed and pulled him under beside her. Neither of them said a word, but both feared that the wild band of hoodlums would burst into their apartment and attack them with clubs or knives. The Nazi thugs might even burn the building down around them. Yet there was nothing they could do but lie there under the bed and pray. Eli was sick with helplessness. His wife needed him, and there was nothing he could do to protect her.

The violence continued through the night and into the next day.

CHAPTER SIXTY-THREE

November 11, 1938

An unnerving silence hung over the little neighborhood. The streets were in shambles. Dried blood left a trail on the sidewalk, spilling into the gutters, and broken glass littered the streets. The shul where the Kaetzels and their friends had worshiped for generations and where Eli taught bar mitzvah classes was hollowed out by fire. The precious Torah lay in ashes, her beautiful scrolls half burnt on the ground.

For the Jews of Berlin, the world as they knew it had ended. But even though time had stopped for those who lived in that little village, somehow the sun still rose that morning. When they could wait no longer, Rebecca and Eli came out of their hiding place. Rebecca could not control her trembling. She thought of her family. Although she longed to go to her parents home and assure herself they were all right, she couldn't even bring herself to look out the window.

Eli peeked through the shades and saw a group of young men, boy's he'd grown up with and his friends from the shul. They were standing in the street looking: their faces still in shock.

"I am going out to talk to them," Eli indicated toward the men outside. Rebecca carefully peered out the window.

"Do you think it's safe?" she asked.

"I don't know. They're all outside. I have to go. My father was their rebbe. They will be looking to me for guidance."

For the first time since they had been married, Rebecca addressed her husband with a tone of sarcasm. "And what kind of guidance do you plan to give them? Do you know what to do? Do you have the answers?"

He shook his head. "Rebecca, I have never known how to lead them. I have never known what to say. And I have no answers. But I know that they need me, so I will go outside and talk to them. I have to try to do my best," he said, broken.

Yousef was outside with the others. As soon as he saw Eli, he ran up to him. "They arrested plenty of Jews last night. Plenty. And for no reason. And from what I understand, it's not over."

"Are you sure?"

"Am I sure of what, Eli?"

"That it's not over."

"I'm not sure of anything," Yousef said.

"How could they arrest people without reason?"

"There is only one reason. The reason is that they are Jewish. We are Jewish, and they hate us. Soon they will come for all of us. Our shul, our beloved synagogue, is nothing but ashes. There's blood, Jewish blood, all over the streets. I'm taking my wife and getting out of Berlin. I suggest you do the same."

"Where will you go?"

"France. My wife has a sister who got married to a French Jew. We'll go and stay with them. Do you want me to ask her if you and Rebecca can come with us?"

"No, no of course not. We couldn't impose like that. No."

"Are you sure?"

"Yes, I am sure. Yousef, it's very kind of you to offer, but you have one child and another on the way. You are moving in with another family. I am sure it will be very crowded. Do they have children too?"

"Yes, three. Two boys and a girl."

"That's a lot of people. Don't worry about us, my dear friend. I promise you that Rebecca and I will be all right."

CHAPTER SIXTY-FOUR

Eli had no idea what he was going to do. The violence continued throughout the following day and night. It was frightening. But what was even more terrifying was that every day more and more Jews were being arrested without cause. Eli had heard that people were taking their families and going into hiding. He thought about hiding in the abandoned warehouse where he and Gretchen had met. But how would he and Rebecca survive if they tried to hide out there? They would have no food. Eli had no idea how to hunt or fish. He did not even have the slightest inkling of how to fire a gun, and that was if he could even get his hands on one. Not to mention that in the winter, the large building with its broken windows would be freezing. Besides, an abandoned warehouse would be the first place the Nazis would look for Jews. The warehouse was not an option.

Before the fire, the yeshiva, or school, had been located in the back of the shul. Now that the building burned down, the yeshiva teachers, including Eli, decided to continue their classes in the homes of several members of the congregation.

Eli didn't teach as often as he had before the night of the broken glass. He was too consumed with worry about the future of his entire community to prepare lessons. But long ago, Eli promised that when

Dovid Finkelstein was ready, he would personally administer his bar mitzvah lessons. Dovid was the grandson of one of Eli's father's best friends, and Eli had made this vow to Dovid's grandfather when he had come to pay his respects at Eli's father's shiva. Even though his heart was not in it, Eli went to Dovid's home twice a week to give him his bar mitzvah lessons. It was a cold night in December, and Eli was on his way home from the Finkelstein's apartment. A strict curfew had been put in place for all Jews, and Eli had stayed out much later than he should have. He lost track of time because Dovid was having difficulty memorizing his Torah portion. Eli wanted to help; helping Dovid Finkelstein was something Eli knew his father would have approved of. And although poor Dovid was not very bright, Eli felt good about his work with the young boy.

It was dark and well past curfew. Eli walked as quickly as he could toward home. The streets were so quiet that the silence was a little unsettling. He felt a chill run through him as he walked past a lamppost spilling yellow light over the crosswalk and illuminating a large poster of Adolf Hitler. As he turned the corner, a black car raced by. The roar of the engine shattered the unearthly quiet. Quickly, Eli hid between two buildings. His heart beat so hard in his chest that he felt dizzy and nauseated. Once the automobile was out of sight, he came out and began to walk even more quickly toward home. When he was almost a block away from the safety of his apartment, Eli felt a firm and authoritative tug on the sleeve of his coat. Pure fear shot through him like a cannonball. *Dear God, not the Gestapo*, he prayed. *I'm going to be taken away. Rebecca won't even know what happened to me.*

CHAPTER SIXTY-FIVE

Rebecca sat at her kitchen table with a cup of hot tea and a blanket wrapped around her shoulders. The chilly weather had never agreed with her. Of all the seasons, winter was her least favorite. If she had a child, she might look forward to the celebration of Hanukkah. She would have enjoyed lighting eight small candles and playing dreidel with her little one. That might have made the winter more fulfilling. But as it stood, winter was a miserable time for her.

Many days she was unable to fulfill her responsibilities of helping the poor or sick because the weather was too bad for her to leave the house. Rebecca knew that most of the people she helped were completely dependent upon her, so her work was very important. Still, if the snow was too deep, she was unable to walk outside, so she could not carry out her duties. This left her feeling guilty and terribly isolated. Eli was either in his study or out teaching at the home of one of his congregants.

As her parents were aging it became more difficult for them to walk to her apartment in the snow. She tried to visit them as often as she could. Visiting them should have brought her joy, but it didn't. Returning to her childhood home was painful. It brought back memories of all her childhood dreams: dreams that had not come true.

Glancing up at the clock on the wall, Rebecca realized Eli was very late. She was keeping his dinner warm; a pot of stew simmered on the stove. *It's two hours past curfew; this is the latest he has ever been. He has never been later than a half hour past curfew and that was when a friend of his mother's passed away, and he was helping the family. But as far as I know, he is only teaching a twelve-year-old boy tonight. I can't imagine what would keep him out so late? I pray that he is safe.* She wrung her hands on the dishtowel.

CHAPTER SIXTY-SIX

The hand tugged the sleeve of Eli's coat and pulled him into an alleyway between two tall apartment buildings.

"Eli."

"Gretchen?"

"Yes, it's me," she whispered.

"What are you doing here?"

"I followed you from your house to that apartment building, and then I waited until you came out. I saw you in the window with that young boy."

"I was giving him his bar mitzvah lessons."

"You shouldn't be out this late."

"I know. It's after curfew. But I can't believe that you waited for hours in the darkness and the cold for me."

"Of course for you, silly. Why else?"

"I don't know. I'm confused. I don't understand why you would do that."

"There's no time for confusion or philosophical discussions. You're in trouble. Your wife is in trouble too. All the Jews in Berlin are in trouble, and I've come to help you."

"Help me? How?"

"You and your wife are going to stay with me. I live in a garden apartment with a cellar. No one in my building even knows the cellar is there. I wouldn't know either had I not found it when I was child. Anyway, I will hide you both in the cellar until all this Jew-hunting nonsense is over."

"I couldn't let you do that. I wouldn't let you put yourself in danger that way."

"I am not asking if you would let me. I am telling you what I plan to do. Now let's go to your flat and pick up your wife. Then we must get back to my apartment before sunrise. You need to put on as many layers of clothing as you can, and do it as quickly as you can."

"I don't know."

"There's no time for this nonsense. You're in danger. They're arresting Jews every day. You don't know when you will be next. I insist that you come with me. Now, let's go."

"Why are you doing this?" he asked.

"Because I think about you all the time, and I can't let you be hurt. I was so angry with you for standing me up that day at the warehouse. I hated you—you fool. But I couldn't go on hating you for very long. As soon as I heard what was going on with the Jews, I knew I had to find a way to help you. But this is bigger than you and I. It is more than just that. I am going to help as many Jews as I can because I feel that what is happening to the Jews here in Germany is wrong. Before my father left for the army, he said something that stuck in my mind. He said that even the smallest crack in the foundation of our civilized nation will grow until it eventually breaks us and turns us all into savages. What I mean is, once we forget our responsibility to treat our fellow man the way we would want to be treated, we become a nation of brutes. And before you know it, the lines between right and wrong are blurred forever."

"Do you believe it will get that bad?"

"I do. And that's why I have decided to fight this outrage against humanity. I am scared, Eli, but I must do this. Even if I fail; even if I am killed in the process."

"I understand your idealism. But you are putting yourself in terrible danger. You're a German, pure German. If anyone is safe right now, you are."

"But what you are not understanding is that as long as there is evil in the world, no one is safe, Eli. No one at all."

"You're a good person, Gretchen. If my father would have given you a chance, he would have really liked you."

"Yes, well, if the Nazis gave your people a chance they might like them too. But people hate easily and without reason. I am not that kind of person. You have taught me a lot about Jews, Eli. And I dare say I think I love you."

"Did I hear you say you love me?" He was stunned.

"Yes, you did. I think perhaps I always have. But I didn't know it. However, I respect that you are married. I would never put your marriage in jeopardy. But please, Eli, let me help you. This is not a matter of pride. It's a matter of life and death. I want to help your wife too.

"How?"

"I want to hide you both."

"But what about my people? I am their rebbe. They need me to show them the way. They need me to lead them."

"You can't lead them if you're dead, can you?"

He shook his head.

"Well, then, come with me. You'll be safe. At least I hope you will. And while you are in hiding maybe you can figure out a way to help the others," she said, then she added, "As long as you are alive there is a flicker of hope for your people, but if you are dead, then who will they turn to?"

"You're right. I'll come."

"And what's your wife's name?" Gretchen asked.

Eli was stunned for a moment. He had forgotten about Rebecca, and now he had no idea how he was going to explain all this to her. How could he explain who Gretchen was, and why she was willing to help them? Although he didn't want to hurt Rebecca by bringing Gretchen to the house, he knew that for Rebecca's sake, she must accept Gretchen's very kind and generous offer. Gretchen was putting her own life in danger to save him and Rebecca. As he looked into Gretchen's eyes, which shone like tiny beacons of light even in the darkness, he realized he didn't just care for Gretchen. He loved her too. He loved her fiercely. She was the reason he had never been able to fully love Rebecca the way a husband should for his wife. Still, he could not tell her. He must never let his feelings show. He owed it to his wife to be faithful even if his heart was aching for another.

"Rebecca. My wife's name is Rebecca."

"Hurry, time is passing. It's long after curfew, and you must not be caught out on the street. Let's get to your apartment. We must convince Rebecca to come with us. The two of you need to be safely hidden in the cellar before sunrise."

"She may refuse. She may not go with us," Eli said.

"But we must try," Gretchen said. "We must try."

CHAPTER SIXTY-SEVEN

Rebecca sat on the sofa in the living room trying to remain calm. The clock ticked quietly, but to her, it sounded like a bomb ticking. Every minute, it was getting later and later. Rebecca was not only worried about Eli, she desperately needed to talk to him. Something terrible had happened. She had gone to see her parents that afternoon, but they were not home. This was unusual, so she went to see her mother's friend next door. She learned that several of the Jewish men in the neighborhood had been arrested on the night of the pogrom. Her mother and father had both gone out to try and help their friends, and they too had been arrested. Her sister had vanished. No one had seen her since.

"Where did they take them?" Rebecca asked.

"No one knows," her mother's friend said.

"This is insane. My parents have never broken a single law. My father has always been very strict about following rules," Rebecca said, her voice cracking.

"I wish I had more to tell you. But this is all I know."

Rebecca walked home in shock. She could hardly catch her breath. On her way, she stopped at the homes of several of Eli's congregants looking for him, but she was unable to find him. She wasn't sure which of his bar mitzvah boys he'd gone to tutor that night, or she would have gone directly there to find him. Eli never told her their names. She only knew that he was privately teaching a few students, so all she could do was wait. And she had been waiting all day, feeling desperate and terrified. She needed to tell him what happened. The day had gone by slowly, but it was late, and he still hadn't returned. So not only was she worried about her parents and sister, she was worried about Eli too. She dared not go out of the house and try to find him as it was too dangerous to be caught outside after curfew. She trembled in fear. *Poor Eli! What if something terrible has happened? With the way things are going, anything could have happened to him. And what about me? Where will I go? What will I do? How will I ever find him or my family?*

The key turned in the door, and Rebecca felt a wave of relief wash over her. But confusion followed when she saw a pretty, young girl enter the apartment with her husband.

"Eli, are you all right?" She looked from Eli to Gretchen, and she was completely puzzled.

"Yes, I'm fine. This is Gretchen Schmidt. She is a good friend of mine. She is going to help us."

"Help us?" Rebecca said as she lifted one of her eyebrows. "How?"

"As you know, things have gotten bad for Jews. Very bad, Rebecca. Gretchen has offered to hide us, so we will be safe. Jews are being arrested all over Berlin," Eli said.

"My parents have been arrested. I went to see them today, and the neighbor told me. My sister is gone. No one knows where she is."

"Yes, it's happening to Jews all over Germany," Gretchen said. "I want to help you both."

Eli and Gretchen glanced at each other. When they did, Rebecca caught the look of understanding and closeness that passed between them, and in that instant she realized she had been right all along. Eli *had* been seeing another woman. She had known it instinctively, and yet she had refused to believe it. She told herself Eli would never break one of the Ten Commandments. And yet he had. She was stunned. As shocking as it was, it was even more surprising to find out she was a shiksa.

Rebecca thought Eli, being the son of a rebbe, would have had more respect for his wife than to bring his mistress home. A quick vision of Shmul passed through Rebecca's mind. She had rejected Shmul because she believed that all the rules she grew up with were absolute. Because of her upbringing, she knew she must never be unfaithful. And yet, here Eli stood before her with another woman.

Rebecca felt a million emotions stir within her. She was angry with Eli, but at the same time, she knew she wasn't in love with him. Her heart wasn't broken: only her pride was hurt. And strangely enough, there was something about this outspoken and spunky shiksa that she actually liked. How was that possible? How does a wife like her husband's mistress? There was a genuineness about Gretchen that Rebecca could feel. Besides, she knew Gretchen was right. She and Eli were not safe in their home. It was only a matter of time before something happened. They had to get away to somewhere safe as quickly as possible.

Rebecca longed to find her family, but she was certain that if she went to the police looking for them it would only result in her own arrest. Perhaps she might find a way to locate them once she and Eli were in hiding?

"Please go now and get ready. Layer as many clothes as you can. Take whatever food or valuables you have, like your photos, but nothing too big. Now hurry, because we must leave as quickly as possible. I have to be sure that you are hidden before sunrise," Gretchen instructed.

"She is putting herself in danger by helping us," Eli said. "We must not do anything to put her in further peril. Please, Rebecca. Hurry," Eli said. He went into the bedroom and began to put on layers and layers of clothing.

Rebecca layered her clothing and then filled her undergarments with the few pieces of jewelry she owned and a picture of her family at a Purim festival taken years before she and Eli were married. Eli was rushing to get ready, so he didn't see Rebecca stop and take a moment to watch him. It was as if she were seeing her husband for the first time. Now everything made sense. She knew why their marriage couldn't work. And for some reason, she was no longer angry.

I finally understand why I have never been able to make Eli happy. It wasn't me. There was nothing wrong with me. It was just that he belonged to someone else. This relationship between Eli and Gretchen may have been going on even before I met him. Well, no matter. After this nightmare of Hitler and his Nazi Party is over, I will leave Eli, and I will find someone of my own. Someone who belongs to me, not because he is forced to by his parents or ancient, outdated laws, but because his heart tells him that I am his b'sheirt, his one and only love.

From this moment on, I will never again follow rules blindly. I did that, and where did it lead? It led to a loveless, lonely marriage. The time has come for me to grow up and stop relying on Eli or my parents to make all my decisions. I am scared of the future, but I am excited too. Because this insight will be life altering for me. I have never had to stand on my own. However, I know that I am stronger than anyone ever realized. I am even stronger than I ever knew I was, and the time has come to prove it, not only to them but to me.

"I'm ready," Rebecca said. "There's a challah in the pantry and some potatoes and carrots. There's also a small bag of noodles. It's a shame to waste the stew that's on the stove, but there is no time for us to eat it, and it's too hot to take. I'll put what I can fit from the pantry into my handbag. Can you take the rest, Gretchen?"

"I can," Gretchen said as she and Rebecca filled their purses with whatever food they could find.

"I'm ready to go now too," Eli said as he walked toward the door. Neither he nor Rebecca carried a suitcase. They dared not bring anything that would draw attention in case they were seen.

"All right, let's get going. It's well after curfew, and we must be very careful, or we'll all be arrested," Gretchen said, taking a deep breath.

Eli took his tall, black hat off the coffee table and put it on his head.

"Don't wear that. If we get caught, I don't want the police to know you are Hasidic. It's bad enough that you have the yellow stars sewn into your clothes."

"After the attack, they passed a law that forced us to sew the yellow Star of David onto our clothes," Rebecca said.

"Yes, I know. I know about the attack. I know about everything. It doesn't matter anyway, because if they did stop us, they would demand to see our papers. They would know you were Jewish anyway."

"The Nazis are ferociously hunting our people. It's terrifying," Eli said, shaking his head.

"Yes, and that's exactly why I am here. Now, we have been wasting too much time talking. There will be plenty of time for us to talk, but that time is not now. Everyone is ready? Let's get going. Stay in the shadows, and be careful to stay out of the light," Gretchen said firmly as she straightened her coat and took a deep breath. Then she led Eli and Rebecca out of the house.

Eli hesitated before closing the door. He kissed his hand then reached up and touched the mezuzah that hung over the side of the front door. For a single moment, he bent his head and whispered a

Hebrew prayer. Then with a sigh, he turned to the two women who mattered most in his life and said, "And may God be with us."

The Darkest Canyon

Book Two in a Holocaust Story series.

Nazi Germany.

Gretchen Schmidt has a secret life. She is in love with a married Jewish man. She is hiding him while his wife is posing as an Aryan woman.

Her best friend, Hilde, who unbeknownst to Gretchen is a sociopath, is working as a guard at Ravensbruck concentration camp.

If Hilde discovers Gretchen's secret, will their friendship be strong enough to keep Gretchen safe? Or will Hilde fall under the spell of the Nazis and turn her best friend over to the Gestapo?

The *Darkest Canyon* is a terrifying ride along the edge of a canyon in the dark of night.

AUTHORS NOTE

First and foremost, I want to thank you for reading my novel and for your continued interest in my work. From time to time, I receive emails from my readers that contest the accuracy of my events. When you pick up a novel, you are entering the author's world where we sometimes take artistic license and ask you to suspend your disbelief. I always try to keep as true to history as possible; however, sometimes there are discrepancies within my novels. This happens sometimes to keep the drama of the story. Thank you for indulging me.

I always enjoy hearing from my readers. Your feelings about my work are very important to me. If you enjoyed it, please consider telling your friends or posting a short review on Amazon. Word of mouth is an author's best friend.

If you enjoyed this book, please sign up for my mailing list, and you will receive Free short stories including an USA Today award-winning novella as my gift to you!!!!! To sign up, just go to...

www.RobertaKagan.com

Many blessings to you,

Roberta

Email: roberta@robertakagan.com

Come and like my Facebook page!

https://www.facebook.com/roberta.kagan.9

Join my book club

https://www.facebook.com/groups/1494285400798292/?ref=br_rs

Follow me on BookBub to receive automatic emails whenever I am offering a special price, a freebie, a giveaway, or a new release. Just click the link below, then click follow button to the right of my name. Thank you so much for your interest in my work.

https://www.bookbub.com/authors/roberta-kagan.

MORE BOOKS BY THE AUTHOR

AVAILABLE ON AMAZON

Not In America

Book One in A Jewish Family Saga

"Jews drink the blood of Christian babies. They use it for their rituals. They are evil and they consort with the devil."

These words rang out in 1928 in a small town in upstate New York when little four-year-old Evelyn Wilson went missing. A horrible witch hunt ensued that was based on a terrible folk tale known as the blood libel.

Follow the Schatzman's as their son is accused of the most horrific crime imaginable. This accusation destroys their family and sends their mother and sister on a journey home to Berlin just as the Nazi's are about to come to power.

Not in America is based on true events. However, the author has taken license in her work, creating a what if tale that could easily have been true.

They Never Saw It Coming

Book Two in A Jewish Family Saga

Goldie Schatzman is nearing forty, but she is behaving like a reckless teenager, and every day she is descending deeper into a dark web. Since her return home to Berlin, she has reconnected with her childhood friend, Leni, a free spirit who has swept Goldie into the Weimar lifestyle that is overflowing with artists and writers, but also with debauchery. Goldie had spent the last nineteen years living a dull life with a spiritless husband. And now she has been set free, completely abandoning any sense of morals she once had.

As Goldie's daughter, Alma, is coming of marriageable age, her grandparents are determined to find her a suitable match. But will Goldie's life of depravity hurt Alma's chances to find a Jewish husband from a good family?

And all the while the SA, a prelude to the Nazi SS, is gaining strength. Germany is a hotbed of political unrest. Leaving a nightclub one night, Goldie finds herself caught in the middle of a demonstration that has turned violent. She is rescued by Felix, a member of the SA, who is immediately charmed by her blonde hair and Aryan appearance. Goldie is living a lie, and her secrets are bound to catch up with her. A girl, who she'd scorned in the past, is now a proud member of the Nazi Party and still carries a deep-seated vendetta against Goldie.

On the other side of the Atlantic, Sam, Goldie's son, is thriving with the Jewish mob in Manhattan; however, he has made a terrible mistake. He has destroyed the trust of the woman he believes is his bashert. He knows he cannot live without her, and he is desperately trying to find a way to win her heart.

And Izzy, the man who Sam once called his best friend, is now his worst enemy. They are both in love with the same woman, and the competition between them could easily result in death.

Then Sam receives word that something has happened in Germany, and he must accompany his father on a journey across the ocean. He is afraid that if he leaves before his beloved accepts his proposal, he might lose her forever.

When The Dust Settled

Book Three in A Jewish Family Saga

Coming December 2020

As the world races like a runaway train toward World War 11, the Schatzman family remains divided.

In New York, prohibition has ended, and Sam's world is turned upside down. He has been earning a good living transporting illegal liquor for the Jewish mob. Now that alcohol is legal, America is celebrating. But as the liquor flows freely, the mob boss realizes he must expand his illegal interests if he is going to continue to live the lavish lifestyle he's come to know. Some of the jobs Sam is offered go against his moral character. Transporting alcohol was one thing, but threatening lives is another.

Meanwhile, across the ocean in Italy, Mussolini, a heartless dictator, runs the country with an iron fist. Those who speak out against him disappear and are never seen again. For the first time since that horrible incident in Medina, Alma is finally happy and has fallen in love with a kind and generous Italian doctor who already has a job awaiting him in Rome; however, he is not Jewish. Alma must decide whether to marry him and risk disappointing her bubbie or let him go to find a suitable Jewish match.

In Berlin, the Nazis are quickly rising to power. Flags with swastikas are appearing everywhere. And Dr. Goebbels, the minister of propaganda is openly spewing hideous lies designed to turn the German people against the Jews. Adolf Hitler had disposed of his enemies, and the SA has been replaced by the even more terrifying

SS. After the horrors they witnessed during Kristallnacht, Goldie's mother, Esther, is ready to abandon all she knows to escape the country. She begs her husband to leave Germany. But Ted refuses to leave everything that he spent his entire life working for. At what point is it too late to leave? And besides, where would they go? What would they do?

The Nazis have taken the country by the throat, and the electrifying atmosphere of the Weimar a distant memory. The period of artistic tolerance and debauchery has been replaced by a strict and cruel regime that seeks to destroy all who do not fit its ideal. Goldie's path of depravity is catching up with her, and her secrets are threatened. Will her Nazi enemies finally strike?

Book Four in A Jewish Family Saga

Coming Early 2021....

The Smallest Crack

Book One in a Holocaust Story series.

1933 Berlin, Germany

The son of a rebbe, Eli Kaetzel, and his beautiful but timid wife, Rebecca, find themselves in danger as Hitler rises to power. Eli knows that their only chance for survival may lie in the hands of Gretchen, a spirited Aryan girl. However, the forbidden and dangerous friendship between Eli and Gretchen has been a secret until now. Because, for Eli, if it is discovered that he has been keeping company with a woman other than his wife it will bring shame to him and his family. For Gretchen her friendship with a Jew is forbidden by law and could cost her, her life.

The Darkest Canyon

Book Two in a Holocaust Story series.

Nazi Germany.

Gretchen Schmidt has a secret life. She is in love with a married Jewish man. She is hiding him while his wife is posing as an Aryan woman.

Her best friend, Hilde, who unbeknownst to Gretchen is a sociopath, is working as a guard at Ravensbruck concentration camp.

If Hilde discovers Gretchen's secret, will their friendship be strong enough to keep Gretchen safe? Or will Hilde fall under the spell of the Nazis and turn her best friend over to the Gestapo?

The *Darkest Canyon* is a terrifying ride along the edge of a canyon in the dark of night.

Millions Of Pebbles

Book Three in a Holocaust Story series.

Benjamin Rabinowitz's life is shattered as he watches his wife, Lila, and his son, Moishe, leave to escape the Lodz ghetto. He is conflicted because he knows this is their best chance of survival, but he asks himself, will he ever see them again?

Ilsa Guhr has a troubled childhood, but as she comes of age, she learns that her beauty and sexuality give her the power to get what she wants. But she craves an even greater power. As the Nazis take control of Germany, she sees an opportunity to gain everything she's ever desired.

Fate will weave a web that will bring these two unlikely people into each other's lives.

Sarah and Solomon

Book Four in a Holocaust Story series

"Give me your children" -Chaim Mordechaj Rumkowski. September 1942 The Lodz Ghetto.

When Hitler's Third Reich reined with an iron fist, the head Judenrat of the Lodz ghetto decides to comply with the Nazis. He agrees to send the Jewish children off on a transport to face death.

In order to save her two young children a mother must take the ultimate risk. The night before the children are to rounded up and sent to their deaths, she helps her nine year old son and her five year old daughter escape into a war torn Europe. However, she cannot fit through the barbed wire, and so the children must go alone.

Follow Sarah and Solomon as they navigate their way through a world filled with hatred, and treachery. However, even in the darkest hour there is always a flicker of light. And these two young innocent souls will be aided by people who's lights will always shine in our memories.

All My Love, Detrick

Book One in the All My Love, Detrick series.

Book One in the All My Love, Detrick Series

Can Forbidden Love Survive in Nazi Germany?

After Germany's defeat in the First World War, she lays in ruins, falling beneath the wheel of depression and famine. And so, with a promise of restoring Germany to her rightful place as a world power, Adolf Hitler begins to rise.

Detrick, a handsome seventeen-year-old Aryan boy is reluctant to join the Nazi party because of his friendship with Jacob, who is Jewish and has been like a father figure to him. However, he learns that in order to protect the woman he loves, Jacob's daughter, he must abandon all his principles and join the Nazis. He knows the only way to survive is to live a double life. Detrick is confronted with fear every day; if he is discovered, he and those he loves will come face to face with the ultimate cruelty of the Third Reich.

Follow two families, one Jewish and one German, as they are thrust into a world of danger on the eve of the Nazis rise to power.

You Are My Sunshine

Book Two in the All My Love, Detrick series.

A child's innocence is the purest of all.

In Nazi Germany, Helga Haswell is at a crossroads. She's pregnant by a married SS officer who has since abandoned her. Left alone with the thought of raising a fatherless child, she has nowhere to turn -- until the Lebensborn steps in. They will take Helga's child when it's born and raise it as their own. Helga will now be free to live her life.

But when Helga has second thoughts, it's already too late. The papers are signed, and her claim to her child has been revoked. Her daughter belongs to Hitler now. And when Hitler's delusions of grandeur rapidly accelerate, Germany becomes involved in a two-front war against the heroic West and the fearless Russians.

Helga's child seems doomed to a life raised by the cruelest humans on Earth. But God's plan for her sends the young girl to the most unexpected people. In their warm embrace, she's given the chance for love in a world full of hate.

You Are My Sunshine is the heartfelt story of second chances. Helga Haswell may be tied to an unthinkable past, but her young daughter has the chance of a brighter future.

The Promised Land:

From Nazi Germany to Israel

Book Three in the All My Love, Detrick series.

Zofia Weiss, a Jewish woman with a painful past, stands at the dock, holding the hand of a little girl. She is about to board The SS Exodus, bound for Palestine with only her life, a dream, and a terrifying secret. As her eyes scan the crowds of people, she sees a familiar face. Her heart pounds and beads of sweat form on her forehead…

The Nazis have surrendered. Zofia survived the Holocaust, but she lives in constant fear. The one person who knows her dark secret is a sadistic SS officer with the power to destroy the life she's working so hard to rebuild. Will he ever find her and the innocent child she has sworn to protect?

To Be An Israeli

Book Four in the All My Love, Detrick series.

Elan understands what it means to be an Israeli. He's sacrificed the woman he loved, his marriage, and his life for Israel. When Israel went to war and Elan was summoned in the middle of the night, he did not hesitate to defend his country, even though he knew he might pay a terrible price. Elan is not a perfect man by any means. He can be cruel. He can be stubborn and self-righteous. But he is brave, and he loves more deeply than he will ever admit.

This is his story.

However, it is not only his story; it is also the story of the lives of the women who loved him: Katja, the girl whom he cherished but could never marry, who would haunt him forever. Janice, the spoiled American he wed to fill a void, who would keep a secret from him that would one day shatter his world. And…Nina, the beautiful Mossad agent whom Elan longed to protect but knew he never could.

To Be an Israeli spans from the beginning of the Six-Day War in 1967 through 1986 when a group of American tourists are on their way to visit their Jewish homeland.

Forever My Homeland

The Fifth and final book in the All My Love, Detrick series.

Bari Lynn has a secret. So she, a young Jewish-American girl, decides to tour Israel with her best friend and the members of their synagogue in search of answers.

Meanwhile, beneath the surface in Israel, trouble is stirring with a group of radical Islamists.

The case falls into the hands of Elan, a powerful passionate Mossad agent, trying to pick up the pieces of his shattered life. He believes nothing can break him, but in order to achieve their goals, the terrorists will go to any means to bring Elan to his knees.

Forever, My Homeland is the story of a country built on blood and determination. It is the tale of a strong and courageous people who don't have the luxury of backing down from any fight, because they live with the constant memory of the Holocaust. In the back of their minds, there is always a soft voice that whispers "Never again."

Michal's Destiny

Book One in the Michal's Destiny series.

It is 1919 in Siberia. Michal—a young, sheltered girl—has eyes for a man other than her betrothed. For a young girl growing up in a traditional Jewish settlement, an arranged marriage is a fact of life. However, destiny, it seems, has other plans for Michal. When a Cossack pogrom invades her small village, the protected life Michal has grown accustomed to and loves will crumble before her eyes. Everything she knows is gone and she is forced to leave her home and embark on a journey to Berlin with the man she thought she wanted.

Michal faces love, loss, and heartache because she is harboring a secret that threatens to destroy her every attempt at happiness. But over the next fourteen tumultuous years, during the peak of the Weimar Republic, she learns she is willing to do anything to have the love she longs for and to protect her family.

However, it is now 1933. Life in Berlin is changing, especially for the Jews. Dark storm clouds are looming on the horizon. Adolf Hitler is about to become the chancellor of Germany, and that will change everything for Michal forever.

A Family Shattered

Book Two in the Michal's Destiny series.

In book two of the Michal's Destiny series, Tavvi and Michal have problems in the beginning of their relationship, but they build a life together. Each stone is laid carefully with love and mutual understanding. They now have a family with two beautiful daughters and a home full of happiness.

It is now 1938—Kristallnacht. Blood runs like a river on the streets, shattered glass covers the walkways of Jewish shop owners, and gangs of Nazi thugs charge though Berlin in a murderous rage. When Tavvi, the strong-willed Jewish carpenter, races outside, without thinking of his own welfare, to save his daughters fiancée, little does his wife Michal know that she might never hold him in her arms again. In an instant, all the stones they laid together come crashing down leaving them with nothing but the hope of finding each other again.

Watch Over My Child

Book Three in the Michal's Destiny series.

In book three of the Michal's Destiny series, after her parents are arrested by the Nazis on Kristallnacht, twelve-year-old Gilde Margolis is sent away from her home, her sister, and everyone she knows and loves.

Alone and afraid, Gilde boards a train through the Kindertransport bound for London, where she will stay with strangers. Over the next seven years as Gilde is coming of age, she learns about love, friendship, heartache, and the pain of betrayal. As the Nazis grow in power, London is thrust into a brutal war against Hitler. Severe rationing is imposed upon the British, while air raids instill terror, and bombs all but destroy the city. Against all odds, and with no knowledge of what has happened to her family in Germany, Gilde keeps a tiny flicker of hope buried deep in her heart: someday, she will be reunited with her loved ones.

Another Breath, Another Sunrise

Book Four, the final book in the Michal's Destiny series.

Now that the Reich has fallen, in this—the final book of the Michal's Destiny series—the reader follows the survivors as they find themselves searching to reconnect with those they love. However, they are no longer the people they were before the war.

While the Russian soldiers, who are angry with the German people and ready to pillage, beat, and rape, begin to invade what's left of Berlin, Lotti is alone and fears for her life.

Though Alina Margolis has broken every tradition to become a successful business woman in America, she fears what has happened to her family and loved ones across the Atlantic Ocean.

As the curtain pulls back on Gilde, a now successful actress in London, she realizes that all that glitters is not gold, and she longs to find the lost family the Nazi's had stolen from her many years ago.

This is a story of ordinary people whose lives were shattered by the terrifying ambitions of Adolf Hitler—a true madman.

And . . . Who Is The Real Mother?

Book One in the Eidel's Story series.

In the Bible, there is a story about King Solomon, who was said to be the wisest man of all time. The story goes like this:

Two women came to the king for advice. Both of them were claiming to be the mother of a child. The king took the child in his arms and said, "I see that both of you care for this child very much. So, rather than decide which of you is the real mother, I will cut the child in half and give each of you a half."

One of the women agreed to the king's decision, but the other cried out, "NO, give the child to that other woman. Don't hurt my baby."

"Ahh," said the king to the second woman who refused to cut the baby. "I will give the child to you, because the real mother would sacrifice anything for her child. She would even give her baby away to another woman if it meant sparing the baby from pain."

And so, King Solomon gave the child to his rightful mother.

The year is 1941. The place is the Warsaw Ghetto in Poland.

The ghetto is riddled with disease and starvation. Children are dying every day.

Zofia Weiss, a young mother, must find a way to save, Eidel her only child. She negotiates a deal with a man on the black market to smuggle Eidel out in the middle of the night and deliver her to Helen, a Polish woman who is a good friend of Zofia's. It is the ultimate sacrifice because there is a good chance that Zofia will die without ever seeing her precious child again.

Helen has a life of her own, a husband and a son. She takes Eidel to live with her family even though she and those she loves will face terrible danger every day. Helen will be forced to do unimaginable things to protect all that she holds dear. And as Eidel grows up in Helen's warm maternal embrace, Helen finds that she has come to love the little girl with all her heart.

So, when Zofia returns to claim her child, and King Solomon is not available to be consulted, it is the reader who must decide…

Who is the real mother?

Secrets Revealed

Book Two in the Eidel's Story series.

Hitler has surrendered. The Nazi flags, which once hung throughout the city striking terror in the hearts of Polish citizens, have been torn down. It seems that Warsaw should be rejoicing in its newly found freedom, but Warsaw is not free. Instead, it is occupied by the Soviet Union, held tight in Stalin's iron grip. Communist soldiers, in uniform, now control the city. Where once people feared the dreaded swastika, now they tremble at the sight of the hammer and sickle. It is a treacherous time. And in the midst of all this danger, Ela Dobinski, a girl with a secret that could change her life, is coming of age.

New Life, New Land

Book Three in the Eidel's Story series.

When Jewish Holocaust survivors Eidel and Dovid Levi arrive in the United States, they believe that their struggles are finally over. Both have suffered greatly under the Nazi reign and are ready to leave the past behind. They arrive in this new and different land filled with optimism for their future. However, acclimating into a new way of life can be challenging for immigrants. And, not only are they immigrants but they are Jewish. Although Jews are not being murdered in the United States, as they were under Hitler in Europe, the Levi's will learn that America is not without anti-Semitism. Still, they go forth, with unfathomable courage. In New Life, New Land, this young couple will face the trials and tribulations of becoming Americans and building a home for themselves and their children that will follow them.

Another Generation

Book Four in the Eidel's Story series.

In the final book in the Eidel's Story series the children of Holocaust survivors Eidel and Dovid Levi have grown to adulthood.

They each face hard trials and tribulations of their own, many of which stem from growing up as children of Holocaust survivors. Haley is a peacemaker who yearns to please even at the expense of her own happiness. Abby is an angry rebel on the road to self-destruction. And, Mark, Dovid's only son, carries a heavy burden of guilt and secrets. He wants to please his father, but he cannot. Each of the Levi children must find a way to navigate their world while accepting that the lessons they have learned from the parents, both good and bad, have shaped them into the people they are destined to become.

The Wrath Of Eden

The Wrath of Eden Book One.

Deep in them Appalachian hills, far from the main roads where the citified people come and go, lies a harsh world where a man's character is all he can rightly claim as his own. This here is a land of deep, dark coal mines, where a miner ain't certain when he ventures into the belly of the mountain whether he will ever see daylight again. To this very day, they still tell tales of the Robin Hood-like outlaw Pretty Boy Floyd, even though there ain't no such thing as a thousand dollar bill no more From this beautiful yet dangerous country where folks is folks comes a story as old as time itself; a tale of good and evil, of right and wrong, and of a troubled man who walked a perilous path on his journey back to God.

The Wrath of Eden begins in 1917, in the fictitious town of Mudwater Creek, West Virginia. Mudwater lies deep in mining country in the Appalachian Mountains. Here, the eldest son of a snake-handling preacher, Cyrus Hunt, is emotionally broken by what he believes is his father's favoritism toward his brother, Aiden. Cyrus is so hurt by what he believes is his father's lack of love for him that he runs away from home to seek his fortune. Not only will he fight in the Great War, but he will return to America and then ramble around the United States for several years, right through the great depression. While on his journey, Cyrus will encounter a multitude of colorful characters and from each he will learn more about himself. This is a tale of good and evil, of brother against brother, of the intricate web of family, and of love lost and found again.

The Angels Song

The Wrath of Eden Book Two.

Cyrus Hunt returns home to the Appalachian Mountains after years of traveling. He has learned a great deal about himself from his journey, and he realizes that the time has come to make peace with his brother and his past. When he arrives in the small town where he grew up, he finds that he has a granddaughter that he never knew existed, and she is almost the same age as his daughter. The two girls grow up as close as sisters. But one is more beautiful than a star-filled night sky, while the other has a physical condition that keeps her from spreading her wings and discovering her own self-worth. As the girls grow into women, the love they have for each other is constantly tested by sibling rivalry, codependency, and betrayals. Are these two descendents of Cyrus Hunt destined to repeat their father's mistakes? Or will they rise above their human weakness and inadequacies and honor the bonds of blood and family that unite them?

One Last Hope

A Voyage to Escape Nazi Germany

Formerly *The Voyage*

Inspired by True Events

On May 13, 1939, five strangers boarded the MS St. Louis. Promised a future of safety away from Nazi Germany and Hitler's Third Reich, unbeknownst to them they were about to embark upon a voyage built on secrets, lies, and treachery. Sacrifice, love, life, and death hung in the balance as each fought against fate, but the voyage was just the beginning.

A Flicker Of Light

Hitler's Master Plan.

The year is 1943

The forests of Munich are crawling with danger during the rule of the Third Reich, but in order to save the life of her unborn child, Petra Jorgenson must escape from the Lebensborn Institute. She is alone, seven months pregnant, and penniless. Avoiding the watchful eyes of the armed guards in the overhead tower, she waits until the dead of night and then climbs under the flesh-shredding barbed wire surrounding the Institute. At the risk of being captured and murdered, she runs headlong into the terrifying, desolate woods. Even during one of the darkest periods in the history of mankind, when horrific acts of cruelty become commonplace and Germany seemed to have gone crazy under the direction of a madman, unexpected heroes come to light. And although there are those who would try to destroy true love, it will prevail. Here in this lost land ruled by human monsters, Petra will

323

learn that even when one faces what appears to be the end of the world, if one looks hard enough, one will find that there is always A Flicker of Light.

The Heart Of A Gypsy

If you liked Inglorious Basterds, Pulp Fiction, and Django Unchained, you'll love The Heart of a Gypsy!

During the Nazi occupation, bands of freedom fighters roamed the forests of Eastern Europe. They hid while waging their own private war against Hitler's tyrannical and murderous reign. Among these Resistance fighters were several groups of Romany people (Gypsies).

The Heart of a Gypsy is a spellbinding love story. It is a tale of a man with remarkable courage and the woman who loved him more than life itself. This historical novel is filled with romance and spiced with the beauty of the Gypsy culture.

Within these pages lies a tale of a people who would rather die than surrender their freedom. Come, enter into a little-known world where only a few have traveled before . . . the world of the Romany.

If you enjoy romance, secret magical traditions, and riveting action you will love The Heart of a Gypsy.

Please be forewarned that this book contains explicit scenes of a sexual nature.